Christa Winsloe was born  1888 into a military family, repressive Potsdam Schoo[l] married a 'new' Hungaria[n] whose wealth came from sugarcane, she was in revolt throughout her life against social and sexual convention. Her marriage swiftly failed and she lived increasingly openly as a lesbian. Christa Winsloe's novels and plays constantly explore the tensions between individual sexual identity and external social constraints, especially as they affect women artists (Winsloe was herself initially a sculptor). She produced her best-known work, *The Child Manuela* (1934) in several forms – as a novel, a play, and the famous film version *Mädchen in Uniform* (*Schoolgirls in Uniform*), directed by Leontine Sagan in 1931.

Later, with the advance of Hitlerism, she settled in France, where she wrote several film scripts, including one for Pabst, *Jeunes filles en detresse*. With her lover, the Swiss author, Simone Gentet, she worked for the Resistance and offered sanctuary to refugees whom they hid in their house. Both women were murdered by fascists in June 1944.

Alison Hennegan, the series editor of *Lesbian Landmarks*, read English at Girton College, Cambridge. From 1977 until its closure in 1983 she was Literary Editor and Assistant Features Editor at *Gay News*. She went on to become Editor of The Women's Press Bookclub 1984–1991 and in 1992 launched the specialist feminist Open Letters Bookclub, which she currently edits.

LESBIAN LANDMARKS

Lesbian writing is booming today – from the most rigorous of scholarly studies to the softest of soft-centre fiction – with special lesbian sections in many bookshops, crammed with volumes from the tiniest lesbian presses and the biggest publishing giants. In the midst of such plenty, it's easy to forget that it was not always so . . . .

Lesbian Landmarks is an exciting new series of reprints which illuminates the rich and eventful history of lesbian writing.

Their politics as varied as their prose and poetry, their ideas on gender as diverse as the genres in which they express them, the writers reprinted here span centuries, castes and cultures. Some were celebrated in their lifetimes but are now forgotten; others were silenced and exiled.

Amongst these authors you will find remarkable innovators in style and content. You may also find women whose far-distant attitudes and assumptions perplex or even anger you. But all of them, in their different ways, engaged in the long struggle to articulate and explore ways of living and loving that have, over the centuries, been variously misrepresented, feared, pathologized and outlawed.

The world these authors knew was often a world apart from ours; yet however unlikely it may sometimes seem, each of these books has helped to make possible today's frequently very different, confidently open lesbian writing. These, in short, are Lesbian Landmarks.

Christa
Winsloe

The Child Manuela

Introduction by Alison Hennegan

English Translation by Agnes Neill Scott

Published by VIRAGO PRESS Limited, March 1994
42–43 Gloucester Crescent, London NW1 7PD

First published in Great Britain by Chapman and Hall 1934

Printed and bound in Great Britain by
Cox & Wyman Ltd., Reading, Berks

Dedicated
in friendship and gratitude
to
Irene Hatvany

Hatvan
Winter 1932/1933

INTRODUCTION

'Don't think, my dear, obey! We Prussians have grown great through obedience. Not through pampering ourselves.'

In these words the Headmistress of Hochdorf, an aristocratic seminary for the daughters of high-ranking German army officers, articulates the values central to herself, her school, and the larger system in the world beyond which she and Hochdorf serve.

'How true, ma'am! How true!', sighs the devoted little Fräulein von Kesten, or Bunny, as she's known to pupils, a name bestowed by virtue of her timid scamperings and her ever-twitching ears, waiting to pick up rumours of scandal and misdeeds which she may bear back eagerly to the Headmistress. The plain and awkward only daughter of an eminent but impoverished General, Bunny had lacked the personal charms which might have won her willing suitors; and her dowry was not large enough to persuade the less enthusiastic.

> So at the age of twenty Bunny donned the grey uniform [of Hochdorf] whose unyielding material apparently hindered her body from developing, and so she parted her hair in the same place to the very end of her life.

Yet surprisingly Bunny – emotionally and physically
retarded, demeaningly subordinate – is the only one
amongst mistresses, pupils and servants who is not
frightened of their formidable Head. That, as Winsloe
chillingly tells us, is probably because Bunny 'was no
longer a person and so had nothing more to fear in this
world.' Such humanity as Bunny ever had has long been
eroded by a régime which operates through fear,
deprivation and denial. Hochdorf is a place where illness is
malingering, starvation is character-forming, numbers are
used instead of names, emotions are deemed weakness, and
obedience is rated higher than intelligence or conscience. It
is a place which has already perfected the vicious arts of
dehumanization which would be given fullest play later in
institutions such as Dachau, Belsen, Auschwitz and
Treblinka.

Above all, Hochdorf is a place where all girls must
remember that just as their fathers and brothers are army
officers, so too should be their husbands and sons.

For the school's young teenage pupils – many of them
constantly homesick, their misery exacerbated by their guilt
at such an 'unsoldierly' emotion – humanity is to be found
only amongst themselves, from the occasional kindly
servant, and from Fräulein von Bernburg, a beautiful and
charismatic young mistress. The adoration she inspires in
almost every schoolgirl breast arouses in the Headmistress a
stinging contempt which masks an inner terror. Passionate
emotions, especially passionate loves, invariably spell
trouble for authoritarian régimes. Yet even Elisabeth von
Bernburg, dutiful daughter of a wealthy military dynasty,
seems to sanction Hochdorf's values:

> 'Whatever is done here is well and rightly done.
> Even although you don't understand why things
> are not different. It will take time before you

> begin to understand. It's not for you to criticize,
> but to obey. The greatest Christian virtue is
> humility. You know that already, don't you?'

Falteringly her pupil, Manuela von Meinhardis, the book's central character, answers 'Yes, Fräulein von Bernburg'. Christa Winsloe, who created both pupil and teacher, would have answered with a long, loud 'no'. This novel, and the play and film based upon it, represent a sustained challenge to Hochdorf, and to the Prussian militarism which nurtured both it and the rise of German fascism – a force which Winsloe recognized early and defied throughout, until the moment when fascists murdered her and her lover in Occupied France, in June 1944.

Readers already familiar with Leontine Sagan's film version, *Mädchen in Uniform* (*Schoolgirls in Uniform*) will be surprised to discover that Manuela's schooldays at Hochdorf form only the second half of the original novel. They may also find their sense of time disrupted. The film and play are set firmly in the years of their making, the film in 1931, the play in 1932; the novel is set much earlier. References to particular historical events make it clear that Manuela is about eight years old in 1895, and comes to Hochdorf in about 1901. In the world of the film and play, the outbreak of the Second World War is less than a decade away. In the world of the novel, the Great War of 1914–1918 has yet to be fought.

The contemporary setting of the film and play links the school's régime more closely to the menacing political events unfolding in Germany in the early Thirties. The school's very existence is now actually dependent on subsidies from the Government: 'How embarrassing to have to accept anything from such people!', exclaims Manuela's aunt when, in the play version, she learns the fact from

Bunny. Yet although *The Child Manuela* was published in
1934, after the film and stage version, Winsloe, as her first
English publishers made clear, 'originally conceived the
story as a novel and so wrote it. The novel, here published
for the first time, tells in more detailed form than play or
film can, the story of the child, Manuela.' That greater detail
and expansiveness is needed for three main purposes. The
first, to chronicle and analyse the corrosive effects of
Prussian militarism on individuals and societies; the second,
to explore the genesis and development of one young girl's
lesbianism; and, the third, to examine the inevitable and
disastrous conflict between Prussianism (and its bastard
offspring, Hitlerism) and love between women.

Two years after *Mädchen in Uniform* was made, and less than
four months after the first London stage production of
Children in Uniform, on January 30th, 1933, Hitler became
Chancellor of Germany. On the face of it there could be
little affinity between the Austrian ex-corporal, born to very
lower-middle-class parents and now backed by a brutal
army of street-fighters, and the aristocratic officers and
statesmen who helped him to power. And, indeed, it's true
that intitially each side believed it could use the other for its
own ends. In fact, however, there were strong psychological
similarities between one particular aspect of German
military tradition and the brash, new, upstart Nazis. The
link was Prussia, that overpoweringly militaristic east
German state, with its grotesque over-valuing of military
virtues, its contempt for civilian life, its love of strictly
observed hierarchies and distinctions of caste, its dubious
'worship' of women which went hand in hand with
contempt for 'feminine' qualities, and an abject terror of
difference which manifested itself in the violent repression
of individuals or groups who ran counter to a narrowly
defined normality and decency.

To sufficiently assured observers, Prussianism could seem mainly risible. Elizabeth von Arnim, Katherine Mansfield's cousin who married a German nobleman, scrutinized the caste from within: she left a devastatingly satirical account of one ludicrous and misogynistic officer's misfortunes in *The Caravaners*, her 1909 comedy-with-a-purpose. Lieutenant Bilse's *Life in a Garrison Town*, which earned its young author a court-martial and a Dishonourable Discharge, and which was suppressed by the German Government in 1903, painted an altogether more sombre picture. Bilse observed the corruption to which Prussianism was vulnerable: the arrogance of the officer caste; the unpayable debts incurred by poorly paid men aping aristocratic extravagance; gambling and drunkenness embraced as a respite from long hours of boredom and inaction; and a tradition of 'gallantry' which put philandering with semi-professional 'ladies' before family life. As Arnold White, a contemporary English commentator, observed in his Introduction to the 1904 English edition:

> It is impossible for Englishmen to grasp the immense effect of Lieutenant Bilse's book, because compulsory military service renders every youth and every parent in Germany personally and directly interested in the facts related to Bilse. [The book] stirred Germany to its very depths, because family life, which is still the dominant note throughout the Kaiser's dominions, was touched in its tenderest spot by the recital of tyranny, debauchery and crime.

Historians of the Third Reich and its antecedents have had much to say about the fear of women and of female sexuality which underlies militaristic and fascist ideologies. They have also traced links between the fear of women and

of other disturbing groups, who become 'feminized' in
fascist perceptions in order to be the better feared and hated.
These groups are dangerous in proportion to the extent that
they 'resemble' women. So Jews, for example, are deemed
to be 'femininely' sensual, greedy and manipulative;
orientals are 'femininely' devious, luxurious and submissive;
negroes are child-like, close to nature (good) but anarchic
(bad), needing the smack of firm government; homosexual
men, according to some of the day's theories, *are* really
women, and homosexual women who *should* actually accept
their femininity, unforgiveably reject it. In contrast to such
social undesirables, a warrior caste abjures physical comfort,
denies the body in order to master it, is 'gallant' to women
but recognizes their basic and contaminating inferiority,
values the group (regiment, nation) above the individual,
and rates obedience as the highest virtue. Much of this
caste's ethos echoes Germany's proudly remembered, pre-
Christian pagan past (an element which Hitler would later
emphasize obsessively). Pagan echoes notwithstanding, into
this perverted religion of blood and iron the Christian God
is co-opted as Commanding Officer whose name is used to
sanction cruelty. And as it is in the officers' mess, so it is in
their daughters' schools. Hochdorf's Headmistress carries
her Bible like a weapon and prefaces public denunciations
with readings from the Gospel of Love. Obedience and
loyalty to the school and its hierarchy become synonymous
with patriotism (loyalty and obedience to the Fatherland),
and spiritual purity (Christian humility to the Heavenly
Father). A challenge to any part of this new Trinity is
immediately construed as a challenge to the whole: as such
it is punished with predictable harshness.

Manuela (or Lela, as her infant tongue first names herself) is
the child of a Prussian officer, Lieutenant-Colonel von
Meinhardis. Her early years are spent in the frontier

garrison town of Mühlburg, taken from the French in 1870,
and still inhabited by passionately resentful French
townspeople who, most reprehensibly, have failed to
become Germans overnight. Those people who pay visits to
the garrison's officers are routinely taken on a tour of the
nearby battlefields and the military cemetery where German
and French dead lie promiscuously mingled. 'Oh come on,
Lela, that's a French grave', says Berti, Lela's older brother,
as she lingers over an enamel-plated photograph set in the
tombstone of a French officer buried there. Only German
dead, it seems, matter. Lela notes the assumption but
inwardly rejects it.

Despite the Germans' crushing defeat of the French in
1870, German fear of France remains intense, and growing.
Even Manuela's gentle mother explains the feverish security
arrangements surrounding the Kaiser's visit to Mühlburg by
saying 'the wicked French might try to hurt him.' Her
explanation brings nightmares for the young Manuela
whose dreams are made hideous by French invaders.
Manuela outgrows her night-time terrors but, years later,
it's clear such dreams also haunt Hochdorf and the parents
who send their daughters there. The play version spells it
out with particular force: the desperately homesick Edelgard
has received a bracing letter from her mother:

> 'Be brave, my girl, and never never give in. Our
> country will soon need men and women of iron again,
> and it is our duty to subdue our feelings.'

As Edelgard explains to Manuela:

> 'At home, you know, they are always talking about the
> time that is coming when we shall need soldiers again,
> and mothers of soldiers. If that is true, I can't let them
> down; I can't be a coward. I must just grin and bear it.'

In perpetual contrast to Papa's military world is Mamma,

'the person who was always there.' From the beginning
Manuela's relationship with her mother is passionate and
sensuous. Even Mamma's discarded clothes continue to
contain her.

> From time to time [Manuela] stole in there [to her
> mother's wardrobe] and buried her face in the soft
> cambric, inhaling its fragrance until her mother
> became palpable to her and seemed to be embracing
> her. It was as if she could feel the warmth of Mamma
> and her gentle hands, and hear her voice saying: 'My
> darling–'

For the whole of her life the scent of a woman's hair, the
line of her neck, the curve of an arm, the swell of a breast,
the perfume of a sweet-smelling hand, will arouse in
Manuela powerfully conflicting emotions – happiness and
security, anxiety and the fear of loss. No one, it seems at
first, can ever dislodge Mamma from pride of place in
Manuela's heart – not even Eva, a precocious schoolfellow
in pre-Hochdorf days, whose mere presence causes Lela's
heart to pound.

Eva recognizes the sexual element in Manuela's feelings
for her long before Manuela herself perceives that it is a
wooing and a courtship she desires to enact, if only she
could get out of the frightful skirts which she hates so much,
and wear knickerbockers instead. Then she would feel 'free
and merry.'

> If she could only wear them at school. Then she would
> simply go up to Eva and make a bow and offer to
> carry her school books, and jump over a fence when
> Eva was looking or climb up a tree and call down to
> her; then she would ask her for a dance and send her
> flowers . . . . People would laugh at her! Oh, if they
> only knew . . . . surely then they wouldn't laugh.

But though happy to play upon that uncertainly dawning
sexuality, and to give Manuela her first distressing lessons
in the possible links between pain and pleasure, love and
fear, Eva sees Manuela mainly as the route to her own,
heterosexual objective – Berti, Manuela's older brother.

Manuela herself briefly shows interest in a boy, after
Mamma's death. But his attractions quickly pale before
those of his mother: 'This woman had Fritz's face! – but
lovelier, more tender, more charming.' Again, it is Frau
Inge's voice, hair and neck, hands and arms which work the
magic. Lela 'could see the opening of Frau Inge's frock and
would have liked to drop a kiss into it, but she did not dare.'
Manuela's enforced departure to Hochdorf separates her
from Frau Inge, but brings her to Elisabeth von Bernburg,
the last and deepest of Manuela's loves.

In the motherless Manuela's devotion for Fräulein von
Bernburg, and in the teacher's equally passionate, but
largely concealed feeling for her pupil, it would be easy to
see an anodyne, desexualized version of lesbianism which
interprets it as 'only' an imitative substitute for mother-
daughter relations. In fact Winsloe is at pains throughout to
reject that view. In this novel it is not that lesbianism is
asexual because maternal, but rather that relations between
mother and daughter always include potentially lesbian
elements. But although lesbian and maternal love may have
elements in common, they can be distinguished from each
other. The fourteen-year-old Manuela can certainly
distinguish them: 'I love you, darling Fräulein von
Bernburg. I love you so much, as much as my mother and
ever so much more.'

For Fräulein von Bernburg (the nearest thing to a mother
that many Hochdorf pupils know) such distinctions come
harder. Paedogogic convention encourages her to maintain
that it is her 'natural maternal' needs which teaching fulfils.
When Manuela asks her shyly if she is happy, Elisabeth

replies 'Yes, my dear, because I have all of you.' Perhaps, Winsloe continues, she should have said to Manuela, 'Because I have *you*.' But to do so would entail acknowledging that Elisabeth's scrupulously impartial treatment of all her pupils conceals the passionate love she feels for Manuela alone. It would also entail breaking with a life-time's Prussian training:

> . . . this daughter and granddaughter of soldiers who had been schooled all their lives to be sparing of their emotions and to despise outpourings of feeling, this virgin daughter of a puritan mother, bred in the fear of God, this young woman who had vowed to herself that she would do her duty truly and uprightly by the children entrusted to her care, could not have brought herself to make such a statement. She had to think here only of 'the children'; she dared not let a single child usurp her heart. And now that she had done so in spite of everything, from the very first moment that her eyes had encountered Manuela's, she dared not contemplate anything but self-discipline and renunciation.

Manuela, it is implied, is not the first young woman to have caused Elisabeth such conflict, even if she is very much the most important. As Elisabeth tells Madamoiselle, the French mistress who questions whether Elisabeth's work can really satisfy her: '. . . some of the children, believe me, Mademoiselle' – and for the first time her well-schooled voice trembled curiously – 'there are *some* who won't ever forget me . . .' Just as Winsloe traces carefully the stages which confirm and consolidate Manuela's development as a lesbian, so too she offers a gradual revelation of the social obstacles which have impeded and delayed Elisabeth's recognition and acceptance of her sexuality.

As so often in lesbian fiction of this period Winsloe leaves open the question of what 'causes' lesbianism: biology or circumstances, heredity or environment? Traces of the biologically based theory of a 'third sex' seem to hover over her descriptions of Manuela's spectacularly slim hips, long legs and seemingly God-given skills of 'leading' her partners in the waltz. After her magnificent triumph, playing the male lead in the school play, her dazzled schoolfellows declare that they're 'inclined to believe tonight that – that you're really half a boy . . . .' Manuela herself is clear that she wants 'to be a boy, I hate being a girl . . . . I don't want to be a woman – I want to be a man'; but her main reason for wanting to be a man is 'to be with *you*, Fräulein von Bernburg.' Here, as so often, female biology is blamed for societal failures. It's not surgery that Manuela needs, but a change in the social system.

Within Hochdorf, that tiny microcosm of the social system, change can come only by overturning its inhuman cardinal 'virtues', chief of which is unquestioning obedience. Winsloe saw its dangers clearly before the Second World War; after it, when the trials of German war criminals elicited that dreary, deadening procession of defendants claiming that they had 'only obeyed orders', its dangers should have become perpetually apparent to everyone.

By the end of 1933, the year in which Hitler had become Chancellor, the entire leadership of his most dangerous political adversaries, and the bulk of those intellectuals who had most outspokenly opposed him, had either fled Germany or were already imprisoned in the Third Reich's first concentration camps. In the play, *Children in Uniform*, Elisabeth, who at last confronts the Headmistress, cries out:

'This house is a rat-trap. It is a house of death. You kill the soul, the spirit! This galvanized suppression is spiritual death. Only women can do such terrible things to women!'

The novel ends less polemically but makes its point no less powerfully. The only people who foresee the final tragedy – the servants, the pupils – are powerless to prevent it. They are, to use a military metaphor appropriate to the establishment, only Other Ranks. It would take a mutiny from the 'officers' to overthrow the High Command. But before that can happen, 'officers' such as Elisabeth von Bernburg must first dismantle in their heads the system which confuses God and the State, discipline and cruelty, love and perversion. For Fräulein von Bernburg, as for hundreds of thousands of 'ordinary, decent people' during the Thirties and Forties, it was a realization that came too late.

Alison Hennegan, Cambridge, 1993

PART ONE

I

MANUELA was a longed-for child. A child passionately loved in anticipation. Manuela had to be born, and had to be a girl. Before she made her appearance in the world a whole household was waiting for her; a father already impatient, a mother who had communed deeply with her child long before it was laid in her arms, and two brothers ready to be their sister's comrades, a little patronizing perhaps, but proud of her once she was actually there.

Manuela could not but be born on a Sunday—and on a Christmas Sunday, too. When her two brothers came home from the Christmas play, there she lay in the cradle, like a newly arrived Christmas gift. The boys were not surprised, for they had just seen the Christ Child lying in a cradle, in the stable of Bethlehem, and the five-year-old Bertram, in a natural confusion of ideas, proposed to the ten-year-old Alfred: "Let's carry her into the stable; she'd like that." Only when it was objected that no ox or ass was in the stable, nothing but horses, which were never seen in Bethlehem, could he be dissuaded from his project.

Everybody said that the baby was a beauty, yet that

3

was not strictly true. For the dark eyes, whose whites were tinged with blue, completely lacked eyebrows; and a little bonnet had to be tied over the infant's head to cover its baldness. Frau Käte caressed the hairless little head uneasily, and when at last a few sparse, silky dark hairs appeared there was a family celebration, and Herr von Meinhardis announced that a bottle of Moselle must be opened.

The child's first years passed like a waking dream, for she could not see beyond the verge of her nest. But she often opened her sloe-black eyes wide when she heard her father's horses trampling in the courtyard, or when her brothers came bursting in from school, throwing their satchels in a corner and shouting "Mother!"

Mother was the person who was always there. It was she who came when Lela screamed, she who brought comfort when Lela cried. Lela was the name the child gave herself as soon as she realized that she was a separate individual: the stately name "Manuela" was too difficult for her small tongue, and so she called herself Lela, and Lela she remained.

A little later she had a crib with high bars around it to keep her from falling out. It was dark in her room at night, except for a ray of light coming through the crack of the door, and the room was lofty. Lela's silky hair was brushed back and tied with a ribbon so straitly that it almost hurt. Outside the door people were running to and fro: the house was disturbed: voices called and answered, and then silence fell again. Lela was supposed to go to sleep. She was lying on her back. Her black Teddy, clasped in both hands, slept on her chest; he felt rough to the touch and his eyes were boot-buttons. He had a bristly moustache like Papa's when one kissed him. But Lela loved "Teddy," and she loved him all the more when other people said he was hideous. On either side of Teddy, with their heads on Lela's shoulders, slept the two Snookies, two white rabbits, or rather two rabbits that had once been white. Snookie Number One had lost his ears, and his leather muzzle was worn quite bald: Mamma had had to make a cross on it with red ink so that one could tell which end was his face. Snookie Number Two was still new and soft to stroke; he had a "real" fell. It was by no means easy to cuddle all three at once.

The clatter of horses sounded from outside and a carriage drew up crunching on the gravel. Lela's heart pounded. She shut her eyes tight. She knew that Mamma and Papa would be going down the steps and climbing into the carriage, and then a door would bang and everything would go dead and the house would be empty. Lela twisted her tiny fingers in Teddy's black velvet coat. "Mamma must come, she must come in and say good night." She put up a secret prayer, although she knew that one really ought not to bother God with such trifles: "Dear God, please let Mamma come in just once more!" And at that very moment the door did open softly. Lela kept her eyes screwed up tight. A gentle voice said: "She's sleeping," and Lela's mother bent cautiously over the crib. A sudden fragrance of sweet-smelling flowers enveloped the child, and the cool blossoms on her mother's naked shoulder touched her face. Lela opened her eyes ever so little. A white satin gown, a glittering diamond brooch. Mamma's slender arms were covered with long, white kid gloves that felt queer. Tenderly a hand made the sign of the cross over Lela's forehead: "God bless you, my darling. . . ."

Then the rustling and swishing of a train. The door creaked a little, and the light that had been coming through the crack was blotted out. Lela opened her eyes wide in the darkness.

II

THE street was wet, the road bumpy; the lamps wavered and rattled in the wind. Nobody was in sight; there was no sound but the beat of iron-shod hoofs. The carriage smelt of old leather. When the lamplight illumined the occupants for a moment it picked out the gleaming badge of an order, bright ribbons arrayed side by side, a red collar with silver braid, glittering buttons.

"What's the matter, Käte? Why are you sighing?" came from one corner.

"Oh, you know well enough; these Court balls are a dreadful trial to me."

"Do you suppose that I like them?" retorted Major von Meinhardis huffily. "God only knows whom I'll have to take in to supper. And the food! These mob-feedings are frightful. Everything served up cold. Some white and flabby fish, and then *filet*—nothing but *filet*."

There was no answer. In the darkness a wryly amused smile flitted over Frau Käte's gentle face but faded almost at once. It would have been so pleasant to stay quietly at home with the children, to do some knitting, write a letter to Grandmamma and go early to

bed.   Not to have to face all these strange people.   She
was apprehensive.   Everything would be so loud.   The
men, tired after the day's routine, always fired themselves
with alcohol and soon had flushed faces above their
tight collars.   They danced till they sweated and
squeezed their partners close.   One grew quite giddy
waltzing.   And yet most of the guests were bored all the
time.   Now, at home . . .

Lela's mother was still a stranger in this garrison town
of Dünheim with its little Court.   Officers are like pawns
picked up by an invisible hand and set down in some
other place; removed and re-arranged without knowing
why or wherefore.   They receive compensation for the
costs of the transfer, but nobody asks them whether they
have left friends behind or whether the new place agrees
with their wives; nobody cares whether a wife is far from
her native air or whether the children are likely to get
on well in the new school.   A man is " transferred " and
that is the end of it.   So his wife's heart turns to her
own old home because she is never given time to make
a new home for herself : she must always be ready to
strike her tent.   Sooner or later, as inevitable as death,
the day of the " transfer " will come.   Until that day
there is nothing for it but to swim with the stream
wherever one happens to be, and that means swimming
in the regimental stream.   Whether one likes them or
not the other officers' wives—the colonel's wife, the
major's, the captain's—are one's intimates.   It is they
who invite one and are invited, they and they alone.
It is "impossible " to strike up a friendship with the wife
of a doctor or of a banker, and indeed one runs no risk
of being tempted, for convention sees to it that one never
meets them.

And so one drives to the Court balls. A Court ball
is an official duty; one cannot absent oneself. A woman
who is seriously ill may indeed beg to be omitted from
the list of invitations, but to refuse the invitation once
received—to disobey a command—is out of the question.

"I'd rather stay at home. . . ." Frau Käte did not
dare even to frame the words. What an absurd idea, to
want to stay at home with the children and knit and
write a letter! And yet it was time she sent a letter to
Pöchlin: she had not yet thanked her mother for the
last consignment of sausage. Nor for the sack of
potatoes for the winter and the barrel of apples. The
ham, too, which would last for a fortnight at least. The
boys could have ham sandwiches for their school
lunches. How much these boys could eat! Really as
much as grown men. And yet they were only eight and
thirteen, but growing fast. Ali's trousers were too short
again. They could be made down for Berti—but Ali
would have to get a new suit. Not this month, anyhow
—unless Grandmamma . . . But Grandmamma was
short of money too. In Pöchlin there was plenty of
everything except money.

And it had been a dry summer. God knew what the
harvest would be like. Frau Käte could see in her
mind's eye her father standing beside the rain-gauge
peering at the scanty rainfall. That gauge, mounted on
an old stump, had been the mysterious bogy of her
childhood, for everything depended on it. Drought—
the terror of her parents, the fear of the farm-servants.
Drought—sickness among the cattle, and poor harvests.
Poor harvests—debts. Debts—mortgages. Mortgages
—ruin. Drought, and a white smother of dust blown
from the high-road lay on the roses and the ilex-bushes:

the trees yellowed in midsummer: the earth gaped: the
horses' hoofs split. And then it was that the unnatural,
leaden-looking agaves in front of the house flourished:
alien and sturdy, they mocked at the thirst of the
geraniums and marguerites. The ears of corn in the
fields remained small, and their husks cracked to scatter
the sparse grain on the hard ground. Gloomy in the
brilliant sunshine lay the house, and gloomily the
occupants avoided each other in silence.

At this moment the carriage halted with a jerk. A
gold-laced flunkey opened the door; a double line of
inquisitive by-standers gaped at Frau Käte's small foot
in its white satin shoe. But she did not have to step
on to the wet pavement, for a thick red carpet had been
laid down, while above her head a canopy stretched to
shield her from the fine rain, and she looked up at it
with gratitude. She had to wait a second or two for her
husband, who emerged from the carriage ceremonially,
being forced to step down sideways because of the spurs
on his patent-leather boots. His lean, brown-knuckled
hand pulled his cloak about him. Resentfully at first
and then good-humouredly his vivacious black eyes ran
over the throng of spectators. He lifted his right hand
carelessly to his cap in answer to the lackey's bow, and
then without any embarrassment, stimulated almost to
geniality by the admiring and envious glances of the
lookers-on, he advanced towards his waiting wife, offered
her his arm and conducted her up the steps to the
entrance door.

This easy assurance was native to Major von Meinhardis. He approved himself and was approved by
others. He liked people to observe that he had inherited
"a touch of something" from a Spanish grandmother.

His yellow skin, his arched instep, his dark, silky hair
were un-German, and when his fellow-officers sometimes
called him " old exotic," he could not suppress a small
smile of gratification. Tenderly protective he led his
wife up the steps, a little affected, as usual, by her obvious
shyness and strangeness. It was this quality in her that
had first attracted him in those early days . . . queer
how at such moments one could not help thinking of
those old times, so long ago. . . .

He had been out on manœuvres then.   Officers' billets.
Heat, dust and fatigue. A troop of strangers on weary
horses, with dusty boots and tanned faces, they had
ridden up the lime avenue of Pöchlin, and the large, cool
white house had received them, and three shy young
girls had conducted the strangers to their rooms. They
had flung off their uniforms, bathed and tumbled into
bed to sleep like the dead, with flies humming round
the chandelier and buzzing at the window-panes. Lieutenant von Meinhardis had blinked in the shadowy
green light filtering through ancient chestnut-trees
before the window. The little girl, the youngest, what
was her name? Käte—he could not help smiling—
Käte. Large-eyed, and had not uttered a word, he was
sure;—a country girl—how could he think of it? He
must be crazy. If Princess Shuvaloff were to hear that
. . . and Madame Shermetyeff in Baden-Baden—von
Meinhardis and a Käte! How they would laugh!
Here everything smelt of apples, he had gone on thinking; smelt definitely of golden pearmains and russets.
Russets got as wrinkled as old women. . . . Käte washed
herself with lavender. He had smelt it, whether it was
from her white frock or her hair or her hands—lavender
unmistakably. Clean and pungent. How funny. . . .

"The devil take this billeting: I can't stand these philandering Hussars," said the old Pöchliner, tapping his barometer. But the day came when all the white doors in Pöchlin were wreathed with thick garlands of blue cornflowers. Red poppies bedecked the table and candles with white frills. And the white muslin curtains were starched, and the parquet floors shone like glass. The parson in his black gown with the little white bands proposed the first toast, and then the officers of the regiment, in their red coats with their blue dolmans thrown over their shoulders, made a crossed archway with their sabres to let the bride and bridegroom pass through, out into the world—under a line of sabres.

All that flashed through his mind as Meinhardis slowly mounted the carpeted steps. Frau Käte shivered and drew her mantle more closely about her.

At the dressing-rooms they separated. The gentlemen were taken in charge by footmen, the ladies by chambermaids in white caps and stiff, black silk gowns. Tall, gold-framed mirrors on the walls of the ladies' room were designed to give confidence to timid beginners, and to reflect the assured glances of beautiful women with stately tiaras of flashing diamonds. Only in the dressing-room could anxious hands let go the long trains that had been held clear of the ground: not until then could one fasten the last little buttons of the tightly fitting gloves. Thick pincushions, needles and cotton stood ready for emergencies. Hasty greetings were exchanged between acquaintances, unofficial greetings, so to speak, for the formal how-do-you-dos were reserved for the *salon* upstairs. A nervous silence reigned in the room; the ladies whispered under their breath.

In the gentlemen's quarters things were different.
There was loud groaning over the tight coats, and necks
were stretched before the mirror to ease them out of the
too high collars, while one cursed a chance cut in the
chin got while shaving, or grumbled at bootmakers who
had lost the art of making high boots of patent leather.
One asked what strangers were expected to-night, and
with a little brush brushed one's moustache before the
looking-glass. A few gentlemen in civilian evening dress
felt effaced in their sober black, which even a red ribbon
could not sufficiently brighten: they could not compete
with all these red collars and green uniforms, blue coats
and white collars, with all that silver and gold and
patent leather and gay cloth. Their faces were pallid
beside the weathered brown skins of the soldiers, and
they tucked their cocked hats under their arms and
silently faded out—the Ministers and Cabinet Councillors
who spent their days no one knew how or where.

A broad staircase, again covered with runners of red
carpet, led the way up. Flowers bordered the steps, and
at the top a chamberlain of the Grand Duke's household
waited, representing his master, to receive the guests.
At this point each guest was given a small, folded card
stamped with a golden crown—the dance programme,
to which a small pencil was attached by a silken cord,
in readiness to note down the names of one's partners.
The programme was unvarying: waltz, polka, schottische, supper; waltz, lancers, polka, waltz, schottische,
Française and cotillion.

All the rooms in the old castle were thrown open on
ball evenings: not a door remained locked. In all the
corridors and doorways stood flunkeys in red liveries
with golden cords over their breasts, knee-breeches and

pumps. Chandeliers with hundreds of warmly glowing candles shed a mild light that brightened faces and made eyes shine. There was no jostling: in spite of the press there was only a gentle drifting to and fro, an exchange of greetings. Frau Käte joined several other ladies while Meinhardis was eagerly inscribing his name on the programmes of the best dancers.

A few taps with a gavel and the room was hushed, the murmur of voices ceased. People drew back, and down the middle passed the Grand Duke in full dress uniform, leading the Grand Duchess towards the great hall. The reception now began. New-comers were formally presented. Meanwhile the orchestra softly struck up a waltz, and the first dancers took the floor. The older ladies slowly settled themselves in groups on the sofas along the walls; the older gentlemen withdrew to the smoking-room. It was still cold; people were still standing about feeling chilly and not very much at home.

Frau Käte had to greet countless acquaintances as politeness required. She sought out the Colonel's wife and paid her respects to the Court ladies, all of whom asked after her children as graciously as if they had been her superior officers. It was Käte's duty to offend no-body and so, one after another, she smiled on the young officers who were her husband's subordinates, as each came up to her punctiliously and made his bow. It must be admitted that none of them looked as if this were a burdensome duty; they literally beamed upon her; they led her out to dance and took her to the buffet for champagne. Little by little the ball-room grew warmer. Already the lace on a lady's train had been torn by the spurs of a dancer. The candles were darting

their flames higher and dripping maliciously upon the
uniforms stationed unsuspectingly beneath them.

Frau Käte flew from partner to partner. Wearily at
last she took refuge on a sofa among a group of the
older ladies, with whom she liked to talk.

"No, I always get my butter sent from North
Germany. I find it much more economical. And it
keeps quite well; I squeeze it tight into a big earthen-
ware pot, and keep it wet. To get a dozen pounds at a
time comes much cheaper."

"Yes, but surely you don't use butter for cooking, do
you?"

"Sometimes I do." She was ashamed of being thought
extravagant, and tried to excuse herself. "You see, 1
come from the country, Your Excellency. Butter is so
plentiful in the country. . . ."

And Her old Excellency nodded understandingly.

But Frau Käte was not to be left in peace. A tall,
officer bore down upon her, and she had to rise.

"What are you doing there among all the old horrors?
They're not the right company for you. . . ."

Frau Käte bent her head in confusion. She could feel
the hard, silver embroidery on the man's sleeve against
the back of her neck. It hurt her. He was holding her
more closely than was needful.

"Don't you know that you are very charming?"

The manly voice coming from so far above her head
embarrassed her. She wished that the music would
stop. She was also blushing a little.

"You keep yourself too much in the background.
You don't come out nearly often enough, a lady so young
and charming as you are."

"Oh, that kind of thing isn't for me. . . ."

"Oh, surely for every woman . . ." and, as the dance was ended, her partner led her into one of the side rooms and settled her under a tall lamp.

Frau Käte was reluctant, but no means of escape suggested itself.

Lieutenant von Kaisersmark sat down close beside her on the small, old-fashioned sofa, which was so low that when he sat sideways his left knee touched the ground, making him look almost as if he were kneeling. And he said nothing, but only sighed.

"Is there anything bothering you?" asked Käte sympathetically. She could see how deeply drawn the furrows were that ran from nose to mouth in Kaisersmark's face. It was a pity; he had such a nice face, she thought.

"My dear lady, I don't really like to alarm you by telling you something that you ought to know nothing about. But I think it will do me good to confess to you. I am head over heels in debt and have no prospect of ever being able to pay up. The Colonel has cautioned me, but I can't do anything about it. . . ."

"And can your father do nothing?"

"He's selling our estate, which is mortgaged already."

"And your friends? . . ."

"That's the worst of it. I'm in debt to all of them."

"Well, the banks then. . . ."

"I'm in debt to them, too. . . ."

"And so . . ."

"And so, my dear little lady, this is the last time I shall have the pleasure of seeing you. This very evening I'm going to shed my uniform "—he gazed at all the silver lace—" and to-morrow I'm going to set off with a suit-case for the other side of the world."

"To America? . . . And what will you be able to do there?"

"I don't know.   Wash dishes, probably."

For a moment there was silence. A few young couples strolled through the room, and an elderly footman came round with a tray of drinks. Kaisersmark took a glass of mineral water and drank it hastily. Käte began again:

"I don't understand it—forgive me for asking—how did it all happen?"

Kaisersmark shrugged his shoulders.

"God, how does it ever happen? My father put me in this expensive regiment, thinking that I would soon make a rich marriage—it was all he could do to scrape up the money for my outfit. But then one has to run up bills at the casino, and appearances have to be kept up: and in any case, after the monotonous routine of the service, and the dull and boring company one has to keep, a man has to have something to cheer him up. So I had a love-affair . . . and that costs money, too. And one's pay is just about enough to buy cigarettes on."

"Yes, but . . ."

"You think I've been reckless? I suppose you're right. But just think of what it means. How can a man drink water when twenty-four comrades are drinking Moselle all around him? Or ride an old hack in front of the regiment? Or wear shabby uniforms, or down-at-heel boots? It can't be done. And then to set one's cap at some rich girl . . . No, I just couldn't manage it. The mess sent me a loaded revolver . . ."

Käte's eyes opened in horror.

"But I sent it back again. I'm not thinking of shooting myself; I want to go on living. . . ."

"Of course you've to go on living, and perhaps in
America . . . who knows? . . ."

Kaisersmark took Käte's hand, bent over it and said:
"Shall we go back to the dance?"

She took his arm and they whirled off to the strains of
a waltz.

In the smoking-room the air was thick. The tables
were laden with fat-bellied bottles of red wine and
countless boxes of cigars. All the faces were shining
and flushed.

"No, that's something he can't do, let him be as gone
on the girl as he likes."

"But, Axelstern, they're very decent people, the
Lowensteins, and rich, my God. . . ."

"That's as may be, but after all they're Jews! And
with his position at Court . . . simply out of the
question. If he were to do it, he'd soon be chucked out;
he'd find himself one of these days in some rotten little
frontier post, in a line regiment. . . ."

"But she's pretty, more than pretty, in fact. . . ."

"Yes," smiled Axelstern, "they have something about
them, these Jewish girls . . . plenty of temperament and
. . . Here's to them!"

In another corner a very young subaltern was laying
down the law to his comrades.

"A trench war? That isn't worth calling war. Just
think of it! You never see the enemy at all, and you're
shot dead before you know where you are. . . ."

"Well, I grant you, there's not much to be said for it."

"Look here, my father was out in the seventies, and

they had regular cavalry charges, hand-to-hand com-
bats . . . that was something like. But trenches? No
place for a gentleman."

Outside in the wet road the carriages began to drive
up. They had been ordered early, regard being paid to
the fact that all the gentlemen had to go on duty again
next morning. But not all of them went home. Their
sabres clanking by their sides, many of them strolled
along to a small bar, where they could comfortably
discuss all that had happened at the ball.

Meinhardis shut the carriage door on his wife, and
with a kiss bade her good night.

'Don't be so late to-night, please."

'But, Käte, I'm only going to have a glass of wine.
All this dancing gives one a frightful thirst. . . ."

Frau Käte laid in a basin of water the armful of
flowers that she had received in the cotillion. Lovingly
she undid the wire that bound them and sprinkled them
with water. The mimosa smelt strong, the white
narcissi mysterious. Noiselessly she opened a door
and stood beside Lela's bed. Lela was breathing
evenly, with both her tiny hands buried in Teddy's
shaggy coat.

III

In her little red slippers Lela tiptoed to the door and
opened it cautiously. In Mamma's bedroom it was
still dark. The curtains were drawn close. But the
door squeaked a little, and from the bed there came
Frau Käte's sleepy voice: "Yes, my love?" answered by

an anxious query from the door: "Mamma, may I come in?" "Yes, darling."

Lela groped her way in the dim light towards the bed. The coverlet lifted to admit her, and like a chicken snuggling under its mother's wing she crept into the warm nest. Close to Mamma, who put an arm around her. Lela's tousled head lay on her mother's breast.

For a while there was silence. Then Lela asked:

"Was it a good party last night?"

"Yes, darling, very good."

"Mamma, were the other ladies as lovely as you?"

"Oh, much lovelier, darling."

"But you're lovely, Mamma, I know you are."

"I'm not lovely, Lela. I don't want to be beautiful. I'd rather be good."

Silence again for a little while, and then came Lela's hesitating assent:

"Yes, Mamma. . . ."

Outside in the street there was a clatter of horses' hoofs as a carriage rattled past. In the house everything was quiet. The boys were both at school, and the governess was away at church.

"Mamma, why does Fräulein Anna go to church every morning?"

"Because she's a Catholic."

"And why do we go only on Sunday mornings?"

"Because we're Protestants."

"Is Fräulein Anna gooder than we are?"

"No, we often go to church in the afternoons, on weekdays, don't we?"

"Yes . . . but, Mamma, it must be really lovely in church in the mornings while it's still dark, or in the evenings when the lights are lit."

"But God is always there, Lela, through the day as well."

"Yes, Mamma."

The fact that God was always there seemed a little uncanny to Lela. She would rather have been told that He was always in the Catholic church, which was becoming an obsession with her. It was for her the most exciting place in Dünheim. This small and pretty town in the South of Germany was clustered round the new castle which the Grand Duke had built for himself. In front of the castle lay an open square with trees and boulevards around it, where a military band played at noon every day and leisured people strolled up and down. From this square a broad and handsome street led down towards a monument to a past Grand Duke, and skirting the Court Theatre and the old castle wound into the Old Town, a labyrinth of twisting little streets surrounding a market-place. But between the new castle and the part of the town where Manuela's parents lived, in one of the detached villas that stood in their own gardens, lay the Catholic church, directly on Lela's route towards the market-place. It was a strange building, quite round. The wall was completely blank, without a window, without any ornamentation. All that one could see were the thin lines dividing one block of stone from another. The whole erection was roofed over by a fairly shallow dome of cold grey slate, and looked much more like a gasometer or an enormous box than a church. And had it not been for a crucifix suspended over the humble entrance, one could have taken it for a kind of circus.

The inscrutability of that hostile wall, the blank and

shut-in aspect of the church, the mysterious, monotonous chanting and organ music that came echoing out of it— and with luck one could get a far-off glimpse of candles gleaming in its dusky depths—excited Lela's imagination. She was sure that Fräulein Anna would have been glad to take her in. But that was something that Mamma would never allow. Lela knew that well enough; she could tell from the tone in which Mamma answered whenever she asked questions about the round church.

When she went past it with Fräulein Anna she said insistently:

" Fräulein Anna, what is it like in there? "

" Oh, very, very lovely, Lela."

" Fräulein Anna, I'd terribly like to come with you sometime. . . ."

" But your mother wouldn't allow you. You have a church of your own, haven't you? "

" Yes, Fräulein Anna."

" Well, there you are. And if you're a good little girl, then your mother will take you on Sunday morning to the garrison church, won't she? "

" Yes, Fräulein Anna."

Silently they passed by and went home.

Just as they opened the garden gate, Papa's black stallion was led out and Papa, beside the horse, called: " Lela! Lela! " Lela rushed towards him, and he swung her high and set her on the horse. The Arab pranced a little, but Papa calmed him down and set himself to lead the horse across the street to the riding-school.

Lela was radiant. This was something she had always dreamed of. Fräulein Anna gasped: " Herr Major, what will Madam say? " But Meinhardis ignored her;

he was proud of his daughter, he was determined to show
her off.

The riding-school, a large, dim hall, was full of people.
Ladies in riding-habits were standing about, gentlemen
in uniform or in red coats were already mounted. And
suddenly, giving Lela a thrill of fearful joy, a band
struck up the Blue Danube Waltz. Somebody escorted
Lela to the gallery and set her on the step. As if the
horses had only been waiting for the signal, they began
to gallop round in time to the waltz music. The riders
ranged themselves in couples, to every gentleman a lady.
They passed quite close to Lela. There was Papa!
Oh, what a lovely lady was riding as his partner! She
had big white pearls in her ears, and a little tricorne hat
and bright golden hair and pink cheeks. Her habit was
a very tight fit, but it suited her very well, thought Lela.
And Papa didn't look as if he were riding at all—he was
laughing and talking to the lady, and it was as if he were
shaking with laughter, not with galloping, so airily was
he keeping time to the music. Both of them, Papa and
his partner, smiled a greeting to Lela every time they
passed. . . .

The horses began to steam. Their hoofs rang hollowly
on the boards of the track; their nostrils snorted. In
the middle of the course stood a man giving words of
command, in answer to which the lines of horses wheeled
and separated to rejoin each other again, describing
circles large and small, sometimes at a gallop, sometimes
at walking pace. Lela saw it all as if it were a dream.
And in the very heart of it rode Papa and the lovely,
lovely lady.

IV

At dinner-time everybody was very quiet. Ali and Berti supped their soup without saying a word. Papa was silent, and Ali glanced anxiously at his mother, who was trying to look unconcerned although her under-lip was trembling and she was eating nothing. Lela had a confused feeling that she was the culprit, that she had committed a crime. It had been glorious at the riding-school—but perhaps to go there was one of the things that one should not do, like going to the Catholic church? Dumbly she went upstairs without venturing to caress her mother as Alfred did after Papa had slammed the door behind him.

She fled instead to Laura, her dove. She thrust her small nose into Laura's wing-quills, and kissed the back of the bird's neck where there was a narrow ring of black feathers. Laura's red claws tightened round her little finger. Laura's feathers smelt warm and pleasant.

"Oh, Laura, how I love you!" she said in a small voice, and a large tear trickled down and dropped on the feathers.

Lela had a cloth in her hand and a blue apron tied round her, and the whole table was crowded with silver. Candlesticks that could be screwed and unscrewed, dishes with gaily ornamented rims, heaps and heaps of forks and spoons and knives. But she was not supposed to touch these; she had to clean a silver bread-basket which was of thin lattice-work that her small fingers could easily poke into. Most of the dishes had inscriptions on them; for instance: " To our dear comrade

Meinhardis in farewell from his Regiment," or: "First prize in Flat-racing, Anniversary Races of Ziethen," and then a date. From one of them Mamma read out: "To my beloved Kammerkatze."

"Mamma, what does that mean, Kammerkatze?"

"That was a horse of Papa's, a very good horse. But he has sold it."

"Why, Mamma?"

"Because Papa can't keep so many horses."

"Why can't he keep so many horses?"

"Because they cost too much. They eat too much."

"But it's only oats they eat, Mamma."

"Oh, darling, that's something you don't understand," and a deep sigh broke from Mamma's bosom.

Lela felt that further questions would be unwelcome. Silently she went on polishing the bread-basket. But there was soon something else to think about.

"We must pull out the table," said Mamma, and that meant excitement for everybody. The two halves of the dining-table had to be seized and simply pulled in opposite directions. Lela helped to pull and Flink barked. Flink was a brown dog of indefinite breed who loved to share in any unusual excitement, and to-day was an unusual occasion, for there was to be a dinner-party.

Board after board was inserted between the two divorced halves of the table; they were supported by props underneath, and Lela and Flink had to crawl in the darkness below the table to see that the props were secure. Then a green baize cover had to be spread over the whole, and then an enormously long, damask table-cloth.

Mamma and Lela went to the linen-cupboard. Lela

watched Mamma's hands as they counted the high
bundles of table-napkins. Mamma had long white
fingers; Lela loved Mamma's hands. If only Mamma
would let her hand stray for a moment over my head,
thought Lela, or inside the neck of my frock—it's
lovely when she does that. Papa does it too, of course,
but his hand is only tickly. She went on looking up
at her mother, thinking that it was dreadful of Mamma
to fasten her hair back so tight in the mornings. She
looked so much prettier with her hair loose and waved
a little. And visitors often came in the morning and
caught Mamma with her hair screwed tight, and that
was so unbearable that Lela had to hide herself, as if
it were her own hair that was badly dressed.

But at the moment Mamma had no time to spare
for Lela. Lela had to carry the table-napkins. Now
there was a clinking sound: Mamma was at the side-
board taking out the crystal bowls one after another.
These Lela was allowed to wipe, and after that Mamma
opened jars of preserves, and thick green fruits went
sliding into the glittering bowls. Looked at from
above they were quite ordinary, but when one peered
through the side where the crystal was cut, how
amusing! Now it was small golden plums, and now
red cherries in another bowl, and black nuts in the
next. One by one they were ranged on the table.
Now it was the big dish of fresh fruit; Lela was allowed
to open the paper bags. Oranges, bunches of grapes,
apples, nuts, almonds and dates—just like Christmas.

"Mamma, why do we have these for visitors and
never for ourselves?"

"Because we're poor people, darling."

Lela said nothing. But she thought: How sad it is

that we're poor people! And yet, how can we be poor? Papa has horses—poor people don't have horses. Mamma has ball-gowns—poor women don't have ball-gowns. And we have silver, too, and lots of table-cloths and a butler. . . .

"Mamma, do poor people always have a butler?"

"Don't be such a little stupid, my darling. You simply don't understand. . . ."

V

On that evening the children were sent earlier to bed. Mamma's bedroom became the ladies' dressing-room, presided over by the washerwoman in her Sunday best. And in Papa's room the gentlemen took off their coats. It was cold outside and the gentlemen's spurs clattered on the steps. Two temporary footmen had been taken on. They were pouring red and golden wine into glass decanters. Lela stole to the door and peeped in. The table looked like something out of a fairy-tale. Candles were burning in the silver candlesticks; flowers were lying scattered over the table without any water for their stalks. The candlelight made twinkling stars in the cut-glass so that it glittered. The footmen were putting on gloves and arranging in what order the dishes were to be offered. First to the Colonel's lady, and then to the next most important lady, and last of all to Mamma. Why must she be last of all? That offended Lela.

Beside each place lay a card with the name of the person who was to sit there. Papa had smoked two

thick cigars to the end before he got the cards right,
and Mamma was cross with him because they were
guests' cigars, and Papa said that if he worked so hard
for the guests he surely deserved the cigars. And
Mamma did not even *hint* that she had been working
all that day and the day before that and the whole
of last week for the guests, and had had only fried
potatoes and a poached egg for supper. Mamma
never said anything at all when Papa spoke to her
in that voice. But Papa always seemed offended afterwards and usually slammed the door very loudly.

The guests did not say much at first when they sat
down at table. From her cot Lela could hear only
the tinkling of many soup-spoons and an occasional
voice. Then the soup was removed, and little by little
conversation loudened, until by the end of the dinner
there was a great noise rising to a roar whenever the
footmen opened the door.

Lela began to get excited, for now Papa's groom,
Karl, would come up, bringing her some of the sweets.
This time it was a great pile of pink spun sugar that
he had saved for her; it looked like a fairy-tale sweet.
And ice-cream, yellow ice-cream with a funny taste.
Karl knelt on the floor beside her cot and held the
dish for her. She stood up and jumped with joy above
the high bars of her cot. The room was almost dark,
only a little light from the corridor shone in.

" What does that taste of, Karl? "

" That's maraschino," said Karl, and then he came
back again on tiptoe and brought her, with an air
of great secrecy, a thin, tall glass. . . . When she
began to drink out of it something prickled all up
her nose.

" What's this, Karl? "

" Champagne."

And Lela drank it off.

Then Karl stole away quickly, peering cautiously to right and left to make sure that no one had seen him. Madam herself was downstairs, of course, but Fräulein Anna, one might be sure, would hardly approve of what he had been doing.

Suddenly there was a terrific din; chairs were pushed back from the table, voices loudly exchanged compliments, and from the dining-room the guests trooped upstairs with flushed faces, heated and exhilarated, towards the coffee, the special cigars and the gaily hued liqueurs.

Frau Käte beamed on everybody, feeling like a general who has just survived a victorious battle. Meinhardis was a little too loud already—but his guests clapped him on the shoulder; good old Meinhardis, a witty fellow, a charming man. . . .

Lela had fallen fast asleep by the time the guests went upstairs. Later the carriages came rolling along, and all sorts of strange footmen arrived to fetch their masters home. One by one the guests took their leave; even Frau Käte had gone to bed, overcome by fatigue; but Meinhardis still sat on with a few of his cronies. The empty bottles had grown to whole batteries, and the ash-trays were filled to the brim. This was real comfort at last. They were at last alone and could say what they pleased. As usual, the main topics were women and horses. Meinhardis had to hear a good few compliments about Frau Käte, and he could not keep the smile off his face.

Lela was still fast asleep when the door was gently

opened. Nor did she waken up even when Papa took
her out of bed, blankets and all, and carried her upstairs.
She opened her eyes only to see a ring of pleasant gentlemen in green uniforms and red collars who were all
laughing.

One of them took her on his knee. Lela tucked her
bare feet underneath her and rubbed her eyes. They
all laughed. She was sitting on Captain Sellner's knee;
she knew him, she liked him, he had a very handsome
face.

"Give me a kiss," said Sellner, and she gave him
one.

But why did the others laugh so much? Now they
all wanted a kiss, but Lela turned from them. No,
not the others, she announced.

Next morning Mamma had migraine, so the house
had to be kept quiet. But at midday Papa brought
home a bunch of violets, and Mamma had to smile
although she had such a frightful headache.

VI

AMONG the bushes the children had erected an Indian
encampment. Papa's manœuvre tent had been pro-
fessionally pegged out with Karl's help, and a few
neighbouring children had arrived in full war-paint.
Berti was Winnetou, with an enormous head-dress and
a tomahawk in his girdle; even Ali, although he was
nearly sixteen, had joined the game, but probably only
because Lela had begged him to. Lela herself was
also decked out with a cock's feather in her hair,
fastened down by a brow band; she was the squaw,

and she had to stay at home and cook while the men
went off on the war-path, rushing off with wild shrieks
to return in triumph bringing scalps and hunting
trophies. Lela sat forlorn in the tent. One of the
boys, Berti's friend, Gerhard, had long Indian trousers
fringed all down the side; he looked imposing and
terrible. Lela felt sad because she was only a squaw.
Once more she brooded over her bad luck in being a
girl and not being allowed to wear Indian trousers.
Why couldn't girls wear trousers, at least for
gymnastics? Fräulein Anna said that it wasn't respectable. But it must be wonderful, all the same, to
stride about like a man with a weapon at one's
belt. . . .

She started with fear. One of the Redskins had come
sneaking up to the tent and now stood grimacing
devilishly, holding out a long spear on which his prey
was spitted, Lela's Teddy. Lela shrieked, a frightful,
heart-rending, long-drawn shriek. But Ali appeared in
the nick of time, seized the unwitting offender, tore
Teddy from him, bleeding sawdust, cuffed the Redskin
violently over the head, and took the trembling, screaming Lela in his arms.

The shrieks had alarmed the household; Mother and
Fräulein Anna were already on the spot.

"It's nothing to worry about, Lela," said Fräulein
Anna soothingly. "We'll soon sew him up again."

But Lela, tortured by this suggestion, only screamed
the louder:

"Not sew him, please, please, not sew him."

Mother gathered her in her arms.

"No, my darling," she said tenderly, "we shan't need
to do that at all. It'll grow together all by itself."

Yet Ali and Mamma had both to sit beside Lela's bed until she had fallen asleep. Even in her sleep she was still trembling and twitching, and her small hand was firmly closed over Teddy's wound. When she was fast asleep, Ali secretly drew the creature out, and Mamma mended the damage by the light of the lamp. Not until Teddy, somewhat less corpulent because of his great loss of blood, was restored to his place on Lela's breast could Ali betake himself to his own bed with a clear conscience.

The brother and sister did not resemble each other. Lela was more like her father, while Ali, clever, quiet Ali, was fairer and more like his mother's people. None the less Ali belonged to Lela. He was always there when Lela needed him. Berti was still a regular boy; he pulled Lela by the scanty pigtail that was a big enough nuisance to her in any case, he hid her Snookies and stole the plates from her dolls' kitchen to feed his white mice in.

"Berti, you're not to do that," wept Manuela. "For now Laura won't eat out of them; she thinks white mice leave a bad smell!"

But Ali always turned up in the nick of time, found the Snookies and removed the dolls' plates from Berti. He sawed away and contrived playthings for Lela; two tiny sets of dolls' chairs magically evolved from the wish-bones of Pöchliner geese. He set Lela on his bicycle and wheeled her round the garden. That was the most heavenly, and at the same time the most terrifying experience Lela could imagine. Her legs dangled on either side of the bicycle, and she had to bend far forward to grasp the handle-bar. Often enough she shook so much that she nearly fell, but

Ali's large, boyish hand was always there to hold her
firm.

VII

MAMMA's birthday. One could feel it approaching.
It was in May that Mamma was born. Long before
the day came Lela was absent-minded, for whenever
Mamma asked her a question she had to think of her
great secret, the gift she was to present to Mamma, and
of how she must not betray it. Because it was to be
a surprise. . . . Her fear of betraying it made her in-
capable of answering a word. Every time that Mamma
came into the nursery, Lela cried: " Shut your eyes! "
Mamma mustn't look until the embroidery was hidden
from sight. "Now it's all right," and Mamma
obediently opened her eyes again.

As soon as Mamma went out of the room the toilet-
mat reappeared. A white mat, on which garlands of
roses were traced in pencil. Lela had gleaming strands
of soft green silk to make the leaves with, and pale
pink and red silk for the flowers. It was frightfully
difficult to get the silk thread into the eye of the needle,
for the eye was small and the silk would untwist and
fray out, and then one had to lick it and twist it up
again between thumb and forefinger. But that always
made the thread rather dirty. Lela sighed profoundly and
grew quite hot with the effort. Yet the day did dawn
at last. From Pöchlin there had arrived a huge parcel
with all kinds of gorgeous things from Grandmamma,
and in the drawing-room a white cloth was spread over

the middle table, on which stood a cake covered with candles—a frightful lot of candles. Mamma had to lie long in bed that morning. The gifts were not to be presented until Papa came back from duty. Flowers upon flowers kept coming in; a whole lilac bush in a pot, gay tulips and anemones. The whole regiment sent its congratulations. Papa had bought some lovely presents—something silver, and something quite small in a case: a ring with a little star of turquoises. Lela's mat, washed and smoothly ironed, lay at the very front. Ali had made a box, and Berti had written a marvellous greeting: a large, double sheet of paper with flowers and angels on it, and in the middle, in fine copperplate handwriting, very unlike Berti's usual scrawl, an inscription wishing Mamma many happy returns. It looked like an important proclamation, and underneath it was written: "From your devoted and grateful son, Bertram."

All at once a troop of soldiers filed into the garden. They ranged themselves in a circle, the bandmaster in the middle, and Papa went into Mamma's bedroom with a bouquet and kissed her, Lela behind him in a white frock with a pink sash, and the two boys in new sailor suits, somewhat embarrassed by the ceremonial. To the strains of the birthday music, Mamma was conducted to her table of presents. She embraced all her family, and her cheeks were quite red, and then ever so many visitors arrived to congratulate her. And Fräulein Anna could not find enough flower-vases. Lela was allowed to cut the cake and take some out to the bandsmen in the garden, while Ali carried the glasses and Berti the wine. In the kitchen a goose from Pöchlin was roasting. And Papa's fingers were all dusty because he had brought up from the cellar a very old bottle of wine, which had to be left unwiped to show that it was genuinely old.

On her birthday everyone had to be very kind to Mamma. And the whole house was fragrant with roses and lilac and wax candles and cakes. And one could run to Mamma at any time, for this was a day on which she was forbidden to do any work. No darning or going into the kitchen or adding up bills; Mamma must only sit on the sofa and look pretty. And Lela swarmed into her lap and put both arms tight round her neck:

" Mamma, Mamma, Mamma, I love you terribly! "

" Ali, give me a ride on your foot," begged Manuela.

Ali knew that that was one of Lela's greatest joys, to sit on his free ankle when his legs were crossed and be swung up and down. But on this occasion he was preoccupied.

" I'd rather not, Lela. I have a headache," he said, and Lela circled round him like a small dog, suspecting something wrong.

Nor did he want to eat his dinner. Nor to go out, or play football. He went to bed instead. And there he stayed for three long days, with leeches applied to him. Lela felt sick to see them; nasty black things with Ali's blood inside.

" What are they for, Mamma? "

Mamma took Lela by the hand. Ali was lying in bed, quite rigid, but his eyes turned to the door. He asked Lela as she was sitting in her mother's lap:

" Is that the teacher? "

" What? " Didn't Ali know that it was Mamma?

Lela hid shyly in her mother's bosom, which was heaving with tearless sobs.

That very night Ali died.

Lela was awakened very early next morning. Berti was standing half-naked in the bright sunshine, weeping soundlessly to himself, and Lela could see the tears running down one after another. His face was hardly distorted at all; he merely forgot to put on his clothes, and stood there crying and crying.

Fräulein Anna combing Lela's hair, told her that Ali was now in heaven.

" Yes," was Manuela's sole comment, and no emotion stirred within her. She felt no sorrow. Only everything in the house seemed different. The front door-bell kept ringing; black-clad ladies rustled into Mamma's room, where everything was very quiet. Many of these visitors laid a hand on Lela's head. " Poor little thing, so young for such a trial! " Lela tried to put on a sad face, for she began to realize that she was being pitied. But it was all very exciting and interesting. Telegrams and flowers kept arriving, and relations, and carriages with nodding laurel trees; the whole house smelt like a florist's shop. The door-bell was tied up, for its ringing worried Mamma.

" Come and see Ali," said someone, and Lela stood beside a large box in which Ali was sleeping. But the room was quite strange, and so was Ali. He had flowers in his hand, and a crucifix; candles were burning, and there were green plants everywhere, just like a wood. It was lovely. Perhaps the Catholic church was something like that.

All the people were crying. Lela was ashamed

because she could not cry. And it was only when she heard her mother sobbing that she rushed to her and clung to her skirt.

"Now we have no Ali any more," said Mamma.

And only then did a violent grief well up in the child's heart.

"Mamma, Mamma," she screamed, "Mamma, you mustn't cry!"

For that was the really unbearable thing, that Mamma was crying. That was what made it seem dreadful that Ali was dead. . . .

"Come, take a last look at him," said Mamma. But Lela trembled—that wasn't Ali; no, she didn't want to look at that Ali.

In the morning he was to be carried away. Lela stood at the window and saw that Ali's schoolfellows were standing ranked along the street and in the garden, like soldiers. She felt proud because they were there. Now they were all standing round the bier, the officers of the regiment, each quite motionless in parade uniform, a helmet with plumes in one arm and hands folded over the sabre-hilt. Just like monuments, thought Lela. Mamma was sitting among a lot of women, invisible behind a black veil. The pastor said comforting words to Mamma, which Lela only half understood—but then the music started to play, long-drawn-out and sorrowful, and at last the child began to cry, violently and unceasingly.

Then came the daily visits to the graveside. The cemetery terrified Lela. It was her task to fetch water from the well to besprinkle the flowers on Ali's grave. On the pump was a warning that the water was not for drinking. It was unclean water; it flowed past dead bodies, explained her mother when she asked about it.

Whenever Lela shut her eyes she could see the dead bodies lying in rows underground, a countless throng, stiff like Ali. "And later there's nothing left of them but some bones," said Berti.

But the worst thing of all was a rubbish-heap outside the cemetery on a low-lying piece of ground that was walled round like the cemetery itself. That was where Lela had to carry the withered wreaths while Mamma stayed behind to pray alone at the grave. This rubbish-heap was always smoking, and for the child it was something neither alive nor dead. The decaying stench of all these bouquets with their satin ribbons, the rusty wires, the slimy brown flowers, with here and there a scrap of crape, a tin basket, a broken vase, made Manuela feel even more panic-stricken than did the well-tended rows of graves under which she knew the dead bodies were lying. She was always glad to get back to Ali's grave, where her mother was either sitting on a bench gazing quietly into vacancy or clearing the withered ivy-leaves from the turf.

It was by her brother's headstone that the little Manuela got her first lessons in reading. She was distressed because she could not read the inscriptions on all the graves, for she needed some occupation during the long hours that her mother, deeply abstracted, spent with Ali. And so she learned to read, and her mother, preoccupied by memories, was hardly aware of the fact.

Frau Käte had changed since Ali's death. Lela's hungry little heart felt the change, and shrank in upon itself every time she saw her mother sitting there, a brooding, sorrowful woman, remote from the living, as if at home in a world that terrified Manuela.

And every evening when the sun set and it was time to go home, she could hear Mamma saying with gentle pathos: "Good night, my boy," as if she were speaking to someone who was listening. . . .

PART TWO

I

"Yes, my dear Meinhardis, it's a bad business."

The old Colonel flicked the ash from his fat cigar, leaned back in his chair and regarded the man opposite him. Meinhardis was also puffing clouds of thick smoke; he blinked a little and stared out of the window to avoid looking his commander in the face. He did not want the Colonel to see what his feelings were. It was decent enough of the old man to have sent for him to tell him privately about his transfer.

"Mühlberg's a rotten garrison," went on the Colonel. "The sweepings of the whole German Army, so to speak. A bunch of criminals, that's what they are. Well, I suppose they need someone there who knows how to keep them in order. And that's why they hit on you. A great honour, of course; and promotion and more pay and all that—but not exactly agreeable. No."

Meinhardis made a gesture implying that orders were orders and must be obeyed. Colonel von Merkel went on:

"The men there are supposed to have been playing up a bit, misbehaving themselves all over the place. But whenever a blackguard gets into trouble they send him to a frontier garrison—it's the same old story. You won't have an easy time of it, old exotic; you have my sympathy. But you'll soon knock the fellows into shape."

Meinhardis felt that he was being dismissed; he rose to go.

"Many thanks, sir . . . it was very kind of you . . .

these things will happen . . . and it might have been
worse. I'd better go home now . . . to tell my wife
. . . women take these things . . . oh, well, no use being
sentimental."

His spurs clicked as he saluted, but the older man
seized his right hand and shook it heartily.

"Keep a stout heart, Meinhardis, and you'll be all
right. . . ."

Outside the door Meinhardis buckled on his sabre
and, catching sight of himself in a looking-glass, pulled
his collar straight. Soon he wouldn't have any more
red collars; he would have to get into a new uniform,
light blue and white. Ridiculous. White collars always
got filthy, and to run round in light blue after being
accustomed to the serviceable dark green would be a
trial. Fancy having to go riding in light blue—
grotesque, he thought, ill-humouredly. And the new
uniform would certainly be much dearer. No doubt
about it. And then, the business of moving . . . Poor
Käte.

He bought a large armful of marguerites and cornflowers from a flower-seller: Käte liked these, they
reminded her of Pöchlin.

But Frau Käte accepted quietly enough the not unexpected news of the transfer, as one accepts the inevitable. She knew very well what it meant to be settled in
a town like Mühlberg, which not so long ago had been
an enemy stronghold. She, too, had a vague intuition
that hard times lay ahead, but she did not want to make
her husband's heart heavier than need be. Besides, she
had still plenty of time: he would have to go on first
and find a house. And in any case, she was wrapped
in a curious serenity, as if she were in a kind of trance.

She went to church much oftener than she had ever done; she always went alone and came back with an expression of profound peace; her eyes were as if turned inwards upon some invisible world. That made her patient, kind and almost cheerful. In the most matter-of-fact way she set about breaking up the household. Silently, like a shadow, the small Lela followed her to and fro.

The last day came. Frau Käte wandered meditatively from room to room. Before the window where Ali's desk had stood she paused for a long time, and then Lela observed her taking her hat and gloves and a few flowers she had bought that morning.

"Mamma, shall I come with you to Ali?" asked Lela, who knew what these preparations meant; but Frau Käte bent down and looked into the child's eyes, for the first time maintaining an air of complete gravity without attempting to give her daughter a tender smile. Seriously she said:

"No, Lela. To-day I must go quite alone—I have to bid Ali good-bye. Ali will have to stay here alone—all alone—without me."

Lela followed her to the garden gate and watched her mother walking quickly and decisively down the street, as if she knew that someone was waiting for her.

Lela found it impossible to play any more that day. She took Flink by the collar and laid his head in her bosom. A strange, sad happiness rose within her. To-day Mamma had spoken to her as if she were grown up—it was a secret between them, and Lela would never tell it to anybody in the world.

II

In front of the station at Mühlberg Lela was standing, her right hand firmly held by Mamma. But Mamma was speaking to Papa, and no one was really attending to Lela. She looked around her. What a confusion there was here! And what a swarm of soldiers! Papa couldn't say more than two words without having to stop and salute somebody. Soldiers were coming and going everywhere. If they were ordinary soldiers they stood to attention before Papa, holding their hands stiffly by their sides, and could not go on until Papa dismissed them. If they were officers they raised their hands to their caps. Even Mamma seemed to find it a strain on her nerves; she looked pale and fagged.

"What's happening here to-day?" she asked.

"Nothing," said Meinhardis. "There are only twenty-four cavalry regiments stationed here, not to mention Bavarians, infantry, artillery and sappers."

Papa was really not Papa at all in that new uniform. Lela tried to ignore it, feeling that she ought not to mention it, but her eyes kept turning back to that white collar.

A landau drove up with a soldier on the box holding the reins, and his uniform, too, was light blue and white. The trunks were hoisted up; the horses set off in a bee-line for a great wall with grass growing on top of it. The entrance into the wall looked like a tunnel.

Lela was scared. "What's that, Papa?"

"The wall of the fort. Mühlberg is a fortress, you see."

"But why does the tunnel bend round? Why doesn't

it go straight through? And why is it so dark that it
has to be lit in the daytime?"

"So that nothing could happen if the French were to
come and shoot their cannon into it."

Lela's eyes widened. There was so much noise in the
tunnel that she could not hear herself speak.

Mamma laid a hand on her knee.

"Don't worry, darling—the French won't come."

Did Mamma say that just to comfort her? Did she
really mean it? When grown-ups spoke in that tone of
voice to children, one never knew. But to disbelieve
what one was told was "rude." . . . However, the child
assured herself at last, Papa was there simply and solely
to see that the French didn't come.

III

THE great wall that had scared Lela so much enclosed
the whole town. There was a moat beneath it, and then
more thick walls and more moats. A broad river
formed a natural protection for the gigantic stronghold.
In the walls were casements, vaults with ammunition
and guns, and vaults that could hold many soldiers.
They were quite dark inside, except for tiny shafts of
light from narrow embrasures, and they smelt musty
and damp. The town was so firmly enclosed that it
could not expand. Ground was dear; the streets were
narrow, the houses huddled and tall. A forest of round
chimney-stacks rose from the countless stoves, straight,
crooked and spiral stacks. The smoke that issued from
them was yellowish and left a layer of soot on all the
roofs, window-sills and pavements. As if it had been

compressed and heightened by the crowding houses
around it, a Gothic cathedral reared itself from the very
middle of the sea of buildings; its spire soared up like
a point into the blue sky.

Meinhardis had hunted all over the town for a house.
But every house was dark and narrow, with all the
windows looking out on walls. And Käte had insisted:
"I must have a bit of sky to look at." As for gardens,
there was not a single garden in the whole of Mühlberg.
Yet one day he discovered a few trees behind a wall
just off the main street, opposite the cathedral. A large,
locked carriage-gate made a break in the blank and
hostile wall, and beside it was a smaller entry with a
bell-handle for pulling and "Concierge" inscribed
upon it.

This house, it appeared, was a private palace dating
back to before the war of 1870, which had interrupted
the building of it. But one wing and a part of the
middle block were still standing, enclosing a wide courtyard, while the unbuilt side allowed space for several
tall trees. An old lady of legendary age lived in the
upper storey of the long wing, and refused even to see
or communicate with an enemy officer, far less to let
the lower storey to him.

Meinhardis had recourse to guile. He doffed his
uniform and called on the old Frenchwoman in his
civilian clothes, merrily twirling his moustache. His
eyes sparkled with glee over this inroad into the enemy's
stronghold, which he intended to capture by his excellent
French, his personal charm and the fairly high rent he
proposed to pay. And indeed the stiff old lady was
taken by surprise. She had never thought that a
"Prussien" could be so courteous, such an amiable

payer of compliments, such a fine-mannered gentleman.
Yet it seemed that she could not digest her defeat after
all, for she went off to France, leaving the upper storey
empty and the Meinhardis family in possession of the
lower.

But she left also " le concierge," Monsieur Girod. He
lived in a small pentagonal lodge built against the wall
of the courtyard between the large carriage entrance
and the small door. Monsieur Girod was anything but
handsome. He had a pointed little beard and a *képi*,
bushy eyebrows and a ferocious glare. He was hardly
ever seen without an old broom in his hand, and Lela
thought that he looked like the husband of the witch
in " Hänsel and Gretel." He never spoke without scold-
ing. His French abuse was incomprehensible to Lela,
but that did not make her fear him any the less. And
Monsieur Girod had occasion to swear from the very
first, for Meinhardis wanted him to leave the carriage
entrance unlocked by day to let the horses pass out and
in to a stable that had been discovered among the out-
buildings. But Monsieur Girod was sixty years old.
Since the surrender of Mühlberg to the Prussians that
gate had not been opened; its bolts and hinges were
rusty and could not be oiled; the Prussian officer and his
attendant could sit their tall horses in front of it and
wait in the street for just so long as Monsieur Girod
saw fit.

Monsieur Girod declared war. All alone in his lodge,
with his broomstick grasped firmly in one hand, he
continued to wage war against this invasion of the
Prussian cavalry.

Lela had a room all to herself with two long windows
looking out on the street. The window-sills were of

white marble veined with grey. Her bed stood in an alcove, on one side of which a door led through a short lobby to a second door giving on the corridor, while on the other side another door, exactly like the first, opened into a cupboard recess. You thought you were going somewhere and found yourself instead in a narrow passage with hooks for clothes on the walls. The passage actually turned round a corner to the right into absolute darkness, but there was no way out.

The whole building was full of such secret cupboards and recesses. You might think that an ordinary door led somewhere and find yourself brought up against a row of shelves for crockery or linen; and if you opened a door hidden by wallpaper, thinking that it gave access merely to a cupboard, you discovered a winding passage that led right through the house into a glass-roofed courtyard.

The living-rooms communicated one with the other, so that when you opened the first door you could see all seven rooms at once, just as in an old castle.

The first room was richly decorated with stucco. Golden angels arched their wings in the rounded corners. Manuela stood on tiptoe and peered over the high ledge of the marble mantelpiece into the mirror. Above her head shone a bronze chandelier with its candles, but she could see a hundred chandeliers and twenty times a hundred glowing candles because there was another fireplace with another tall, gold-framed mirror above it at the other end of the room. Manuela found it difficult to think of being " at home " in a room like that. With a sigh she took her French grammar from under her arm, lay down in front of the log fire, opened the book and stared into the red glow.

She saw little of Berti in these days. But she was fully occupied with herself and her own experiences. After having had only private lessons in Dünheim, she was now attending a school with all the other children of the town. Many of the little girls in this frontier region were French, and looked quite different from all the children she had previously known. But that was just what interested Manuela, and their names, too, sounded interesting and beautiful. In front of her, to one side, sat Jeanne Amos, who had dark red hair hanging loose with a large, gleaming white bow of satin ribbon in it: beside her sat Andréa, whose hair was cut short and stuck out rebelliously. Andréa had a very thin neck and frail arms, and wore rings and bracelets. Amélie, on the other hand, looked like a dirty, untidy boy; her black hair hung in strands over her face, covering her enormous grey eyes. But Lela liked her almost best of all, and yearned to ask her a question which she did not yet dare to put. Were all the French very sad because the Germans had conquered them? Lela felt that it was her duty to be very nice to the little French girls, because it must be a dreadful feeling to know that one was conquered. Berti, when she asked him for his opinion, said: "Not a bit of it, they're all much too cheeky. Besides, it was so long ago. . . ."

However, he went on to expound, there might, of course, be another war at any time, just like 1870, and in that case all women and girls would have to clear out of the town within twenty-four hours. Only the men would be allowed to stay.

Lela, with round eyes, asked:

"Where should we go to?"

"Oh, anywhere. Only you couldn't stay here. Because

there would be shooting. Each of you would get a box,
like a soldier's box, and you would have to pack in it
whatever you needed."

Lela, with anxiety: "The Snookies, too?"

"I should think not," was Berti's decided reply.
"Only useful things, of course."

And next day in school there was actually a rehearsal
of "mobilization." When a bell rang in the playground
you had to stand up. The teacher counted: One, and
then you packed your books; Two, and you left your
seat; Three, and you put on your coat; Four, and you
formed up in twos by the door. You weren't to run
along the street, but to make for home in an orderly
manner at a double quick pace. And when you got
home you had to pack your box.

The thought of this box, and the question whether all
that she treasured would find room in it, obsessed Lela.
Whatever was left behind would probably be seized by
the French. And a soldier's box was so small! And
Mamma would want heaps of underclothes and stockings to go in it, and school-books and frocks and shoes.
At table she asked Papa, simply to find out how much
time she had to make up her mind:

"Papa, are the French coming soon?"

Papa laughed uproariously. Mamma said she
shouldn't ask such silly questions, there was no
likelihood of it at all. But Papa defended her.

"It's quite a sensible question, for war might well
break out. But war," he said, "isn't so terrible as you
think. I've been in a war myself, and it was great fun."

"Papa, have you really killed a Frenchman? Have
you jabbed one with a sword?"

"Oh, yes—but one has to do that kind of thing when

there's a war. They killed your Uncle Helmuth, you know—the red-shanks."

Yes, of course they had. In Papa's room Uncle's sash hung over the sofa, a silver sash with a tassel, and there was a patch of dried brown blood on it. And his helmet hung there too, and his dagger. Lela hardly ventured to go on asking "silly" questions. But there was one thing she could not understand; what would happen to Amélie, Andréa and Jeanne when the French began to shoot. Would they have to go too, and where would they go? Or would they be killed on the spot by the Germans?

"Rubbish," said Berti. No German waged war on women and children. . . .

None the less Manuela felt that she had to be extra nice to Amélie, Andréa and Jeanne.

She invited them all to tea, which seemed to Meinhardis a little uncalled-for. This time it was Mamma who defended Lela. Her daughter should invite whom she pleased. And Mamma was very kind to Lela's little friends, who were at first somewhat scared by the military caps, sabres, riding-whips and officers' mantles that hung all over the cloak-room.

Amélie in especial had to come again and again. It was she who helped Lela to construct her fairy-tale. For Lela wanted to have a fairy-tale, a *real* fairy-tale, not one merely written in a book without a single picture to look at, but a fairy-tale of her very own making. In her toy-box there were ever so many little dolls, and Amélie had a knack of producing all kinds of marvellous scraps of stuff to dress them in, gorgeous stuffs such as Lela had never seen before: white and silver brocades, silk ribbons with roses and garlands, veils and laces, gauze

—bright green for a Nixie, thick red satin for a royal train, white silk for a fairy, tulle for elves; minute bits of fur, tiny feathers both green and turquoise blue, yes, even starry spangles for a diadem. And all of it, every bit of it, came from clothes belonging to Amélie's Mamma. Lela longed to see Amélie's Mamma even once, but Amélie never spoke about her, and Lela did not venture to say a word. With a burning face she sat there dressing her dolls. A little table and chairs, some of them a still-surviving legacy from poor Ali, were fished out, and in the darkest recess of the cupboard—to make it as mysterious as possible—a fairy palace was set up. The whole scene was supposed to represent a Round Table of fairy knights, a royal banquet. But it was not easy to arrange the banquet; there were far too many elves and too few princes, not to mention the fact that it all had to be done in the dark.

Amélie, however, thought of a device. Next time they met at school she brought Lela a small round roll of thread dipped in wax as thick as a pencil, rose-coloured and fragrant. It smells like something Catholic, thought Lela. The two children cut it into tiny candles, which they ranged on the table of the fairy king.

The candles burned bravely and crackled a little. The effect was stately and beautiful, certainly much more beautiful than anything in the Catholic church; and in the flickering light the brocade and the silk shimmered and the red satin of the king's mantle glowed duskily.

Long after Amélie had gone home, Lela was still sitting devoutly in the closed cupboard regarding all this gorgeousness when Sofie, the chubby servant-girl

with red arms and a snub nose, sniffed the candle reek
and suspiciously opened the cupboard door. Goodness,
how she screamed! And then, pushing the trembling,
shrieking Lela against the wall, she fell upon the Round
Table, blew out the candles and shouted:

"You'll set the house on fire, you naughty girl! I'll
tell the mistress at once, and then you'll hear about
it. . . ."

One after the other she snatched the dolls out.

"And just look at the trash they're got up in—downright heathenish. Half-naked, all of them! Aren't you
ashamed of yourself? But you've got a bad conscience
all right, that's why you've crept into the sinful darkness
with them where nobody could see you. . . ."

Lela gaped at her as if petrified. She did not shed
a single tear. Mamma would have understood—but
Mamma was not at home; she had been invited out.

Dumbly Lela let herself be put to bed. She could
not eat any supper, otherwise she seemed unaffected. It
was only when her room was dark and she lay thinking
of the ruined chaos behind the cupboard door that she
began to weep. Quietly, without a sob, without a sound,
tear after tear rolled down on her pillow. And then all
at once Mamma's sweet-smelling hand was on her hair,
and arms enfolded her, and she could press her head
on Mamma's bosom and kiss Mamma's soft face with
her trembling lips. It was so pleasant to be able to cry
like that, and she had to go on crying because it was
so comforting; and, indeed, to be able to cry was much
more satisfying than all the fairy dolls in the cupboard.

IV

THE fairy-tale faded and reality broke in again.
School was always there, and now something happened
that gave Lela much to think about. It was only a
few days later that Berti, showing himself uncommonly
chivalrous, presented a large piece of chocolate to Lela
and drew her into a corner of the dark corridor.

"I say, Lel, I want you to do something for me "—
and then quickly: "Do you know Eva von Mahlsdorf
who goes to your school? "

Lela tried to remember. Yes, she knew the girl.
A tall, ash-blonde girl with long hair and a red tammy.

"Yes, what about her? "

"Well, when you see her give her my best regards.
Will you? "

Lela was willing enough. That was quite easy! Eva
was in a much higher class than herself, of course; she
was one of the "big girls"; but they all played during
the interval in the same playground, so that she saw
Eva every day.

"Thanks, Lel. That's nice of you. And will you
keep an eye on her to see what kind of a face she
makes when you say 'my brother Bert' . . . ? "

Lela promised. That wasn't difficult, and in any
case she was glad to do something for Bert. She had
a kind of admiration for her elder brother, especially
now that Ali was dead and Berti had stopped tormenting her. He was very fair, with clear blue eyes. He
had a winning smile and people took to him readily.
The servants and grooms loved him, and so did his

schoolfellows and his relations. Lela had often to submit to hearing people say: "Oh, Berti is such a pleasant child . . ." and then, only after a long pause, "and so is Lela. . . ." She felt that her dark hair and eyes were in some way inferior to the fairness of her brother. So she was all the happier to be able now to do him what was obviously a great service.

Next day her eagerness to fulfil her mission sent her much too early to school. In her first lesson she was inattentive; in her second she muffed every question. But then at long last the bell rang for the interval, and, forgetting her lunch, she rushed out and posted herself opposite the door from which the girls of the other classes issued.

The stream poured out past her; she grew quite giddy watching. There came Eva, at last, shaking her fair hair and laughing—oh, how she was laughing! She had a girl on either arm, and she seemed to be telling them something very funny, for they were all bursting with laughter, and then they put their heads together and whispered. Lela suddenly felt that she was frightfully ugly. Her face seemed yellow, her legs too thin, her straight frock so shabby, her hands so bony, and her black pinafore hideous. She stood where she was, and she went on standing . . . until the interval came to an end and the playground was empty.

Berti was waiting for her at home, in the very doorway.

"Did you tell her?"

"No—to-morrow . . ." and she pushed him quickly aside.

For the whole of that day she was restless,

gazed at herself in the glass and examined her face.
No, she was certainly not pretty. Her skin was
naturally pale, her neck scraggy; the hanging frock
was too awful. If she could only wear trousers like
Berti she would feel more assured. Sometimes
Mamma allowed her to do gymnastics in dark blue
knickerbockers, and then she felt free and merry. If
she could only wear them at school! Then she would
simply go up to Eva and make a bow and offer to
carry her school books, and jump over a fence while
Eva was looking, or climb up a tree and call down
to her; then she would ask her for a dance and send
her flowers. . . . But that was something she *could* at
least do, it dawned on Lela. Yet as soon as she considered it from a practical view-point there seemed
to be insuperable difficulties. Where could she get the
flowers? Money she had, but how to escape from the
house, buy flowers and then hide them? . . . And
would she have the courage? . . . People would laugh
at her! Oh, if they only knew . . . surely then they
wouldn't laugh.

In one of the long dark corridors some gymnastic
apparatus had been rigged up for the use of both
children. There was a trapeze bar hanging from two
ropes, and Manuela could easily reach it and swing
herself up on it. She circled it in the air and let herself hang by the knees with her head down, flying
back and forward; and away beneath her she saw an
enormous audience, and she was swinging high in a
circus and all the limelights were on her and the band
played a sustained chord while she did the Grand Loop,
and sounded a flourish when she leapt off in a lofty
curve to land on the mat with bent knees and with a

final spring stood upright. Then there was a storm
of wild applause, and Manuela, who was, of course, a
man, in close-fitting silk tights, bowed to the audience
with a smile as if to say: Don't mention it, that was
nothing. . . .

V

NEXT morning came. Lela kept herself well in hand
during the long interval; arm-in-arm with Jeanne Amos
she drifted round the playground, peacefully eating
her bread and butter as if nothing had happened or was
likely to happen. She stole glances at Eva, who had
come slowly out of the door with an apple in one
hand and a book that she was reading in the other.
Now Eva was leaning against the wall; standing on
one leg, her other leg drawn up, she saw and heard
nothing; she was reading her book and taking an
occasional bite from her apple. Every time Lela
passed her she had palpitations. When other children
ran across her path and blocked her view of Eva she felt
irritable. Eva had on a red frock with a short pleated
skirt and a white boyish collar. As she read, her soft,
fair hair fell over her face; it was loose hair that waved
without being curly. Her hands were white and her
fingers pointed.

Lela knew which way Eva went home. When
twelve o'clock rang she carried out her plan and was
the very first girl to rush out of the school. Not to
her own home, for she turned to the right round a
corner and ran on for a bit till she came to a broad
house entrance that she had noted. There she pulled

the ribbon from her pigtail and undid it, as if it had
loosened itself while she was running, for she hated
to have her hair screwed up. She pitched her school-
bag on the ground and rumpled her hair with both
hands; then she shook herself like a dog shaking himself to rights after a romp and rammed on her sailor
cap again.

Now she could look out for Eva, who actually came
in sight, walking alone and swinging her school-bag.
Lela's heart rose into her throat. But she plucked up
courage to advance and asked Eva shyly: "May I
carry your bag for you?" She blushed as she spoke,
and felt hot. Without looking at Eva she seized the
school-bag and walked beside her.

Eva laughed.

"Where have you sprung from? Have you really
been waiting for me?" she asked, obviously flattered.

Lela could only nod. Eva's bag was heavy.

"There you are," said Eva, "that's what you get.
Why have you got a craze on me? It'll only be a fag
to you."

"I haven't got a craze on you at all," said Lela
defiantly.

"Oh? Well, let's see . . ." Eva made a side-step,
bringing Lela between her and the wall, then she
forced her against the wall, putting her hands on Lela's
shoulders and thrusting her backwards until her back
was against the house.

Lela had a school-bag in either hand and could do
nothing. Slowly Eva ran her hands up Lela's throat
and played with her ears. It was the first time that
Lela had ever been at anyone's mercy, and tears of
fright stood in her eyes.

"Look at me! Look me straight in the eye!"

Instead of doing so Lela flung the bags to the ground in raging shame and seized Eva's arms.

"Oh, you're going to stand up to me, are you?" laughed Eva. "That would be a fine how-do-you-do!" and she gave her a light cuff on the ear. "You wild Red Indian. . . ."

Lela felt her knees weakening. But Eva suddenly let her go.

"All right, if you won't, you won't. I can get on well enough without you, my dear." She picked up her school-bag and turned to go. "Adieu," she called, but Lela could not return this far from friendly salutation because something was tightening in her throat.

Now she had spoilt everything. Now Eva would never, never speak to her again. Why had she been so stupid? Brooding, with hanging head, her eyes on the ground, she trotted slowly home.

Of course Berti was on the look-out for her. Berti was very tall for his fourteen years. Although Lela was the biggest girl in her own class, she always felt small beside Berti.

"Well, have you spoken to her? What happened?" he asked quickly in a low voice, following her to her room.

Manuela quietly deposited her bag.

"Have you really got a craze on her?"

Bert was insulted.

"A craze!—that's what girls do—I'm an admirer of hers."

Lela said calmly: "Indeed . . ." and relapsed into silence. Not another word could he get out of her, and he finished up by calling her a sulky, stupid thing

who understood nothing, and it would be the last time
he ever told her anything.

The door slammed behind him. Lela remained
curiously unaffected. Usually when she had a row with
Berti she wept her heart out, but to-day something made
it all different.

She was almost cheerful as she went in to dinner.

VI

"THIS is going to be difficult," said Karl the groom,
coming into Lela's room with a box of tools and gazing
out at the street.

"What is it, Karl?"

Although Lela would have preferred to be alone just
then, best of all to retire into the dark cupboard where
her fairy-tale had once glimmered, and there, holding
her hands over her ears, to think of Eva and Eva's
hands, she did not mind being disturbed.

"Oh, the flagstaff has to be rigged up at this window.
And it's fairly long. And the window's not very high."

Thoughtfully he inspected the wall beneath the
window-sill.

Manuela was delighted to hear it. Flags always
meant sprees of some kind. And this time it was to
be a grand celebration: the Kaiser was coming. And
there would be a school holiday with flags everywhere
and military music and parades, and Papa would wear
his helmet with the plume, which she would be
allowed to comb, and the bells would ring, all the
marvellous bells in the cathedral.

Even the "Mutte" would be rung! The "Mutte" was a very old bell, huge and thick, and because it was cracked it was rung only on very rare and very grand occasions. And even then it was rung all by itself, and its chimes came at long intervals because they took a long time to sound and die away. One had to wait a long time before the next one sounded.

Karl was hammering iron staples into the wall below the window-sill. He laughed as he hammered.

"What are you laughing at, Karl?"

"I was just thinking that the Frenchmen won't be too pleased to see the Prussian flag hanging here, the black-and-white. If it were even the German flag——"

Apparently that reflection had occurred to Frau Käte too, for she hastily stitched together a broad band of black and white and red stripes as a pendant to the Prussian flag. The flagstaff was also black and white and had a golden point at the top.

"You won't be able to shut the window quite close to-night, because the staff will be there. . . ."

"Oh, that doesn't matter, Karl." Manuela was proud because the flag was in her room, hanging from her window. She had indeed begged to have it, and now her wish was granted.

"Karl, will there be illuminations?"

"Of course. The mistress has bought a lot of candles. And there's to be a tattoo as well."

That afternoon preparations for the great event began in all the houses. Fir garlands were looped from window to window. Carpets were draped from balconies. Ladders were set up and decorations of black, white and red stuff nailed over the doors. In the large shop-windows stood busts of the Kaiser crowned with

wreaths of paper oak-leaves. Small flags were bought.
All the window-ledges were filled with candles.

Manuela had a burning candle in her hand and was
holding the bottom of another one in the flame to heat
it. When it was soft she pressed it down on the window-
sill and held it steady till it was cold. There were twelve
candles in each window. She could hardly wait for darkness to set in. The torch-light procession was to come
through the main street, right past the Meinhardis'
windows.

While Manuela and her mother were lighting the
candles along the whole house-front they could hear in
the distance shouts of command from the military tattoo.
Then the music began.

"Mamma," said Lela, peering anxiously down into
the dimly lit street, "there's a man down there who's
always looking up—he's been standing there all afternoon."

"Oh, that's probably a detective on the look-out."

"Is he watching us, Mamma?"

"No, stupid darling; he's watching to see that nothing
happens to the Kaiser, that nobody tries to make an
attempt on his life. Wherever the Kaiser goes he has
to be guarded. That's why Papa's here too—he has
to be on the look-out as well."

Lela felt sorry for the Kaiser. How dreadful it must
be! To think that whenever people wanted to entertain
him he was really scared all the time!

"Mamma, is the Kaiser scared?"

"No, darling. The Kaiser is never afraid. Only we
are afraid for him, afraid the wicked French might try
to hurt him."

In the distance there sounded a roll of drums. Then

for a moment absolute silence, and then a threefold
cheer, rising hoarsely into an uncanny roar: "Hurrah!
Hurrah! Hurrah!" and the band began to play a
march.

Down in the street people jostled and crowded. The
soldiers who had been drawn up along the kerb for a
long time now lowered their weapons and fended the
crowd back on to the pavement. The candles in the
windows flickered uncertainly. A damp evening wind
stirred the gay flags. There was a smell of green fir.
The people in the street grew still. The band came
nearer. Bandsmen on horses. The big trumpets flashed
brassy rays of light. The horses were wearing red tassels
at their ears and gold-embroidered caparisons. The
street was so narrow that the horses brushed the soldiers
in passing.

And now came an uncanny flare, red and yellow over
everything. Lela grasped her mother's hand: the
torches! A sea of flame. High aloft in their hands
hundreds of students were brandishing flaring staves,
and the flames spired over their heads in red tongues
of fire among clouds of thick black smoke. Side by side
they went, close packed, keeping step in their ranks.
The band vanished in the distance and now the bells
drowned every other sound. Slow to begin, they were
soon ringing out from every side.

Lela gazed up into her mother's face that looked unreal in the glow from the torches. Mother said something. She moved her lips. But Manuela could not
hear the words. She could only see Mamma's flickering eyes. She clutched her mother's hand as tight as she
could, as if she had to hold on to her and keep her from
being carried off. On the other side of the street the

walls of the houses were lit up by a glare that looked
as if some building were burning near by. One could
not help thinking: You might catch fire too. Why not?
Fire is impartial: it spares no one. For this once you
are safe, but next time . . .

In the streets the flaring torches illumined the people's
faces, and they looked wooden. One had the feeling
that the great celebration which had been planned had
somehow fallen a little flat. The bells stopped ringing
now, and from the neighbouring cathedral, from high up
in its tower, notes came floating, first softly, then swelling
louder. Borne by the wind over quiet roofs outlined by
the glow of torches and candle-light, over thousands
and thousands of listening people, there came the sound
of trumpets and trombones proclaiming with strength
and assurance:

> " I reverence the power of love
> Revealed to us in Christ. . . ."

Lela folded her hands. It was *her* hymn, her favourite hymn, the hymn that was played in the Evangelical
church and was now resounding from the tall Catholic
cathedral. As the last echoes of it died away the old
cracked " Mutte " began its awesome clang, solemn and
uncanny.

The candles on the window-ledges flickered out: the
street grew darker. " Now they're throwing all the
torches into a pile," said somebody, and the " Mutte "
clanged and clanged, and its tolling reverberated threat-
eningly, rattling all the window-panes and vibrating on
one's ear until it was like a pain. Various people in the
street who had been looking on indifferently now raised
their heads and glanced up at the tower as if the

"Mutte" were calling them. The "Mutte" is French, of course, thought Lela, and probably Amélie is thrilled at this moment to hear it. . . . Lela was glad to think that Amélie and the others had something to rejoice about too, but she kept her thoughts to herself.

When she went to bed her eyes closed almost at once. The street was now empty, but one window directly opposite remained bright. It was the window of a drinking-bar, where there was plenty of din and smoke, hubbub and argument, with an occasional voice recommending less noise. Policemen were on patrol and passed the bar every now and then; they were keeping a watchful eye on it; they halted and took counsel with each other, but then slowly went on down the street.

Frau Käte slipped once more into Lela's room and peeped out of the window. At the moment all was quiet. Then she bent over Lela, but the child was sleeping soundly. That was not always the case. Frau Käte had remarked for some time that Lela had bad dreams and tossed about, as if she were afraid of something, as if she were running away from something in a nightmare. Sometimes she even screamed aloud, irrelevant nonsense such as: "The French are coming!" or "They're shooting, they're shooting!" When that happened her mother awakened her and whispered comforting words, stroking her forehead gently until Lela fell quietly asleep again; she never referred to her nightmare next day, indeed, she never seemed to remember it. Silently Frau Käte made the sign of the cross over Lela's brow. Noiselessly she shut the door, and Lela was left alone in the deep sleep of childhood, with her two beloved Snookies, as of old, clasped in her arms.

Loud, husky voices in the street did not awaken her. A few drunken figures came staggering out of the bar. Their hiccuping French was incomprehensible. There was not a breath of wind stirring and the flag hung down motionless, right down, almost touching the ground. Who grasped it? Who pulled it? Who helped? The heavy butt-end of the enormous flagstaff in Lela's room suddenly rose into the air. With a loud crack the iron staples tore out of the walls and flung against the window-panes. Something fell clattering, and somebody shrieked in the street. Was it a shriek of joy, or of pain?

The end of the flagstaff was still lying on the window-sill. A confused hubbub arose. Tearing of cloth, splintering of wood. And Lela was standing deathly white in the middle of her room. " Mamma, Mamma, Mamma . . ." But her voice died in her throat, not a sound would come out. The door of the bar flew open, disgorging man after man, dark figures waving their arms, leaping, snatching at shreds, stamping them in the wet mud of the street. Lela heard only one thing: " A bas les Prussiens! A bas les Prussiens! "

That was a phrase she knew. These were the first French words that had impressed themselves upon her: " Prussiens " and " à bas." . . . The flagstaff was gone. Splinters of glass lay before her bare feet. The window was wide, wide open. Slowly and fearlessly Lela advanced towards the window. There was no one left down there—nor the flag either. Far in the distance there was a riotous roaring of the Marseillaise.

When Lela awoke in the morning she was in her mother's bed. Her hand was firmly clasped in Mamma's Only her eyes were so heavy and would not open; they

were swollen as if from long weeping. Had she been
crying in the night? How did she come to be in
Mamma's bed? Something or other had happened—
the flag, oh, yes, that was it. She snuggled closer to her
mother. Nothing could hurt her here. Papa kept on
saying that she was too big now to creep into Mamma's
bed; it was only babies who did that; but here she was,
anyway, and it was lovely. If only she could stay where
she was! This was where she belonged and nowhere
else. It was so cold to lie all alone in one's bed. There
were the Snookies, of course—but they were threatening to take even the Snookies away from her; she was
supposed to be too big for Snookies. What did happen
to the flagstaff? Frenchmen had torn it down. Now
why did they do that? Lela sighed.

That woke Frau Käte.

"What's the matter, darling?"

"Mamma, if we were all very kind to the French,
don't you think they would feel better about having lost
the war?"

Lela, it was decided, was not to go to school that day.
She was overjoyed. "Lazy little pig," said Mamma—
but it wasn't only getting out of lessons—Mamma didn't
know, of course—it was because of Eva; Eva would be
furious—Eva would see that Manuela didn't care a
button. Only, it was impossible to explain that to
Mamma. Now why was it impossible?

She was given a small basket to carry and was allowed
to go with Mamma to the market-hall. What kind of
a market could it be that was held in a hall? Lela had
always liked going to market with the cook when she
was quite tiny, but the market in Dünheim had been
an ordinary affair, with fat countrywomen sitting about

who spoke an awful dialect and had words of their own
for fruit and potatoes and flowers that one had to
learn.

Many of them had had nothing to sell but a few
beetroots and radishes and heads of lettuce laid out on
a piece of sacking spread on the pavement. The flower-
sellers sat round the old well in the middle of the
market-place. One visited them last of all if there were
twenty pfennigs left over to buy a few forget-me-nots
for Mamma. Here in Mühlberg, however, everything
was quite different—the market as well.

The market-hall was not indeed a hall such as
Manuela had imagined. She felt a little disappointed
when she saw the great building: it looked much more
like an enormous barn. But inside there were lively
doings: shouting, shrieking and gesticulating. Lela
clutched her mother's hand nervously as they entered.
At first, coming in from the sunlight, she could not
see properly. Only gradually did her eyes adjust themselves to the half-light.

"Eh, bien, Madame—Madame désire? . . . Madame
est déja servie?" rang out from all sides.

Lela stood rooted to the spot, holding her mother
tightly by the hand. As if she were recording a miracle
that defied every law of Nature she cried:

"Mamma, the market-women are speaking French!"

Frau von Meinhardis had already moved towards a
stall and was surveying a mountain of asparagus.

"Mamma, how have the countrywomen learned to
speak French?"

"Because they are Frenchwomen, you silly darling."

There was nothing more to be said. Frenchwomen,
of course, were different. And the market-women here

were so well-mannered, so courteous—not at all like
market-women. . . .

She could hear her mother chaffering in French.
About the asparagus. There were huge round drums
of asparagus with bundles upon bundles in them,
asparagus with pinky-blue lilac heads. There were
other bundles, quite small, as if for a dolls' dinner, and
these were grass-green and not very long and had sprout-
ing heads. Then there was ordinary asparagus, such as
she had always seen, in pound packets, and an array of
blanched, thick, fat asparagus with fat, lily-white heads
—and that was the dearest kind. On the floor beside
Lela there was a pyramid of radishes. A regular tower
of them, broad at the base and tapering to a point, as
high as Lela herself. The green leaves were turned
inside so as to be invisible, and all that one could see
was a mass of tiny tails sticking out from the red little
bullet heads. She could not help laughing—it was too
pretty. It was almost a pity to spoil it, she thought,
when a few wet bundles were taken off and laid in her
basket.

Then she caught sight of something new.

"Mamma, look, cucumbers, cucumbers already!"

"Yes, but these are too dear for us."

Mamma had bought the very cheapest asparagus.
The fat white button mushrooms that were piled high
in a spotless chip basket Lela merely looked at longingly;
Mamma must certainly have seen them too, but if even
the cucumbers were too dear . . . ! Slowly they made
their way farther. There were all kinds of fruit and
vegetables that Lela had never seen before. Fat purple
aubergines, queer salad that was called "Chicorée" . . .
but Mamma bought none of them, although it would

have been interesting to try them. . . . Lela thought it better, however, to say nothing. One must not be greedy and always want to have the best of everything. All these fine things were for other people. Somebody or other, of course, would be sure to buy "the best." These young geese, for instance, hanging up there, the roasting capons, the pigeons and chickens. Although Lela was quite glad not to have to put anything bloody in her basket, she could not help gazing at them.

The enormous salmon and other silvery fish that lay in cold, slippery cuts on wet slabs did not attract her at all, but that was just where her mother called a halt and bought a haddock. Lela looked the other way, for the haddock, too, came out of an overflowing barrel that was marked with the lowest price. Fortunately Mamma herself took charge of the blotched brown-paper parcel.

The fishmonger was by no means so polite as the vegetable sellers. He rolled up Mamma's purchase at great speed and almost flung it in her face. He did not say "thank you," or even "adieu" when they turned away. Lela did not know whether that was because Mamma did not know the French for haddock or because it was only haddock she had bought.

On the way home, walking beside her mother, she threw stolen glances into the shop-windows to get a glimpse of her reflection beside Mamma's. She was already a big girl and reached almost up to Mamma's shoulder. But it was frightful, the speed with which she was growing out of her clothes. Mamma always had to be letting down hems and lengthening sleeves because her thin wrists were sticking out. And then once more she felt the small, hot ache in her breast. Eva. To-day she had not seen Eva. But to-morrow.

To-morrow she would certainly deliver Berti's message.
She would speak to Eva. Why not? Even if there
were other girls there. She shot a sidelong glance at
her mother. What would Mamma say if she were to
ask her now whether she could put on some other frock
for school to-morrow? . . .

But Mamma was thinking of other things. She had
paused before a confectioner's window, remembering
that visitors were due next day. Her sister and her
brother-in-law from Berlin were coming to have a
look at Mühlberg. So it would be as well to order
some tea-cakes.

Monsieur Calignan was no hater of Prussians. When
he saw Lela's open-mouthed, yearning gaze at the tall
glasses of variegated sweets, he thought nothing of
tucking a handful, wrapped in paper, beside the lettuce
and radishes in her basket. Lela thanked him with a
shy "merci bien." But inwardly she was agog with
excitement to discover what could be in these funny
little eggs that she had admired hundreds of times
already in the window. She was no sooner home than
she tried a white one between her teeth. It was frightfully hard. Then it cracked, and an almond appeared.
With some disappointment she regarded the others:
pale lilac, mauve and brown. Queer colours. Yet
quite pretty outside, but terribly hard, and inside only
an ordinary almond. Slowly she dropped them, one
after another, into an open drawer; they rattled just
like stones.

And she had omitted again to say something to
Mamma about the straight, hanging frock. . . .

VII

"Go and brush your hair smooth—what do you think you look like? And put your new shoes on, and a clean pinafore. Aunt Luise will notice it at once if you're not tidy—do it quick; they'll be here any minute!"

Manuela ran to her room. She dipped her hairbrush in water and began operations on her head. Aunt Luise Ehrenhardt was not popular in the family. "She means well," Mamma kept on saying, but Berti remarked that when she kissed you it was like a bite, for you felt all her teeth. "She has never had children of her own and so doesn't understand very well," said Mamma excusingly. . . . Uncle, however, was a different matter. The children delighted in him. Uncle Ehrenhardt was merry and friendly. A grey little gentleman with a rather high voice, which he often had to moderate in order to soothe Aunt Luise, who was always up in the air about something. On these occasions she addressed Uncle by his surname: "Ehrenhardt, believe me, it was as I say." And General Ehrenhardt, who had the title of Excellency and heaps of decorations, even an order to wear at his neck, always said yes. It was no trouble to him— it was the habit of a lifetime. He usually smiled a little as he said it—but occasionally he refrained from smiling and said with cheerful finality, hoping that he need never say it again: "You're always in the right, aren't you?" Then he would fling his newspaper on the table and his pleasant, bony little hands

with the crested signet-ring would tremble a little.
Aunt Luise, however, never turned a hair. In any
case she had a high, smooth coiffure that could not be
disarranged: two rolls that looked as if they were
lacquered into shape, pinned down with steel hairpins.
Her face was rosy, rather chubby, and her nose
obstinately small, which made it difficult for her to
look as dignified as she desired. But her high corseted
bosom and the double chin above her high, closed
collar certainly helped her to make good these defects.
She was not really tall but she seemed tall: it was all
in the way she carried herself. And the same was
true of the old General, who carried himself so as to
look small although he was not really so very small.

And now here they were again, Uncle Ehrenhardt
and Aunt Luise, and of course they had again forgotten
to bring any presents for the children.

"But if we haven't gone and forgotten something! "
said Uncle at dinner. . . . "All the same, Luise, it's
really your business."

Berti and Lela did not dare to look at each other,
but stared at their plates like well-conducted children
although their mouths were twitching. Of course it
was Aunt Luise's business to remember the presents.
But one always knew what the result of that would be.
They usually turned up on Christmas Eve, when Lela's
birthday was also celebrated; and although Mamma's
other sister, Aunt Irene, who had lots of children of
her own and no time to spare, sent Lela every year
two parcels in pretty paper with golden ribbons and
a sprig of fir, and two cards, one of which said " For
Manuela on her birthday " and the other " For
Manuela's Christmas," Aunt Luise never brought more

than one trifling gift and always said: "That's for both together, my dear, for Christmas and for your birthday. . . ."

This time, however, they had arrived in the middle of summer, and it was decided that Papa should get one of the regimental carriages to drive them all to the battlefields, the children too. Lela and Berti exchanged despairing glances. They knew the battlefields already by heart, but there was no getting out of it, visitors were always taken to the battlefields. Soon they were both sitting patiently on the dickey-seat behind Uncle and Aunt Ehrenhardt while Papa was up on box beside the soldier who was driving. It was a light curricle and it rattled terribly through the streets. Mamma had stayed at home; she had escaped the picnic by pleading a headache.

Aunt Ehrenhardt gazed round her like any tourist in a strange town.

"This looks exactly like a French town still, not at all like a German town."

"Well, well, my dear, it isn't so long ago, you know —twenty-five years, what's that? You can't expect anything else. It'll change in time," remarked Uncle Ehrenhardt.

"But that kind of thing shouldn't be allowed—all these French names, how horrible! That sign-board shouldn't be 'Charcutier,' for instance; it should be 'Metzger.' If I had my say these French words would all come down and good German names would go up!"

Aunt Luise grew quite excited thinking of all the things she would do if she had her say.

They were now bowling through a suburb that had something of a village air. All the men were out

smoking their pipes in blue jackets and wooden clogs
before the low-fronted houses. Discreetly the horses
went skimming past them; Meinhardis himself was in
civilian dress, but the soldier on the box appeared somewhat uneasy and sat very straight, looking neither to
right nor to left.

If one smokes a pipe one has to spit a lot, thought
Lela, until she suddenly realized that these men were
all spitting on purpose. An ancient creature shook his
fist after the fleeing curricle, spat on the ground and
shouted fanatically in a furious, penetrating scream:
"À bas les Prussiens." Berti was looking the other
way and the rest of the occupants had their backs to
the old man: it was only Lela's terrified eyes that he
could meet, and he held them insistently with a wild
and threatening glare. Lela felt sick with terror. She
clung to the little iron rail beside her seat. I mustn't
fall out! she thought. They would tear me to pieces!
Quick, quick, away from them, away. . . .

"Manuela seems terribly pale," observed Aunt Luise.
"Is there anything wrong, child?"

"Oh, nonsense!" Meinhardis on the box had overheard the question. "She's always pale. She takes
after me. A pale complexion in a girl of her age
makes her look interesting."

"Red cheeks are much better for children," said Aunt
Ehrenhardt dictatorially.

Manuela felt snubbed. Of course she would have
preferred red cheeks and fair hair like Eva's. It was
not surprising that Eva didn't care for her. This was
Sunday, and she hadn't seen Eva at all on Saturday.
But next day—to-morrow she would show Eva once
and for all that she didn't care either. She was finally

resolved not to bother any more about the girl. She would simply cut her dead, and Berti could find somebody else to deliver his message. . . .

The curricle stopped. "Le cheval blanc"—a fat, galloping white horse on a black sign-board hung over the inn door. They clambered down, for this was where the horses were to be stabled and where they themselves would return for dinner. Valiantly the little company set off down the sunny, dusty road. Aunt Luise opened her parasol. The two gentlemen came to a halt, for they had to take their bearings, and Meinhardis waved an arm largely towards the swelling landscape. Yonder the Crown Prince's army had been stationed. Ehrenhardt knew all about it, for he had been "through it" too: he had been there during the attack and the evening after the victory.

"Yes, I had a very funny experience that evening, do you know——"

When Papa began to relate this story Berti and Lela quietly sneaked off. They listened to Papa's war anecdotes only when their mother's stern eye was on them. For they knew every word that was coming. But Aunt Luise was all ears.

"Oh, do go on. It's so interesting to hear all about it, on the very spot, this sacred spot. . . ."

"Well, it's nothing at all, really. We Hussars had been lying in reserve all day and were wild with rage because we were being left out of it. The battle had been going on since early morning, and there were we sitting in a barn with nothing to do but smoke our pipes. It was already dark when the signal came and we were suddenly bidden to mount and away. One second and we were in the saddle, and I just stuck my

pipe in my breast-pocket, and we charged in full cry
against the enemy. That was a cut-and-thrust business!
These damned Turcos, you know"—he glanced at
Ehrenhardt, who nodded—"they always slashed at one's
wrists with those scimitars of theirs. But I had silk
handkerchiefs wound round both my wrists; my mother
had sent me them for that very purpose; and—well,
it was a mad affair altogether. A terrible massacre,
but my fellows were simply grand; they roared like
lions and we hacked our way through.

"Suddenly the enemy had vanished. Wiped out. As
for us, we'd had about enough. We dismounted at a
farm near by, and just when I was sitting down I felt
a frightful pain in my breast. I got a regular scare
and said to the others: 'I'm wounded!' They tore off
my tunic and out came a great cloud of smoke, and
my shirt and I were simply charred. And what had
happened was this: I had stuck my burning pipe in
my pocket, and in the fury of the charge the smoul-
dering tobacco had fallen out and roasted me alive.
My chest looked like a beefsteak. And how they
laughed!"

Aunt Luise squeaked with delight and Uncle
Ehrenhardt clapped Meinhardis on the shoulder.

"You're a comical chap, my dear fellow."

"And now I'll show you where that all happened
and how the battle went. Well, here on this side
stood the artillery . . ." and Meinhardis pointed east-
wards.

Lela and Berti had strolled off together. They were
standing before a grave in the very middle of a bare,
fallow field. The grave was enclosed by an iron railing
and marked with a cross and two thuya trees—trees of

life. The cross and the whole of the grave-mound were covered with bead wreaths—beads of every colour —and there was a photograph on an enamel plate in the centre of one of the wreaths. A man with a turned-up moustache and a black frock-coat.

"Oh, come on, Lela, that's a French grave," said Berti, pulling her away.

They were already being shouted for. "Berti, Lela, come along!"

A wide plain opened in front of them. Here and there in the middle of a field or on a stubble patch there rose a monument. Their first objective was a newly consecrated memorial to the Rifle Brigade. From the distance it looked simply like an ink-pot, thought Lela. An enormous stone pedestal with steps leading up to it; it gleamed snow-white in the sunlight; broad and comfortable-looking, tapering towards the top where rose the colossal figure of a more than life-size rifleman. The statue looked as if it were striding forward, and one arm was stretched out as if indicating a distant hill. The whole figure seemed to be made of pure gold: the rays of the sun flashed on it in a thousand sparkles. It was so blinding that one had to keep one's eyes half-shut and peer at it through one's eyelashes to make it bearable.

When Lela and Berti arrived, the grown-ups were busily deciphering the names of the fallen and the dates. Most of the names were known to them. "Oh, Lassow, a fine chap he was—a pity about him. He was always cracking jokes. And Grüne—do you remember him? That was the chap whose girl followed him, a pretty, fair girl—yes, yes."

Then they went on again. The land was nearly all

fallow, covered with weeds—thistles and nettles, shepherd's purse and dandelion, a riot of small pale poppies. Lots of stones and dust. Not a tree, not a bush. A barren desert. As if the ground were so oppressed by memories and monuments that it could not remember its proper function; derelict it lay, parched with drought and heat. Farther along a fierce and heroic-looking eagle spread its vast bronze wings over the dead land. Yonder an angel pointed a dying soldier towards heaven; in his fall he was clinging to a gun that was also toppling. A few solitary graves darkly punctuated the blank desolation. Covered with dust, dragging their weary feet, silent and fagged, the little party returned to the inn.

VIII

" Le vin gris " is something special; a light red wine that looks like a mixture of red wine and water, much water, you would think, and very little wine. But if you swallow it unthinkingly you soon discover that there cannot be much water in it, if any. Possibly you do not make this discovery until you try to stand up. Then the curious fact emerges that there is something wrong with your legs; either you have great knee-boots on, or you are wading through water, or there is lead on your foot-soles, or your knees are made of cotton-wool. But that is only the effect of " le petit vin gris." A " little " wine it might call itself, but Uncle Ehrenhardt remarked at once that there was " something to it." And Aunt Luise had flushed cheeks and laughed at everything Papa

said, like an old turtle-dove. It was too funny, it was,
that story about the French lying in a ditch, and how
Meinhardis simply jumped his horse over them and
shouted to them in French to clear out of it, and they
were taken in, thinking he was a " Guide de Napoleon "
because his hussar uniform looked much the same. Too
stupid, these fellows.

" Well, they did let off a shot or two behind our bunch,
but they didn't hit anybody—we were galloping like
hell," Meinhardis concluded.

There was every excuse for a toast. The small glass
tumblers of brightly gleaming wine were raised and
clinked together, giving off only a dull sound, and then
carried once more to the lips. Uncle Ehrenhardt carefully wiped his white sea-lion's moustache and laid his
arms comfortably on the table. His forehead was almost
white, while the lower half of his face was weather-
tanned, with a fine network of tiny blue veins running
over it. His well-shaped nose was now a little red, and
his eyes looked moist.

" Tell us another story, my dear chap. I've had experiences myself, but I'm not much good at telling them.
I'm no talker; I've left the talking to other people my
whole life long—mostly to my dear Luise," with a cock
of the eye towards his wife, who was a little embarrassed
but could not on this occasion take offence at anything
he said. For this was a red-letter day, a day sacred to
pleasure. One was on a tour, one was among relations,
one had gone on an excursion and seen the sights; and
all that for Aunt Luise came under the head of
"pleasure." Yes, one was even kicking over the traces
and drinking red wine by broad daylight.

" Come along, out with a story," she said cheerfully.

Meinhardis did not need much urging.

"Well, if you insist, I'll tell you something that happened after the war. I was in the Army of Occupation then, in France"—turning to the children: "The French had to come across with the cash after peace was signed, and until it was paid a good few of our troops stayed on in the country. It was great fun, it was."

Overcome by memories, he puffed thick clouds of smoke around him so that for a moment he was quite invisible, then he carefully shook off the ash into a tray and went on:

"You see, we had double pay and no end of entertainment — racing, hunting, and all that kind of thing. And nothing at all to do. Well, one day a girl turned up to see me, Laurence was her name. Laurence," he repeated dreamily, smiling to himself. "Yes, Laurence. She had fair hair and clear grey eyes. She was sobbing her heart out, and at first I couldn't get a word out of her, but at last I found out what was her trouble. Her sweetheart had been taken prisoner and was in Berlin. She was very touching in her black frock with a locket on a golden chain, and his photograph inside the locket. A hideous creature he was, too, I can assure you. Well, I comforted her as best I could, poor girl. I sat down on the spot and wrote to the Commander-in-Chief, whose brother was in charge of the prisoners' camps. We had been at riding-school together and had had many a merry time there. I didn't really believe that anything would come of it; but Laurence turned up every day to ask if I had had any news, and so forth. Well, she soon stopped crying. But one fine day her sweetheart did come back, and, believe me or

not, by that time she wouldn't have anything more to
do with him."

In vain Meinhardis tried to suppress a smile of
triumph. Berti and Lela had been listening with
interest; this was a story they had never heard before.
And Luise shot a guilty glance at the two children who
were sitting there with hot cheeks and glistening eyes.
Berti acted as if he had understood nothing, but Lela,
in strange excitement, jumped up and kissed her father
of her own accord, a thing she never did, in the very
middle of his moustache.

Joyously her father seized her hands.

"Well, did you like that story? The story of the
lovely Laurence?" he asked with pride.

Lela only nodded and beamed upon him.

"That's not really a story for little girls," said Aunt
Luise, with an attempt at severity.

But Uncle observed: "Tut, she's a young woman
already, our Manuela, isn't she?" And he, too, drew
Lela to him and embraced her for a moment.

IX

LELA had stuck to her resolution. She had really "cut
Eva dead" during the interval. Amélie had helped to
do it. They both went off to a distant corner of the
playground and Lela had ostentatiously turned her back
when Eva and the other girls went by. But suddenly
her pigtail was pulled so violently that her head was
jerked right back. Blissfully she felt the grasp of a well-
known hand on her shoulder, and some hint of fragrance
from the beloved hair told her well enough who it was.

None the less she shrieked and fought, but was answered only by a cheerful laugh from above her head. Eva let her go and said: "That's what happens to infants who can't say good morning." But she did not go away; she stood there enjoying Lela's discomfiture.

"So you haven't a craze on me, haven't you?"

"No," asserted Lela defiantly.

"Then why did you wait for me, and carry my books, if I may ask?"

"Oh—that! I only had a message to give you from my brother. . . ."

Eva was astounded.

"What's your brother's name?" she inquired quickly.

Manuela hung her head.

"Berti," she said, half whispering.

Eva pushed aside her friends and Amélie, and, taking Lela's arm, led her away to a private corner.

"Now you'll just tell me the whole truth," she said in a voice that was actually severe.

"I won't," said Lela, strangely resentful of this newly awakened interest that left her out of account.

Eva's grasp tightened.

"You will, do you hear me? Go on, now; what did he say?"

Lela told a lie.

"Nothing."

"That's not true. Out with it. I suppose it was something nasty?"

Lela shrank in alarm.

"No—of course not. . . ."

"Well then, what was it?"

Lela's arm was now really hurting.

"Let go!" she said, her teeth clenched.

" Only if you promise to tell me exactly . . ."

Under Eva's stern eye Lela promised. Her newly
laundered frock was all crushed where Eva had seized
hold of her. She was really glad to have that as a
remembrance to take home with her, and wanted to spin
the interview out as long as possible, for to be standing
in this corner close to Eva, all by herself, was a bliss
that should never come to an end. . . .

But at that moment the bell rang and the interval was
over. Hastily Eva told her:

" Listen, do you never go to the Powder-garden? I'll
be there this afternoon. Meet me at the roundabout,
you and your brother, and then he can tell me himself
what he wants to say; he won't be like you, and I won't
have to twist it out of *him*."

It was high time to go; the playground was nearly
empty; Eva had fled.

The Powder-garden was a park on the other side of
the river, which formed one of the town boundaries.
Somewhere thereabouts were powder magazines, and
since houses could not be erected near them, a park
had naturally come into being. Lela did not care for
this park; she suspected every small building in it of
containing explosives, for notice-boards of white enamel
were everywhere, inscribed with the warning, in red
letters: " No Smoking! " A military band played there
regularly, and there was also a restaurant, where one
could drink coffee, and countless sports grounds for
children and grown-ups. Lela had often enough walked
in the Powder-garden with her mother, but the fact that
Berti now condescended to take his little sister there
astounded the household. Indeed, he would much rather
have gone alone, but for this one occasion decency for-

bade leaving his sister behind, and she would soon pick
up some friends of her own, he hoped.

They were both sitting on a narrow wooden bench,
without exchanging a word. In front of them was the
roundabout, a kind of maypole with four rope-ladders
attached to a wheel round the top. You hung on to a
rope and ran fast and soon you were flying in the air.
It was a lovely feeling to swing so high with your legs
flying over the heads of the spectators.

Lela and Berti were watching a figure with a red frock,
streaming hair, and an impertinent smile that flashed
out at them every time the red skirt whirled past. Lela
was holding a red tammy in her lap. The roundabout
had three more rope-ladders, but these were occupied
by other children. Lela was pining to join in, and when
Eva suddenly stopped and called: "Do you want a
turn?" she hastily dropped the tammy on the seat and
ran over.

Eva handed her the rope.

"But don't let anybody else get it, or we'll never have
another chance."

Lela was full of ardour. She felt honoured by Eva's
attention—Eva might well have left the ladder dangling
without bothering whether she wanted a turn or not.
Her eyes lit up with gratitude, and she accepted the rope.
Now she was setting off, now she was flying high, much
higher than the other children. Growing reckless, she
put her left foot on the lowest rung of the ladder and
held on with her left hand only, leaving her right arm
and leg waving free to greet Berti and Eva—but Berti
and Eva were no longer there.

In her disappointment Lela stopped short. The seat
was empty. Of course she couldn't go looking for the

pair of them, since she had promised Eva to keep her
place on the roundabout. All she could do was to go
on swinging. But her delight in the game had vanished;
she simply went on to avoid hindering the others, letting
herself fly in the air and again running on the ground.
The palms of her hands began to hurt; it was easy to get
blisters; the rope was hard and when you grasped it
firmly your skin was compressed in ridges. The place
became deserted. The air grew chilly. One after
another the rest of the children went home.

Lela quitted the roundabout and sat down on the seat
where Eva and Berti had been stationed. They were
bound to come back. Berti couldn't possibly go home
without her. And so she waited. The band had stopped
playing, and now the plashing of the river was audible.
A bat flapped past her. Lela was not afraid; she liked
bats; yet she got up, for she was shivering. She ran
at random along a path crying timidly: "Berti . . .
Eva . . ." But there was no answer.

The path she had hit upon was narrow and wound
between high bushes. She came out into a clearing, and
there, beneath her feet, silent and swift, the river eddied
past in a succession of small rapids. A sleepy duck
quacked among the reeds. Far on the horizon the sun
was setting. The sky was yellow and the meadow on
the farther bank of the river looked an unnatural green,
like the artificial grass on which the wooden sheep are set
in a Christmas crib.

Lela had never been out so late by herself. A cold
shudder went down her back, and suddenly, haunted by
an uncanny premonition of fear, she took to her heels
and ran. She ran with her mouth wide open as if she
were going to scream, but she uttered no sound. Her

mouth was parched: the tears dried on her cheeks.
Once she had started running real terror clutched her,
and everything looked ghostly: the buildings full of
gunpowder, the trees, the railing that enclosed the park,
the high bridge over the river and the mighty fortress
walls.   In the town the street-lamps were being lit, giving
out yellow rays against the greenish sky.   The jostle of
people in the streets hindered her as she ran; her knees
ached; she was nearly reeling.

Frau Käte had not yet turned on the lights.   She
loved the dusk of twilight that slowed down the restless
activities of her day; she sank into a deep, comfortable
chair and rested.   The house was empty; Meinhardis
and Ehrenhardt had gone out for an evening glass of
wine, and Luise was shopping.   The children should be
home soon.   Indeed, that was Lela's footfall outside; the
child was running up the few steps leading from the
courtyard to the house door, two steps at a time.   Lela
pulled at the bell, which jangled loudly, rushed in and
threw herself round her mother's neck.   Too breathless
to speak, she could only nod in assent to questions.

"Have you left Berti behind?"

Manuela nodded.

"Did you run home all alone?"

After that, however, Frau Käte put no more questions;
she could not but feel that it was no mere fear of the
darkness which was agitating the child.   Soothingly she
passed her hand over Lela's head; the child had buried
her face in her mother's bosom as if she were ashamed.
Her breath was still coming in gasps.

"Steady, darling, steady!"

The beloved voice was tender and comforted Lela;
she pushed closer to her mother, seeking shelter from

her own pain.   She dared not think about it all, but she
could not help thinking—Eva and Berti—Berti and Eva.
Somewhere in the darkness of the park they were both
together, leaving her . . . leaving her alone.

"Oh, Mamma, Mamma!"   At length the tension
broke within her, and Lela sobbed like a baby.   And
her mother, as if she knew everything—and perhaps
mothers do know everything—caressed the child and
said secretly in her ear:

"Never mind, my darling, I'm here, and I'm always
with you, and I'll always stay with you."

Then there was silence in the dark room, and the noise
of street traffic was audible only as an indistinct murmur.

X

THE school-bag was heavy, and the road long.   Manuela
would have liked to stay at home and not go to
school.   But perhaps all that had happened yesterday
had been sheer accident; perhaps the other two had
really lost their way, as Berti had protested in the evening; perhaps they had really looked for Lela.   She should
have waited for them a little longer.   Yet, to be honest
with herself, Lela could not help feeling that she had
been deliberately shaken off, that they had probably
found it a great joke to think that she was still hanging
on to the roundabout, keeping a place for Eva, who had
no intention of returning.   Perhaps Eva was passing the
story on to the other girls; that was possible enough;
and they would all be laughing at her.   Lela desired
only one thing, to sink into the ground where she was
standing, and not have to go to school.   Anything but

that! Most of all she feared to see the impertinent
light in Eva's eyes, to hear the mocking laugh that came
so naturally to her. Eva, however, kept out of sight,
and it was only when Lela was going home that she
caught a momentary glimpse of a red skirt whisking
round a corner in the distance, and felt a stab of pain
in her heart. . . .

Aunt Luise and Uncle Ehrenhardt departed, and
with them there went the holiday excitement that
visitors always occasioned in the house. Papa once more
was gloomy whenever he came home, and most of
the meals were taken in silence. Sometimes the grown-
ups spoke English to each other so that the children
could not follow what they were saying. Papa was
kept very busy: he was seldom at home in the evenings,
and even then he was writing at his desk and everybody had to be very quiet. Mamma was always going
to church.

One day Berti did not come home from school at
dinner-time. Dinner was postponed, but still he did
not come. When a message of inquiry was sent to
the school, the answer came back that he had been sent
home with a headache at ten o'clock in the morning.
The agitation in the house mounted higher. Lela was
sent running to all sorts of people who were friends
of Berti's, but nobody had set eyes on him.

When she came back Berti was lying in bed in a
darkened room. Mamma was with him. Lela was to
make no noise, they said, for Berti had fallen in the
playground and hurt his head: he had not been able
to find the way when he was sent home. He had
turned up in church, at the hour of the confirmation
class, and the sacristan had brought him back.

Berti was supposed to have concussion. He was delirious, said Sofie. He was lying in Mamma's bed, and Mamma stayed beside him. Lela was not allowed to go in. Papa came home for a moment or two and went away again. Mamma did not budge. A sofa was taken in for her to sleep on, and she did not come out for supper, either. Lela had to sit all alone at the large dining-table; her eggs grew cold in the glass, and she chewed mechanically at a ham sandwich.

The dining-room was large and high; the lamp on the table gave but little light. Blankly Lela slipped down from her chair and went out at the door. There were six steps leading down to the courtyard, and a vine grew beside them. Lela sat down on a step with the feeling that everything was unreal. The dry tops of the acacia trees in the courtyard waved to and fro and shed tiny leaves on the ground.

Monsieur Girod was sweeping the yard. With his brown, knotted, old hands he parted the vine-trellis behind which Lela sat, and whispered hoarsely:

" Est-ce qu'il a mal, le petit? "

Lela started in alarm. Yet it was a relief to have somebody speak to her, and she answered with friendliness, in French:

"Yes, I think he's very ill."

And Monsieur Girod slowly removed himself, muttering:

"Ah, quelle misère, pauvre Madame, quelle misère. . . ."

The days stretched out grey and grudging. Eva had not a glance to spare for Lela. Not even a word of greeting passed between them. Not a word of inquiry for Berti—not a message for him. Lela hung about in

the house, in the kitchen, the stable, the courtyard.
Papa was still in a bad mood: sometimes he yelled
at the groom, and once he even shouted at Mamma.
Berti was getting better, but very slowly; Lela could
visit him only once in a while, and he was easily upset:
light hurt his eyes and he could not bear the slightest
sound. Mamma did not move from his side; she
had on a white apron, and over the bed was hung a
black crucifix with a white Saviour on it.

Mamma was to go away with Berti for a holiday.
Grandmamma was to come in her place. Frau Käte
explained it all to Lela as if she were grown-up.

"Berti must go into the country. He has to get
quite better."

"Far away?"

"No, not far at all. You can pay us a visit with
Papa or Grandmamma. It's very nice of Grandmamma to come here. A long way for her. . . ."

Manuela nodded a dumb assent to everything.

A dreadful, oppressive fear weighed on her heart.
Mamma was to go away and she was to stay behind.
She was to be left alone.

XI

GRANDMAMMA was supposed to be very kind. Lela
wouldn't deny that: she was kind. Grandmamma gave
a real gold coin to each of her grandchildren at
Christmas and on their birthdays: a ten-mark piece.
She always brushed it first in warm soapy water with
an old tooth-brush and then wrapped it in white tissue-
paper; it was intended to shine brightly, and shine it

did on the white-decked birthday table in the light of
the lamps.

Grandmamma wore a white muslin bonnet that
framed her face with a thickly frilled ruche. Under
her chin two broad ribbons of starched and snow-white
cambric were tied in a great bow. Grandmamma still
looked young. She had a clear skin, a small mouth,
a round face and light blue-grey eyes. She took
possession of Mamma's bed and Mamma's room, and
there was no longer a scent of lavender there and
Crème Simon. Mamma's clothes had been removed
from the wardrobe, and the footsteps that Lela could
hear on the old parquet did not go tap-tap like the
heels of Mamma's house-slippers but shuffled slowly
from door to window, from window to bed, punctuated
by sighs.

Grandmamma always had money, and was always
willing to let Lela run into the confectioner's to buy
the most marvellous cakes. Grandmamma ordered a
large roast of veal because Papa liked it. Grandmamma was jolly. And Papa was in a much better
temper because he enjoyed drawing her on, for she
was always scandalized by him. Shocked at the dirty
boots with which he came into the salon, at the half-
smoked cigars lying all over the house, at the way he
put salt into his soup before he even tasted it.

In Pöchlin Grandmamma had been accustomed to
lavish housekeeping with great quantities of stores, and
the modest, economical way of living in the town
seemed niggling to her. But she did what she could to
keep Papa and Lela happy. Yet Lela was not happy
as she should have been: she sat silent, and left un-
touched the large piece of chocolate Grandmamma gave

her. She told Grandmamma that this was the kind of chocolate Mamma liked so much, and that she was going to save it for her homecoming.

Lela now began to come home late from school. She had always been wont to appear not a second later than ten minutes past twelve, pitching her school-bag into a corner with a mighty crash, in emulation of her brother, and shouting as soon as the door was opened: " Where's Mamma? " before rushing in to kiss her good day. If by chance mother happened to be out, that was the greatest disappointment the children could experience: they used to wander from room to room as if they did not know what to do with themselves, peering out all the time to see if their thoughtless Mamma was coming back to her duties. But now Lela made no haste to return: she sauntered slowly through the streets and stared at the shop-windows, or she went home to lunch with Amélie, who had actually invited her to come and see her mother.

At first sight Lela found it difficult to believe that Amélie's mother was really a mother. She did not embrace her daughter; she hardly looked at her at all, and only glanced with mild interest at Lela and asked if she spoke French. She smoked cigarettes and was very simply but very elegantly clothed. The rooms were filled with photographs of herself, and the whole flat was dark, crammed with all kinds of furniture and yet not very friendly. She gave both the children some money and told them to run out and play, although Lela had come expressly to do home-work for school with Amélie. When the two of them worked together they got on more easily and quickly, for Amélie was good at arithmetic and history, which were Lela's weak subjects, while on the other hand Lela could help Amélie with natural science and all the German exercises. Nor did Amélie's Mamma say, as Lela's did: "Now go and wash your hands and brush your hair and come to dinner"; she only said: "Viens manger." But Amélie's Mamma had lots of illustrated journals, and that was really what induced Lela time and again to mount the dark, unfriendly staircase. Madame Bernin used to give them a whole pile to look at in the nursery, where the two nine-year-olds would sit poring over *La Vie Parisienne*, *Le Rire*, various art magazines and fashion journals. Amélie translated the French jokes for Lela, although even in German they were incomprehensible. Lela delighted, however, in the elegant clothes, and was firmly resolved to dress exactly like Madame Bernin when she grew up.

These visits were never mentioned at home by Lela. But she was once rather surprised when Papa cut a lot of pictures out of an illustrated catalogue and threw them in the waste-paper basket with the remark: "Not for children," for she had caught a glimpse of them and they were only the kind of pictures she had seen by the hundred in Madame Bernin's. Statues without clothes and pictures of real women with nothing on.

She was allowed to look at all the pictures save these. Lela did not regret their loss, but she could not understand why they were forbidden. Only there was so much that one could not understand in the grown-ups' actions. Grandmamma, for instance, had forbidden her, on the spot, to visit the stable in her gym knickers. Why not the stable, of all places? Karl was always amused to see her and lifted her high up

on the horses' backs. She was much too big for that
kind of thing, said Grandmamma. One was always
either too small for something or much too big; it would
be a good thing, thought Lela, to be really grown up
at last.

Lela could not bear to see Grandmamma sitting in
her mother's chair at table. Could not the place be
kept empty? Lela ate nothing, learned her school
lessons badly, and looked dishevelled. One evening
when Sofie came in as usual to wash her feet she ordered
her out in a fit of rage; she would have no more of
Sofie, she wanted to be left alone. She threw a glass of
water quite deliberately at the marble chimney-piece.
She wanted noise, discord, strife—the worse the better.
Of course they all came running in, Grandmamma
protesting: "But, child, child!" and Papa asking:
"Misbehaving again?" Then a buffet landed on Lela's
ear, and Papa slammed the door and left the house.

"What would your mother say if she knew how
naughty you are?"

Lela remained mute and sullen until Grandmamma
went out muttering to herself. There! There they
were! That was what they got! Why, oh, why did
they let her be left all alone? Why did they take
Mamma from her? Berti had her all the time, all to
himself, and that was unjust. It was she—she who
needed to have Mamma sleeping next door.

She couldn't go to bed all by herself. Yes, she did
get up too late in the mornings, but what was there
to get up for, now that Mamma wasn't there to say
good morning? What was the use? Oh, to go into
the dark bedroom while Mamma was still asleep—to
creep quietly up to the bed, where Mamma snuggled

warmly and passed her arm round Lela without opening her eyes, and kissed her on the forehead, saying:
"Good morning, darling—come back again soon!"
That alone made it possible to go to school and come
home again. How Lela longed for a kiss from Mamma
—to be with her for one moment, only one! There
was nobody who knew so well as Lela how lovely
Mamma was. Grandmamma didn't know, nor Papa
either, for he sometimes made Mamma cry. Nobody
knew but Lela. And she simply could not go on living
if Mamma didn't come home. Now, at once. She
simply must come. With all her clothes on, Lela flung
herself on the bed. No, she would not undress. Nor
would she wash, or eat any more food, until they gave
her back her mother.

Perhaps her father, after all, had an inkling of what
was troubling the naughty child. At any rate he
ordered Lela to get ready for a visit to Mamma and
Berti. Outwardly Lela remained unchanged until they
were actually in the low-roofed room with the two high
beds, and Mamma rose from a low wicker chair by the
hearth. Then something within her dissolved, something that had been like a stone in her bosom for days
—for two whole weeks, ever since Mamma went away.

Frau Käte soothed the sobbing child. Papa did not
mention that she had been naughty, and in the letter
they had brought from Grandmamma not a word was
said about it. As soon as Lela discovered that her
fears on both these counts were unfounded, she was
overwhelmed by sheer bliss. Papa stayed with Berti,
and Lela was permitted to go for a walk arm in arm
with Mamma.

The trees were yellow and red; pheasants scurried

over the road; there were lots of berries, both red and
black. The sun shone down on the wet leaves as if
through a veil. Lela came and went, dancing round
her mother as a little dog dances round its master.
She picked a pretty nosegay and laid it on her mother's
arm. Through the growing dusk they walked home
without speaking, back to the small village with the
humble houses and the tiny, bright windows that
looked like peace on earth.

XII

THERE are people so afraid of death that they never
cease talking of it. " When I die . . ." they keep on
saying, imagining that they are giving proof of their
indifference. And there were officers, too, who kept
on saying: " When I send in my papers. . . ." If they
were poor men their voices trembled a little, for they
saw nothing in prospect but a small pension and a
large family. If they were wealthy, however, they
saw themselves able at last to travel about the world,
to go hunting, to find time at last for all the amuse-
ments that had been hitherto impracticable. But sometimes when a man retired from the service it was said
of him: " He's had to send in his papers," and that
had a hint of unpleasantness about it. Yes, there was
a retirement which was far from honourable, preceded
by a court martial and a verdict. Courts martial were
of frequent occurrence, and were composed of officers
of high rank who sat in judgment on their fellows as
officers and gentlemen. Meinhardis disliked the days

on which he had to attend a court martial. Always
some stupid affair or other, he said, that they were
asked to discuss. Whatever the offence, to him it was
only "a stupid affair." And he hated sitting there
and ruining some young officer's career because of a
stupidity. Sometimes it was never known whether a
man had been dismissed the service or had resigned:
occasionally a man was asked to send in his papers,
and then he had really been dismissed although he
had apparently resigned.

Lela never knew the grounds of her father's retirement. The fact that he had retired simply became
clear one day. Mother and father had to decide where
they were to go: after a lifetime of being transferred
from one town to another, they now had to choose
for themselves. Frau Käte was drawn back to Dünheim, their old home, where Ali's grave was; Meinhardis hankered for Berlin, but the objection that
Berlin would be too dear for a half-pay officer nipped
that desire in the bud.

"You might try your hand at doing something,"
said Frau Käte.

Quite so. Earn some money. But how? What
was there that a retired officer could do? It had to
be a gentleman's occupation. A man who had been
giving orders for thirty years could hardly begin to
take orders from others—and from civilians at that!
From shopkeepers! From bagmen, as the fellows
were called! No, Meinhardis would rather break
stones.

Still, if a man was barely fifty, sound as a bell, and
lively, what was he to do with himself? What could
he do of a morning, for instance? What did people

do of a morning when they were off duty? They slept. Quite so. Riding was out of the question, for the horses would have to be sold off. All four of them. There wasn't enough money for the luxury of riding. How did one live without horses? Well, it had to be faced. But it might well have waited until later. If only he hadn't had that row with the Colonel. . . . However, there was no point in going over that again. The army didn't care what happened to him now: the army was concerned only with men in uniform and didn't give a bean for civilians. And Meinhardis was now a civilian, although his whole wardrobe was full of uniforms; although his harness-room was full of saddles and stirrup-leathers; although a battery of riding-boots stood on their trees beside his wardrobe. He had a fine fur-lined cloak with a beaver collar, and a brand-new tunic, but soon he would have nothing to wear except his old grey-green suit, with a tie round his neck. How he hated ties! A soft hat instead of cap and helmet. Grey gloves instead of white. No longer would he be plagued in the street by privates standing to attention before him. All the officers he did not know would pass him without a glance, and for those he did know he would have to take off his hat!

Something to do. What could he do? He could do only one thing: give orders. What else? Strategy, tactics, shooting, riding. . . . He knew some foreign languages, but only enough to carry on a conversation in a drawing-room. He could pay compliments to a woman in every language, let her be a princess or a waitress or a shop-girl. But what to do. . . ?

Frau Käte's eyes rested on her husband in his childish

grief. She stretched her hand across the table and patted his as if he were a child.

"Lots of men become directors of a spa, or something like that; wouldn't that be fun for you? "

No, an entertainment merchant he would never be. Besides, they always expected a man to sit in an office adding up accounts. In short, he could not orient himself towards the future: he had not yet digested the fact that he had been discarded from his profession before his powers were on the wane. Other men had their country estates where they could plant cabbages, but he—he had nothing. Nothing but a military rank and a microscopic pension.

Frau Käte sighed. She saw well enough that she must seize the reins. She must make the decision. And so she resolved to return to Dünheim, where Meinhardis still had friends, and where she herself had Ali's grave.

XIII

THE decision was made, but there was still time before it had to be carried out. For a few weeks Meinhardis had to remain at his post until a successor could be appointed. Meanwhile the preparations had to be made. Officers and horse-copers and neighbouring squires all came to see the stable: the horses were put through their paces in the courtyard, at a walk, a trot, a gallop. One of the riding horses was to be turned into a carriage horse, another to be trained for racing. Wordlessly Meinhardis patted their necks.

"Old thing . . ." was all he whispered, and drew a
last piece of sugar out of his pocket. Without a single
objection Monsieur Girod opened the large gates to let
them out one by one. The sparrows in the courtyard
got their last scattering of oats. Only one horse, which
belonged to the regiment, was left in the deserted stable,
and his anxious whinnying echoed from the high walls.

The orderly, a soldier who came daily with the
regimental orders, brought Meinhardis a large yellow
envelope on which "Night Manœuvre" was inscribed
in German characters, in spidery official writing, and
beneath it the instruction: "To be opened at 8.15 p.m."
Then an added note: "All officers of the regiment are
to assemble on horseback in field marching order at
8 p.m. before the lodging of Lieutenant-Colonel von
Meinhardis."

It was his last official duty. Thoughtfully he
regarded the thick envelope. He signed the requisite
order, as he had done for thirty years, but this was
for the last time. The orderly stood to attention as
usual, received the order, clicked his heels and marched
out. Monsieur Girod opened the small door for him
almost with a bow.

In the evening the large yard was full of horses, the
officers, holding their bridles, standing beside them.
Conversation was subdued. A hint of excitement was
in the air, for the horses were as unused to being out
in the darkness at this hour instead of standing in a
warm stable or lying down in straw, as their masters
were unaccustomed to desert their homes or their evening glasses of wine at the Casino.

Meinhardis advanced to the window and called in a
steady voice:

"Captain von Allersleben."

A "Yes, sir," came out of the darkness. The trampling of hoofs, the sound of someone mounting, and a
sharp click of the tongue were heard. Then the Captain
received his marching orders.

"Main road over Montjury. Then turn off to the
south-east. Leave the forest on your left and pass the
farm. Four milestones to the east Sergeant-Major
Reichelt will meet you and you will link up with him.
Further instructions will be handed you there."

Another "Yes, sir," and Captain von Allersleben
rode off with composure. He still had his electric
pocket-torch, his map and his compass to help him.
But Sergeant-Major Reichelt would relieve him of these
when they met, giving him a new route of march, and
sending him on without anything at all, so that he
might quite possibly wander about all night and be
thankful if he managed to get back to barracks in the
grey light of dawn.

Twenty minutes later Meinhardis dispatched the
next officer. At regular intervals, one by one, they
vanished. Manuela could hear the hoofs of the single
horses slipping on the wet stones outside her window.
She knew how many there were, and counted them.
Then she followed them in imagination. There was
moorland, where they might sink in mire. There were
water-ditches. Roots, over which horses stumbled,
branches that whipped riders' caps from their heads.
Pitch-black forests, where a man might be thrown and
nobody would find him. Were the horses scared? To
be sure they were. Now and then they whinnied in
the courtyard: Lela could hear them. She could hear,
too, Papa's firm, resonant voice calling the names and

reading out the orders. Now the last man was sent off, and Papa could go to bed. For Papa did not ride out when he had to start the others. She could hear him going into his room in his heavy boots; it was next door to hers. Then he stood still, then he pottered about, and then . . . he went right out again. She could hear him go down the stairs and into the court-yard. Shortly afterwards the carriage-gate creaked yet again.

This time Monsieur Girod actually saluted, raising his hand to his cap. Meinhardis rode out with bent head. The horse's footfalls rang hollow in the deserted street; it had no guidance—it merely went straight on —anywhere. At first street-lamps twinkled past, and then the ground underfoot became soft. Tall chimney-stacks of factories were smoking in the night: a melting furnace glowed. Then nothing at all. The wind blew fresh through willow-bushes beside the track. Then the horse gave a start that wakened his rider up. Steady, steady. . . . Oha . . . don't be nervous, old thing; to-morrow you'll go back to barracks and then you'll sleep sound every night . . . every night. . .

PART THREE

I

A LONG row of little villas stood side by side. One
could see them easily enough, for there were no buildings opposite: the street was finished only on one
side, and the road was steep and miry, so that every
vehicle left deep ruts behind it. On the open side of
the street stretched potato patches, orchards, and fields
upon fields, away back to the forest. This was the very
end of the town. They were not dear, these closely
ranged little houses that gazed over tiny front gardens
and railings into the fields. The fine stucco whorls above
their windows had mostly fallen off already and lay in
ugly yellowish heaps on the scant turf of the gardens.
Hardly a finger was lifted to clear them away. The
yellowish-grey house fronts had suffered too; there were
scaling patches where the country storms had been
too much for these urban buildings, unfit for such
exposure.

It was hard to accustom oneself to living here. The
rooms were small, the floors of unseasoned wood; the
doors would not shut, and the stairs creaked—this was
what annoyed Meinhardis most, for Frau Käte always
woke up whenever he came home late. Frau Käte slept
very lightly, although she was really tired out. The
exertion of moving in had obviously been too much
for her. All the packing and unpacking. Porcelain
swathed in paper after paper, yards of shavings, wooden
boxes. Furniture smashed, glass splintered out of

picture frames. Curtains to be altered, large carpets to be made smaller—everything seemed too big for this tiny house.

A cold wind whistled through the closed windows. Frau Käte tried to keep it out by hanging thick rugs before the window. She was shivering. Her hour of rest at twilight grew longer and longer, for she felt weary. Whenever she came back from the cemetery she sank exhausted into an armchair and shut her eyes. Then the household went on tiptoe so as not to disturb her, and she said in a low voice: "But, my dears, I'm not sleeping—I'm only keeping my eyes shut."

Meinhardis had hunted out his old wine-bar, where he found some of his former associates. In a dark corner there stood a round table with a nickel flag in the middle announcing that it was reserved. This was where the "old men" sat. There they sat in the mornings when the youngsters came in dusty and thirsty from their duties, and in the evenings as dusk wore on, and at night until supper-time, when each of them went home to a waiting family. Even then many of them slunk back again after wife and children had gone to bed. This was the circle which now admitted Meinhardis. What else could a man do? At home it was deadly dull. No social life of any kind, for Frau Käte did not care to see anybody. All he could do was now and then to take a thick walking-stick and tramp out to the nearby mountains.

Manuela had to rise early to get to school in time. When she was awakened in the morning she felt as if the back of her head were glued to the pillow, as if her eyelids were of lead, and her limbs logs of wood. She disputed every extra minute with the maid whose

task it was to drum her out of bed. In the cold, grey
light of early dawn, nibbling at a roll and with her
tongue still scorched by boiling milk gulped hastily,
she set off for school half-drunken with sleep. She
hated her new school, for she had been transferred
in mid-term to a class that was following an entirely
different plan of studies from her old one, and she could
not catch on to what was being done. Her schoolfellows were cold to her: she was " a new girl." Frau
Käte exerted herself in every conceivable way to help
her daughter, and went over the school tasks with her
daily. But Lela was fagged and listless; she had lost
the thread of things and her spirit failed her. For
the first time there were disagreements between mother
and daughter. Lela secretly blamed her mother for
all her troubles. Her bedroom was cold and school
was a long way from home: she had no friends of her
own age. She was almost impatient when she saw
Mamma crying so often.

Lela knew very well why Mamma cried: it was
because Papa always came home so late. And if
Mamma said a word about it, however gently, he grew
furious and raged at her. He raged at everybody.
What would he not give for his own man, whom the
regiment had always provided for him, instead of these
stupid maids! They knew nothing and they could do
nothing. They couldn't even put a stud in a man's
shirt-collar, not to speak of brushing his boots . . .
Frau Käte looked wan, but nobody remarked it, at
least nobody mentioned it: yet once when Lela saw
her mother's hand quite close to her holding a pen,
she had the feeling that her bones must soon come
quite through her skin, and she began to feel scared.

Mamma kept on sighing too, not as other people sighed, but in deep gasps, as if she had not the strength even to expel air in one breath.

She said to Lela: "When I'm dead and gone you must be very kind to Papa. . . ."

Lela did not take these words seriously. Her mother wasn't going to die; she said that kind of thing just because she was tired and because she was thinking more about Ali nowadays. It would be Grandmamma, of course, who would die first. Mamma was fairly old, but it would be a long time before she died. Still, she never laughed now. On the other hand, there wasn't anything to laugh about. . . .

Not far from the house a long chestnut avenue led to the forest, and Lela was walking there arm-in-arm with her mother. As soon as they came to a seat Mamma sat down. An infinite compassion overwhelmed the child as she looked into her mother's wan, unsmiling face. The chestnut trees sent broad yellow leaves fluttering down upon her. Mamma never spoke, except for an enigmatic phrase now and then, such as: "When the leaves come again we shan't be walking here together." Lela's blood ran cold, although she did not accept the words literally. Mamma had been saying that kind of thing too often lately. But if Papa heard her at it he simply grew angry. One day he had brought in a doctor, and ever since then Mamma had to swallow tiny pills in a mouthful of water after meals. Anæmia, overwork, said the doctor. Frau Käte was to take care of herself. But she was taking care of herself; she was doing nothing in the house and did not get up until midday. When she came home from school Lela often found her mother still

in her dressing-gown, which she did not want to discard
for a less comfortable garment. Even her journeys to
the cemetery became more infrequent. "It's too much
for me," she kept on saying.

On this day, too, Lela walked slowly and silently
beside her, holding in her hand a few late red poppies
and some wild snap-dragons, yellow and bleached.

"I like autumn," said Mamma. "It's good to see
Nature going to rest."

Mother's hands felt cold. Yes, they were turning
quite blue.

"Let's turn home," suggested Manuela timidly.

Her mother went to bed. No, there was nothing wrong
with her, she only needed a sleep, a long sleep. Her
room was darkened and she was left alone. But she did
not get up again. Lela's heart palpitated, and slowly a
measureless fear welled up within her. What if . . . ?
But that was what one must not say; that was the kind
of thing it was a sin to say, the kind of thing one must
not even think. . . . And how beastly she had often
been to Mamma of late!

When she awoke in the morning Lela listened at her
mother's door, and if she heard no sound she opened
the door softly and did not go away until she was
assured that Mamma was breathing. Coming home
from school she ran the last part of the way as if
hounded, fearing that there might be dreadful news
for her when she reached the house. Breathlessly she
raced up the steps and flung herself beside Mamma's
bed. Her mother smiled. Thank God! Lela breathed
freely again.

She sat on the edge of the bed.

"Mamma, have you a pain anywhere?"

"No, darling, I'm quite comfortable. I'll soon be with Ali."

"No, Mamma, stay here. . . ." And in Lela's bosom everything knotted itself into a terrible, heart-rending sob.

"Don't, darling, don't. It's good that it should be so. It's peaceful and beautiful. Whatever God wills is good, and we must obey Him. His will be done."

Meinhardis came in softly.

"Lela, go downstairs to your dinner."

And Lela went.

Meinhardis remained standing by his wife's bed.

"I must go," she whispered.

"Oh, nonsense, Kitty. What a thing to say. All you need is a good rest and plenty of good food. Then you'll be as right as rain."

"When did you come home last night?"

"Late, I'm afraid," he admitted ruefully.

"Must you always go drinking in the evenings?"

"What else am I to do with myself?"

"Can't you find some occupation, some work?"

"Well, if you like, I'll put in an advertisement. . . ."

He really intended to do it, but somehow it was never done. What was the use, anyhow? Everybody was putting in advertisements, all the other fellows in the wine-bar too, and it was no good at all. He only said that he would do it to avoid vexing Käte. Until she was better he would have to be patient.

Lela got up after a bad night's sleep, and her head felt empty. And yet it was late, and she would have to hurry. The room was cold and she had to put on the light to see. Before the tiny mirror she combed her hair and regarded her large, unslept eyes. She

felt ill. She always felt ill in the mornings. Before
she went downstairs she paused as usual at her mother's
door. All was quiet in there. Gently she opened the
door, the smallest possible crack. There was no sound.
She strained her ears to listen, and waited to hear the
slightest movement. Her heart stood still. She did
not dare to move. In the dimness she could see her
mother's hair like a dark shadow: her hands were
folded on her breast. The door creaked. Of course
that would waken mother. Why hadn't the hinge
been oiled? She had been meaning to do it for a long
time. . . .

But from the bed there came no sign. Lela could
not move. Her hand on the brass handle grew icy.
She could not stir a step, she could not even utter a
cry, for boundless, frantic, senseless terror. She felt
that all she had to do was to say: " Mamma ! " and
Mamma would waken up, but she could not bring it
out. This was a sleep from which none might be
awakened. This was a holy place, where none might
break the silence. As in the cathedral, an invisible
hand was laid upon Lela's mouth. She must not speak.
No answer would come from the bed. Never again.
But when she thought " never " she screamed aloud.
A wild, piercing scream, frenzied by the unbearable-
ness of finality. That " never " was too much for Lela.

Berti dashed upstairs, the maid and Meinhardis came
running. Lela held the door against them. Nobody
should go in. That was her mother, and nobody
should touch her and nobody should turn on the
light. She struggled as if she were out of her senses
and had to be dragged away from the door. The
child's body can't stand this, thought the cook, a new

maid recently come from the country, and she took
Lela on her lap, holding the child to her broad, ample
peasant bosom, rocking her like an infant. She wept
herself and rocked to and fro in her own grief. Lela
resisted, but the peasant woman's arms were too strong
for her and she had to submit. Her shrieks died away
in wailing sobs that came from her small chest like
the long-drawn howls of an animal. "Mamma, Mamma,
Mamma," cried her tear-wet, shaking lips, and her
hands clutched convulsively at the solid flesh of the
strange woman. "I can't, I can't . . ." but a hard,
rough hand was laid insistently over her face.

Suddenly she fell quiet and sat listening. Upstairs
Berti was screaming. She jerked herself free and raced
up to her brother, who was holding both hands to his
temples, and running round and round a table, crying:
"Oh, my head, my head, my head."

"The children must be got away, the children must
get out of the house," said Meinhardis. He showed
but little emotion. He had too much to do. A doctor
had to be fetched, his wife's sisters must be wired for,
also Grandmamma. There was a great deal that
simply must, must, must be done. Somebody dressed
Lela and took her away; some woman or other, a distant
cousin. Lela was exhausted and unresisting. She was
in a strange room: people were fitting a black frock
on her. She wanted to go home. "You're going
home. To-night."

Candles were already set round mother's bed, and
flowers. Mother looked lovely, like a waxen figure.
Lela stood by the bed.

"Say good-bye to Mamma," urged Meinhardis. It
seemed to Lela that his voice had changed. His hands

were on her shoulders. How could she say good-bye
to Mamma, when Mamma no longer heard her? The
candles flickered up and threw a warm glow over the
dead face. Lela went softly up, carefully put out her
hand and made a cross over the white forehead of her
dead mother.

"Good night, sleep well, Mamma, God bless you!"

II

LELA was standing at the window, her forehead
pressed against the glass. With a wet handkerchief she
kept wiping away the misted patch that her breathing
left on the pane. The solemn funeral service was over.
There had been few to attend it, only Frau Käte's two
sisters and one or two acquaintances from the town
besides the servants, for after such a long absence the
Meinhardis were almost strangers again in Dünheim.
A new parson had conducted the service. The coffin
was now being carried down the narrow staircase, and
outside in the wet road a black hearse was waiting to
receive it. Four solemn men pushed it home in a
matter-of-fact manner. Then the flowers and wreaths
were piled on top; there were not many of them.
Berti and Papa were walking behind the hearse, then
a few more people. Slowly the cortège moved off:
the hearse jolted a little, for the road was bad, but it
advanced very, very slowly, as if not to disturb Mamma
in her sleep. Last of all came an ancient cab with
the parson inside. The route lay up-hill and there was
no band: they only moved on very slowly and silently.

Lela suddenly felt broken in two.   Until now Mamma
had been in the house, but this was her final, her real
departure. Now she was gone, and the house was empty.
The stupid, senseless house.   Empty.

On the stairs lay scattered leaves and trodden flowers.
The house-door was still open—wide open.   A damp
draught was blowing in; all the windows had been
thrown open to air the house.   It was no longer a house
at all.

Manuela had only one desire, to get away, to escape
—to be alone.   Here all was bustle and noise; people
were clearing up, washing floors, making beds, cooking
and stoking the furnace.   Both the aunts were busy in
the drawers and the wardrobe: they had to be quick
about it, for they wanted to get back to their homes.

" This under-linen's no good to the child—everything's
much too big for her," said Aunt Luise Ehrenhardt.
" And that Persian muff would do very well for you,
Irene; it matches your stole."

" Yes, thank you.   When Lela's grown up I'll let her
have it again."

Lela heard what they were saying.   The beloved muff
in which Mamma had snuggled her cold, thin hands!
Lela used always to put her own hand in too, and to lay
her head on the soft lambskin.

" This had better all go to the wash," she heard a voice
go on.

That made her run to stand beside the two women,
with a wild, pale face.   She did not venture to make
any objection; she merely watched where they put the
bundle, and as soon as she got the chance she seized it
and hid in her own bed all the clothes her mother had
been wearing.

From time to time she stole in there and buried her
face in the soft cambric, inhaling its fragrance until her
mother become palpable to her and seemed to be em-
bracing her. It was as if she could feel the warmth of
Mamma and her gentle hands, and hear her voice
saying: " My darling——"

Aunt Irene's caresses were a comfort to Lela, for Aunt
Irene was a dear and rather like Mamma. From a
distance her voice sometimes sounded exactly like
Mamma's voice, and her hands were like Mamma's
hands. But Aunt Irene had to go at once, back to her
own children; she had no time. Aunt Luise departed
too, with a trunkful of Mamma's things: Aunt Irene
had let her take the lion's share. . . .

They were all kindness to Lela, but she did not feel
it as kindness; it was merely a burden to her. She
wanted to be alone, for only then could she recover her
mother. She wanted to go to the chestnut avenue and
sit on the seat where she and Mamma had always rested;
she felt that Mamma must be waiting there for her.
She was not allowed to go, however; it was almost as
if a watch were set about her. She fled to her school-
books, and there on every page were pencil-marks
made by Mamma, and Lela remembered exactly what
Mamma had said about this passage and that in her
reading-book.

If she laid her hands over her ears Mamma was
beside her, quite close, speaking to her. But somebody
always came in just then and turned on the light
and laid a hand on her head and said: " Poor
child! "

It was only at night that she was left in peace. She
fell soundly asleep, for Mamma had always told her to

sleep soundly. She almost believed that if she were asleep she would be nearer her mother.

Once, in the depths of night, she had the impression that there was a dark shadow standing by her bed trying to take her hand. Wildly she started up shrieking, and in a trice the room was full of people and the light turned on. Only after they had all gone did Lela realize that it was Mamma who had come to her, and she, like a fool, had been scared, had frightened her away with shrieks and the switching on of lights—her own mother. In sorrowful despair over her foolishness she forced herself to lie quiet and waited with staring eyes, but nothing came to visit her again. Not that night, nor any other night.

PART FOUR

I

A BRIGHT and sparkling sheet of ice. The cold rays of
the winter sun made a path of gold across it. A band
was playing a waltz, and the keels of countless skates
were scoring fine lines on the hard, polished surface.
All the people had gay faces: some were skating hand-
in-hand, and children were playing follow-my-leader
across the ice, holding on behind each other, until the
leader came to a sudden stop and the whole tail rolled
up around him except for the last child, who let go and
went flying far off at a tangent.

Couples were skating with crossed hands, and in the
more quiet corners, away from the music, experts were
practising figures, circles, eights, threes, reversing and
jumping. With both arms outstretched, his head turned
sharply over his right shoulder, hands flexed outwards
and upwards, Fritz Lennartz stood on his right leg,
swinging the left leg out as he finished a dazzling curve.
For a moment his body relaxed, and then with fresh
energy, that came from one could not tell where, tautened itself to execute another curve on the left leg. A
fur cap sat on the back of his head and a fair lock of
hair fell over his brow. His dark blue jacket was tightly
buttoned and revealed at every movement the lines of
his slim, elastic body. He was wearing knickers fastened
below the knee and long black stockings. His skin was
soft as a girl's and his cheeks were reddened by the cold
air. Now he paused and gazed at the close-packed

throng circling round to the band music; he passed all
the girls in review with half-shut, somewhat arrogant
eyes. Without letting his interest be remarked he
watched one in particular, a slender girl with long legs,
a sailor cap carelessly stuck on the back of her head
and soft waving hair flying in the wind. She was
apparently enjoying herself very well and laughing up
at the partner who held her crossed hands firmly and
securely. She looked as if she had not seen Fritz at all.
Now the pair of them, swinging in time to the music,
passed right in front of him. Fritz assumed the air of
one looking for somebody else.

Joachim, Lela's partner, could not contain himself.
" Did you see Fritz? "

And Manuela replied: " Yes; cocky, wasn't he? "

Joachim was appeased by this answer; a benevolent
grin overspread his good-humoured countenance.

" Well, he can do plenty of stunts. But he always
goes off by himself," he remarked, casting a sharp side-
glance at Lela.

" Let him, if he likes it."

Joachim had a twinge of conscience. Obviously Lela
disliked the way that Fritz always stayed by himself.
He felt all at once that it was hardly fair to keep on
parading past Fritz, and so he invited Lela to have a
hot drink in the restaurant.

The restaurant was a wooden booth containing a few
tables covered with red-checked cloths. There was no
need to take off one's skates. Balancing awkwardly, one
steered a course across the wet wooden floor to the
nearest chair and fell into it. Lela wanted tea, and
Joachim ordered it—tea with rum. It was smoky and
steamy and noisy enough in there, yet Lela enjoyed

sitting at a table with a boy, although the boy was only
Joachim.   She sipped her hot tea in contentment, as she
sat facing the door, to which Joachim's back was turned.
Joachim was almost her next-door neighbour.   Joachim
whistled at midday in the street and then Lela came out
and they went off skating together.   That was a matter
of course.

The haunting memory of his wife's death had driven
Meinhardis out of the house on the outskirts of the town.
He could not bear to go on living there, and it did not
take him long to engage a housekeeper and remove to
a more central district.   The family was now settled
in a street of villas, with trees in front and gardens all
round.   Lela and Berti had not far to go to school,
and Meinhardis was only a few minutes' walk from
his wine-bar.

Fräulein von Helling was the housekeeper.   She was a
rather severe-looking lady.   Her collars were all high so
that she had to hold her head very erect, and she preferred to dress in dark colours, indeed, mostly in black.
Her complexion was fresh, her mouth pinched and a
little embittered.   She was extremely thrifty, which
pleased Meinhardis.   He had never learned to be careful of money and usually carried it loose and uncounted
in his pockets, a habit that scandalized Fräulein von
Helling.   Meinhardis delighted in shocking her with
his bad habits—he would roar with laughter over her
head-shakings until she had to join in timidly, as if
out of politeness.   To do her justice, however, Fräulein
von Helling enjoyed a laugh.   She was pleasantly
fluttered by the teasing attentions of the Lieutenant-
Colonel.   All her life she had had but little luck in her
affections, and as the daughter of a large family on a

small, poverty-stricken country estate she had been forced to earn her living by housekeeping.

Manuela could not bear the sight of her. She could not forgive her for sleeping in Mamma's bed and using Mamma's wardrobe. Fräulein von Helling had been quick to feel the child's hostility, and, having learned wisdom from experience in many strange families, she made no attempt to overcome it by direct means. Her cherishing care was devoted rather to the male inhabitants of the house; Berti enjoyed all his favourite dishes, and Meinhardis could always depend on her for pleasant companionship if he wanted to sit over a glass of wine after dinner and recount his old stories to a new and grateful listener. On these occasions, after much pressing, she would drink a small glass with him, although she insisted that she never drank wine; Meinhardis, however, would not suffer anyone to remain "dry" in his company. Besides, it amused him when a flush mounted to the Fräulein's cheeks and she could not help laughing loudly in spite of her upbringing and her principles. He called her "Helling," and sometimes, when in a good mood, he even ventured to address her as "Du," while she stuck firmly to her "But, Herr Lieutenant-Colonel . . ."

So Manuela was left to her own devices and could sit quite light-heartedly drinking tea with rum at Joachim's invitation. With both elbows propped on the table, she let the grateful warmth of the beverage do its work. She was glad to be sitting down, for her slim ankles soon ached from skating. As if by chance, she kept her eyes fixed on the doorway while she listened to Joachim's account of a journey to Berlin. And, as she had expected, Fritz came in. He did not stagger about so

awkwardly as the others but went with easy assurance
to the buffet and asked for cigarettes. Composedly he
pocketed them after lighting one, and went out again
without so much as a glance at Lela, exactly as if he
had not seen her. Lela grew restless.

"Come on, let's skate a little more," and Joachim
obeyed her at once. When they emerged into daylight
again the sun was just setting behind the dark fir forest.
The band had stopped playing and the throng of skaters
was gradually dispersing.

Joachim and Lela skated singly, side by side. Lela
wanted to learn figure-skating, and with her right foot
she managed to swing round on the outside edge so that
she experienced a little of the unique exhilaration of the
flying curve. She felt a burning ambition to learn more
and more—but at that moment she saw Fritz gliding
along quite close to her, linked to Hella Andreas. Hella
was radiant, laughing with affected excitement, and Fritz
was carelessly holding her hands, condescending out of
mere politeness to skate straightforwardly like anyone
else.

All at once Lela shivered and felt tired. Joachim
knelt before her and unstrapped her skates, which he
carried home. Lela caught a last glimpse of Fritz and
Hella disappearing into the restaurant together.

When she got home Manuela rapidly finished her
home lessons and then withdrew into a sofa corner with
a book. Fräulein von Helling was darning underwear.
Lela hated the smell of it.

"If you were the right kind of girl you would be
helping me."

Lela felt exhausted. She could think of nothing but
how she would learn figure-skating next day. She was

restless. She couldn't read, and shut her book. Just
then Meinhardis came into the room.

" Well, are you being good? "

He moved the lamp nearer to Fräulein von Helling.

" You're ruining your eyesight.   Isn't she industrious,
Lela? "

Fräulein von Helling bent her head over her work,
and the lamplight illumined the thick blonde plait
braided into a bun on the top of her head.   Meinhardis' hands were lying on the back of her chair, and
he could not resist making a quick pounce and removing
the two large hair-pins that held the erection together.
The plait tumbled down over Fräulein von Helling's
shoulder.

" But, Herr Lieutenant-Colonel! "

Scandalized and blushing she sprang to her feet,
putting up both hands to hold the plait on the top of
her head.

Meinhardis chuckled and then laughed. Lela laughed
too, for Papa was always playing tricks; there was
nothing unusual in that. His next move, however, was
unusual; he seized Helling and gave her a kiss. Lela
had an idea that Helling could quite well have pre-
vented him if she had only let go her silly plait of
hair. . . .

Next day Lela evaded poor Joachim. She raced
down the steep road to the ice-rink, buckled on her
skates with feverish haste, and struck out at once
towards a vacant corner where she began to practise.
She grew hot with exertion: she fell, too, one or twice,
and her coat was glistening white with powdered ice.
At last she threw the coat away, then her gloves and
her muff. That was much better. She was just

beginning a loop when she felt two strong hands seizing
her from behind, by the belt, and propelling her across
the ice.   In less than two seconds her speed was
terrific.   The ice crackled and whistled under her feet;
the black firs round the rink went flying past in a blur;
the icy wind cut her face like a knife.

"Don't waver, Lela, keep steady; you can do it well
enough!   Are you scared? "

"No, Fritz, no.   It's glorious. . . ."

"Oh, you're as light as a feather.   I can hardly feel
your weight.   I'm much too strong," he gasped from
behind her.

It was like a wild hunt, and she was the quarry,
and she had to keep still, and that was all as it should
be.

"Lel? " he asked after a while.   "Can you go on? "

"Yes, Fritz, of course.   I can go on as long as you
like. . . ."

She hardly knew what she was saying; she was aware
only of the wide berth given them by the other skaters,
and that the hands holding her were guiding her
within a hair's breath of the frozen verges of the rink.
She felt herself instinctively throwing her weight to
one side at the turns.   Her shins were aching; she was
trembling a little—but if she had been steering straight
for hell she would not have given up.

Finally Fritz gave her a strong push, and Lela flew
on alone across the dazzling, smooth surface.   A curve
—a few lumps of ice in her way—she bent forward to
avoid losing her balance, fighting wildly and in vain
to prevent the inevitable tumble, but in the very nick
of time Fritz caught her.   Although her feet had shot
from beneath her she did not fall, she remained upright,

her cold cheeks pressed against the rough cloth of
Fritz's jacket, his hard buttons icy-cold on her skin.

"You did that beautifully, Lela."

"Not I. If you hadn't been there I'd have gone
down flat. . . ."

They both laughed.

They had to wipe their noses and set their caps on
straight. Lela pulled her dress down, for it had got
rumpled up in her wild career, and Fritz combed back
with his fingers the lock of hair that was falling over
his face. They were really quite dishevelled.

Fritz took off his boots, skates and all, hung them
on a strap round his neck so that they dangled on his
chest, and put on another pair. Then he knelt on the
ground before Lela and unstrapped her skates. His
untidy fair hair was close to Lela's face. But she
quickly put her hands in her coat-pockets, as if she
were searching for something.

II

MEINHARDIS had come to terms again with his life.
There were days on which he was dejected and went
about looking conscience-stricken or set off for a long
tramp in the mountains: days on which he could not
shake off the thought that he had not been good enough
to "Kitty." Every moment of that last year, when
he had vented on her the ill-temper that regimental
friction had provoked, now kept coming into his mind
and haunting him. But in a little he seemed to recover
from his melancholy, as if he had conquered it, and

then he would plunge into gay company where no one could tell better stories than he, no one could be so charming to the ladies, no one could think of such merry jests.

The thought of his children sometimes bothered him, but he hoped that Helling would manage them all right. He watched Manuela's looks closely: his friends had told him, among other pleasant things, that she was going to be a beauty, and he was delighted because she had his eyes and his build. He would enjoy having a good-looking daughter; besides, a girl had to be pretty if she was to marry a rich man. And that his daughter was going to make a wealthy marriage was a settled affair in Meinhardis' mind. "Some fellow with a deer-forest," he used to say. He liked to think of himself as papa-in-law on some fine estate in the north of Germany, sauntering in the garden or entertaining the shooting guests over red wine and fat cigars. The money left to him at Käte's death was melting away, and his pension was damned small. He had always hoped to travel a bit when he retired, but now he couldn't afford it. Secretly he consoled himself by reflecting that "the girl," as he always called Lela among his friends, would "set the family on its feet again."

It was with greater apprehension that he considered Berti's future. The boy must go into the diplomatic service. That meant, after his matriculation this year, his joining some exclusive corps, perhaps in Heidelberg, so as to make the right connections. A boy needed to be well connected. To be on a friendly footing with good families, rich families, was the most important thing. That was how a man got on. Well, Berti was

a smart young fellow. It was amazing how the women
had begun to run after him already. He would make
his way all right. It was no time since he had met
Berti out walking with a damned pretty woman. Of
course he looked the other way; on such occasions a
father has to be discreet. And the whole table roared
with laughter. Yes, Meinhardis wasn't like other
fathers; he didn't interfere with his children. Anyhow, one got no further by always coming down on
them. He himself had never been dragooned by his
parents; probably if they had tried it he would have
put them in their place.

They drank to this ideal father, and called a toast:

"Here's to the future of your little beauty! Long
may she live!"

And Meinhardis gladly honoured it.

III

NEXT day a bunch of lilies-of-the-valley and a note
were delivered to Lela:

"I must practise my violin for the Christmas bazaar
on Saturday, and so I can't come skating.
                    "Best wishes,
                            "FRITZ LENNARTZ."

Lela's small brown hands carefully undid the tissue-
paper. The flowers had a lovely scent. She filled a
vase with water in the kitchen. The cook stood by
with a meaning smile.

" From an admirer? "

Lela made no reply.

" Why not? " remarked the cook. Marie was open-minded. All the same, she took it upon herself to warn others against love, since her own experiences had been unfortunate. Lela had heard all about them. Marie's sweetheart was a sergeant, but hardly an admirable one. Her room was crammed with curious knick-knacks concocted of some greyish-brown substance—a photograph frame, an ink-pot, even a naked girl, who looked rather like a gingerbread figure, and stood beside a palm made of the same mysterious compost—which was nothing more nor less than army bread kneaded into a paste with water. Marie's Karl was an artist, and apparently spent most of his time in the cells, since that was the only place where he had leisure to indulge his passion for modelling. In " clink " one had bread, water and leisure, and out of these three Karl conjured his art.

Marie was proud of his productions and embarrassed by them. She was a kindly woman who loved Lela, and Lela spent much time in the warm kitchen and acquired much useful information there.

" Don't let the gracious Fräulein see the flowers, Fräulein Lela! " advised Marie benevolently. " She'll pull another long face about them—besides, she doesn't need to know everything."

Lela carried her flowers upstairs, careful to spill no water. She had been feeling so happy, and now all at once a sense of dejection overcame her. Helling . . . true, Helling hardly ever came into her room, and so would not be likely to see the lilies-of-the-valley, but still. . . . A shout from below that dinner was ready interrupted her, and, glad to stop thinking about the problem, she ran downstairs.

Berti announced that there was going to be a thaw and studied Lela's face to see the effect of his words.

A searing pain cramped her breast, and she bent her head over the chair-back on which her hands were folded. They all stood like that round the table while Berti said grace: "Come, Lord Jesus, be our guest, and share with us what Thou hast blessed." Everybody joined in the Amen, and not until then did they sit down to eat.

IV

LELA had crumpled up the programme on her lap, holding it fast in her hot hands. Fräulein von Helling beside her was dressed in her "best"—a black taffeta gown—and was busy discussing the various items of the performance with her neighbour, a lady she knew. Once more Lela smoothed out the programme; it was quite true, the next item actually read: "Violin solo—Friedrich Lennartz."

In her imagination she pictured Fritz having to stand quite alone on that high, wide platform while ever so many people stared up at him, all alone, and she trembled with agitation as if the ordeal were to be hers, as if she herself would have to mount up there and stand forlornly in her poor little frock and have a violin thrust into her hands and hear the audience shouting at her from the expectant silence: "Play up! Play! Play! . . ."

A light shone on the dark curtain, and a hush came over the room. The curtain flew apart, and there stood a huge, black grand piano with a stool in front of it. From the little side-door emerged Fritz, with his violin under his left arm; he paused in the middle of the stage and bowed. He showed no signs of fright; he seemed to take it quite simply, as if he had never done anything else but bow to gaping audiences.

Lela's agitation subsided, now that Fritz was actually there. A little sigh of relief escaped her and was remarked by Helling. She and her neighbour were keeping a sharp eye on the unwitting Lela, for to-day Helling was firmly resolved to " take the place of a mother " to the poor child, and save her from improper ideas. Of all this Lela was utterly unaware. She had eyes only for Fritz, who now turned towards the piano, where a blonde young woman was sitting looking up at him. As soon as Lela caught sight of that up-turned face she stiffened to attention, and involuntarily leaned forward in her chair to get a closer view. This woman had Fritz's face!—but lovelier, more tender, more charming, and now she was smiling to him in encouragement, and he was returning her smile with a little nod. There was perfect understanding between the two, and suddenly Lela realized why Fritz was so confident. Of course; *she* was there, and her being there made everything all right.

The pianist settled her sheets of music, and Fritz, with an almost arrogant look, turned towards the audience and waited while the two white hands at the keyboard evoked the prologue, which went sweeping past him down into the hall, until he joined in, with an energetic stroke that shook his hair into disorder.

Now he was the leader, and the piano accompanied him, up and down, pausing to wait for him, suggesting a theme for him to develop, and both of them, the woman and Fritz, had the same movements of the head. A lock of hair kept falling over her eyes just as Fritz's hair did; she tucked it back quickly, but it fell again, and so did Fritz's whenever he tossed his head. They had no time to bother about their hair; they had to go on and up and forward, and the prisms of the chandeliers trembled and tinkled, and the audience sat as still as death, as if holding its breath.

Lela's mouth was open, and her eyes fixed on the stage. She did not know that she had grasped the back of the chair in front. Her ears burned, her face paled with the intensity of her emotion; her mouth was parched dry, her palms were damp. What was it— what could it be? It hurt dreadfully, and then it stopped hurting. Those two up there were not two but one, fused into unity, loving together and feeling together and not to be separated from one another. Fritz was dissolved, he was no longer there; he was only a part of something else, and yet he was there as never before. For he filled the whole hall, and he was quite alone in it; but he was guided by the woman, upborne by her, and without *her* neither he nor the music could have come into being. Something was seizing the listening people and shaking them and drawing them out of themselves, and they were all submissive, letting themselves be drawn. And then something laughed at them in mockery, and turned caressing again, and soothed and calmed them until it was as if everybody sang together, in full chorus, and Lela was in the

middle of it, a part of it all. Without her it wouldn't
have been there either—but *what* was it really? . . .
That was the end.

For a moment the audience remained in stupefied
amazement. There was a dead silence. Fritz had
time to lay his violin on the piano while the pianist
rose to her feet: only then did the applause burst out.
As if the people felt a need to yell and stamp to keep
themselves from suffocating, they shouted with all their
might. With a soft step the young woman went up
to Fritz and laid her arm round his shoulders. Fritz
wasn't at all embarrassed; he beamed at her and bowed
gratefully to the audience. Again and again he had
to come forward, hand-in-hand with his mother, while
the audience shouted at them. His mother—he has a
mother, thought Lela. . . .

She began to push her way forward, but Fräulein
von Helling made a grab at her.

" You're to stay where you are."

Lela started round and looked into a strange, angry,
jealous face.

" Girls don't run after boys. It isn't decent! "

An ice-cold hand closed on Lela's heart. Mechanically she turned back and sat down in her place.

Suddenly the hall was again darkened, and everybody had to sit down. There was some disorder, and
a few chairs beside Lela were left empty, right up to
the gangway. Now the main item of the programme
came on, the Christmas Play. Lela's eyes followed
the scenes but without any understanding. Figures
appeared on the stage and went off again, both children
and grown-ups. People in the audience coughed now
and then or nibbled at chocolate. A chair was scraped;

someone whispered; someone crackled a programme, trying to decipher the next number.

All at once Lela caught sight of Fritz slowly making his way along the wall towards her. He threaded noiselessly through the rows of chairs and sat down at her side. Lela did not know what she was expected to say to a successful violinist, and gave him an anxious look. He seemed to understand and smiled encouragingly to comfort her. He took her hand in his, as if to say: "No, I'm not so bad as all that. . . ."

Then they had to sit silent. Her hand remained where he had laid it, on his knee, with his hand closed over it protectively.

"What do you think of my mother?" he whispered.

And Lela, without looking at him, replied:

"She's wonderful."

For nothing in the world could she add another word; she would have had to burst out crying. She fought and fought against a lump in her throat, and blinked rapidly to control the tears that were so stupidly, so absurdly gathering, all unasked-for, in her eyes. She swallowed them as best she could, and Fritz put his mouth quite close to her ear so that she could feel his hair.

"I'm going to take you to her afterwards, she wants to see you——"

Lela bit her lips in agitation. Her mouth grew dark. She had fought back her tears, but her eyes were still glistening. Her hair was parted and fell on her shoulders over her bare arms that looked so thin and helpless. She was ashamed of her arms. Fritz's mother had soft, white arms and lovely hands—lovelier than Fritz's. Indeed, Fritz's hand was beginning to hurt her, for it was bony. His mother's hands were certainly very soft and gentle in their touch: one could see that by the way she played. And her feet were quite tiny. Fritz had enormous feet.

Now the stage grew as bright as day, brighter still, and yet brighter. A great staircase stretched right up to heaven, covered with angels. An organ was playing, and the countless angels were all singing a Christmas carol.

" Now she's coming! " said Fritz.

He did not need to say who was coming; he knew that Lela was thinking about his mother. . . . Far up at the top of the staircase a glittering figure appeared, so dazzling that at first one could not see who it was. A hushed melody was played, and a marvellous, triumphant voice took up the angels' tidings. A finely pleated long gown fell down from a close-fitting silver bodice with tight sleeves over the arms, leaving only the throat free. Her blonde hair was loose, and a silver helmet sat firmly on her young head. All the lights, playing upon her, sparkled in her blue eyes.

Clear, pure and confident, her voice took possession of the hall. It was a voice that made one feel good and happy, it carried one up, right up. Lela held on to her stool as if in resistance. Fritz had forgotten her: he was staring up, spellbound and lost. He, too, felt that there was no one so lovely as his mother— no one.

" And on earth peace, goodwill toward men . . ." came the ringing voice from above; the angels joined in, and the orchestra; drums thundered, carrying the voices with them: " Goodwill toward men . . ." and the dark curtain rustled down.

V

With a grown-up, cavalier bow, Fritz greeted Fräulein
von Helling and her friend, old Frau Professor Metzner,
and led the three of them to a small table in the side
room where he helped the two elder ladies to tea and
cakes.   Then he took Lela by the hand and said quite
simply: "Come along, Mamma's waiting for us."
There was a frightful crowd; people stood jammed in
the doorways.   There were stalls all round where things
were being sold for the benefit of poor children.   Fritz
held Lela firmly by the hand and drew her behind
him. He had often to stand still while some old
gentleman clapped him on the shoulder and said:
"Well done, my boy! " or some old lady gushed over
him: "A great talent, yours, a great talent. . . ." Lela
was proud of him.   But it was all merely a hindrance
to Fritz: he was only anxious to push on.

"Mamma's at the flower stall," he said, and they
hunted through the press to find the flower stall.   There
it was—over there.   But she wasn't waiting for them
at all; she was surrounded by people and had both
hands full of work.   The two children crawled into
the tent behind her and found just enough room on
a box for Lela to sit down.   Lela felt happy, however,
glad to be out of the throng and glad that Frau
Lennartz was occupied for the moment. Masses of
flowers were heaped on all sides, and small sprays made
up of three roses or three carnations lay tied up and
ready on the table.   Frau Lennartz reached out a hand
towards the wet flowers and the bast.

Without being aware of her own action, Lela pushed the hand away.

"No," she said firmly, "let me do that."

Amused at the decisiveness of the girl and surprised by this unexpected offer of help, Fritz's mother bent down, put her hand under Lela's chin and raised the bent head.

"This is Manuela von Meinhardis, Mamma," said Fritz shyly.

For a moment Lela looked into the blue eyes above her, held her breath, and then returned the smile that greeted her.

"It's delightful of you to offer to help me, but I can't possibly accept the sacrifice—you must be wanting to run away and enjoy yourself."

Lela energetically shook her head.

"No, Mamma, Lela would rather stay here. Is there anything I can do?"

Lela, relieved to be no longer a subject of discussion, set herself to work.

"Yes; will you be so good as to change this money for me . . . ?"

Frau Lennartz gave Fritz a handful of notes and he turned to go. His mother pushed the lock of hair off his forehead before he went. Lela shook her own hair over her face, hoping that Frau Inge, as she had heard her called, would run a hand over hers too, as she had done to Fritz. Eagerly she tore at the rusty wire till her fingers smarted; recklessly she seized the thick-stemmed, thorny roses; with her teeth she bit off the recalcitrant bast, and plunged her hand so often into the icy water that her fingers grew stiff with cold. She breathed in deeply the bitter fragrance of the leaves and did not venture to look up at Frau Inge; she only listened to her voice and her laugh.

‘

VI

"THERE you are, Frau Professor," said Fräulein von Helling to her friend. "That's what the child is like, she thinks of nothing but boys. It's simply dreadful. And how am I to look after her? I can't always go chasing about at her heels. This Fritz is paying her attentions and she welcomes them. She's head over ears in love with him, and at her age, too! I ask you —a girl of thirteen and a half. What would her mother have said? It's a good thing she's not alive to see what a hussy her daughter is turning out." Helling sighed profoundly. "I have a hard time of it, I assure you. Her aunts write that I must keep an eye on her. Keep an eye on her! And she takes to her heels and runs out of the door and nobody knows what she's up to. I've tried to talk seriously about it to her father, but you know what men are. . . . Well, she takes it off him, you see; he's just the same, dangling after every petticoat—one can't really be surprised. But now I've seen her at it with my own eyes, and I'll be able to tell him exactly what his 'pretty daughter' is doing. I won't be responsible for her. And I'll write another letter this very evening to Her Excellency von Ehrenhardt. In my opinion the girl must be sent away from home. What she doesn't see and hear!—she's for ever gossiping in the kitchen. As for Bertram—do you know that the boy sometimes

doesn't come home all night? Yes, you may well look
surprised. That's what children are like in these
days. . . ."

VII

FRITZ was chartered to carry rolls and hock cup. The
press of people was exhausting. Frau Inge was at last
relieved by another lady and had a breathing-space.
She sat down on the box among the flowers, and, as
there was no other seat, she drew Lela, quite as a matter
of course, on to her lap.

" Come here and rest."

A warm, bubbling happiness welled up in Lela. She
did not dare to stir a finger. She had to put her arm
round the strange lady to keep from falling; she could
feel her warm neck and soft hair against her hand.
She could feel Frau Inge's breast. In that blissful
moment everything sank away, the flowers, the bazaar,
Fritz—the flood rose and covered them all: it was
Lela's twilight hour; the evening hour with her mother.
She shut her eyes and revelled in the stranger's warm
fragrance. It was as if she could hear the sounds
coming up from the street, and in a minute the evening
bells would ring out from the Cathedral—and the
Powder-garden was shrouded in dusk—and . . . Eva,
yes, Eva had had hair like that too. She suddenly
realized it. And perhaps Eva's arms were just like
these—her hands had a firm enough grip. . . . Unconsciously Lela let her head sink wearily on Frau
Inge's shoulder. She could see the opening of Frau

Inge's frock and would have liked to drop a kiss into it, but she did not dare.

Quite involuntarily she began to tremble. Frau Inge looked down at her and twined her left hand in Lela's hair. For a second she laid her head beside the girl's and said in a low voice:

"You silly thing, you're still just a baby. Is it true that you're such a brilliant skater?"

Lela tried to regain her composure, but she could not speak until she slipped down from the embrace and stood on her feet to show that she wasn't a baby.

Fritz paused at the champagne stall and drank a glass quickly. Then he went out to the artistes' dressing-room. Fading flowers were lying on the table beside his violin. Carefully he opened the case and picked a little at the strings, as if to see whether they had suddenly lost their voices. Then he took the white silk handkerchief that his mother had given him, tucked it under his chin and laid the violin on it. Softly, for his own pleasure, for nobody else, he drew the bow across the strings. He stood quite quietly, and his hand was confident as never before. Yet something was rising in his throat, and he shook his head to get rid of it, but it would not go; it swelled, it goaded and oppressed him. His jaws moved, grinding upon each other. He would not give in to it, no; he would play, play, play.

VIII

Lieutenant-Colonel von Meinhardis was pacing up and down the room, puffing thick clouds of cigar smoke

and growling to himself from time to time. He was
apparently ignoring Fräulein von Helling who sat
sewing by the window, bending industriously over her
embroidery. The light was fading, but this evening
he did not care whether Helling was ruining her eyesight or not; he had other things to think about.
Suddenly he halted, and bending forward swiftly to
emphasize his words, said, as if continuing a conversation:

"Well, what do other people do with their girls?"

It appeared that Fräulein von Helling did not know,
or, if she did know, that she had already provided the
information, for she merely shrugged her shoulders.

"It's enough to drive a man crazy," he went on. "I
can hardly confine her to barracks, can I, as if she were
a defaulting private?"

The lady at the window made a gesture as if she
saw no reason against such a measure, but she said
nothing.

"God, what does it matter if she is smitten with some
boy or other? There's nothing very terrible about
that. . . ."

Now the figure by the window roused itself.

"People are talking about her, Herr Lieutenant-
Colonel. Her reputation . . ."

"Oh, well. Yes, yes. Quite so. And women like
you can think of nothing else but to lock the poor
child up in some convent or other, what? Just to get
rid of her. That's about your mark. To get some
half-witted old wives to make the child's life a burden
to her. I know the kind. Do nothing but snuffle
prayers all day . . . no . . . Lela . . ."

"We're only suggesting what's best for the child,

Herr Lieutenant-Colonel. And Her Excellency von
Ehrenhardt agrees . . ."

Helling was rudely interrupted.

"Don't you try to come over me with *her*. She's
never had children of her own. She hasn't the faintest
notion . . ."

"Well, Frau von Kendra, Frau Irene . . ."

"She's a right enough woman. Has six daughters
and not one of them away at boarding-school. . . ."

Helling saw an opening.

"Yes, an excellent mother. But that's just the point;
Lela has no mother, and a stranger can't have the
same influence over her. Manuela is old for her years,
and very independent; she does exactly as she pleases—
and she's not fourteen yet."

Meinhardis began to prowl again. He was beginning to hate the creature by the window. She was
actually stitching away at a curtain that Käte had
begun shortly before she died. He must get rid of
her. And, of course, if Lela were out of the house
—Bertram was due to go up to Heidelberg in the spring
—he could shut the place up or sell it outright and
travel about a bit on his own. He had visions of himself in Italy or on the Riviera. God, he was an old
crock already and had seen nothing of the world yet:
he had surely earned a bit of a holiday.

"What reply am I to send to Her Excellency von
Ehrenhardt?" came from the window.

Meinhardis awoke.

"Oh, yes, about Lela. Well, you'd better just tell
her that I don't much like it, but God knows I'm not
to be trusted with the education of young girls. Let
her look round and see what she can find. But let

it be somewhere near Frau von Kendra, so that she can at least keep an eye on the child."

Helling rose and carefully laid her work aside, then left the room. With a sigh Meinhardis went up to a small cupboard, drew a bunch of keys from his pocket and unlocked the cupboard door. He laid his cigar down and took out a bottle and a small glass. Carefully he filled the glass, gazed at it sadly, emptied it at one draught, throwing his head back, then replaced it empty on the shelf, wiped his moustache first on one side and then on the other, and with another deep sigh locked the cupboard.

IX

LELA was standing before a florist's shop. Alpine violets, she wondered? No, too frivolous. But if she were to give Fritz's mother a present it would have to be flowers. Admirers always gave flowers to their adored ones, to let them know that they were beloved. But mother said —in secret Manuela thought of her only as "mother" —that Lela was still a baby. Why? And why wasn't she grown up yet? She was burning with impatience to be grown up. Fritz, who was older than she, was just a great child, for he had cried on that day, although he was a boy. He had tried to hide the fact, but Lela had seen that his eyes were red. In the evening they had gone home together, all three of them, after wringing a grudging permission from Helling, and the two children had each taken an arm of Frau Lennartz, who, before they parted, had invited Lela to come to her that afternoon. That was why Lela was now examining the shop-window for some gift to take with her. Carnations? No, they had wire rings round their necks to keep their petals from falling, and their colour was a loud and hectic red. It should really be lilies, but there were no lilies in the shop. Pompous, conceited-looking tulips there were, with fat, crackling leaves; no, they wouldn't do. Mimosa? Yes, if one could buy a whole armful of it, so that Mamma might think Lela was bringing in a forest of golden sun-balls; but a mere spray or two? No. And to buy an armful was more than she could afford.

She dived into her pocket and hovered undecidedly before the window. The azaleas were too dear, and, anyhow, they fell very quickly. But suddenly she caught sight of a tall white candle lurking in a corner; a half-blown hyacinth of remarkable size, a tall, full head of blossom on a firm, square stem, with magnificent dark green leaves. A strong, pure fragrance rose from it. They wrapped it in layers of white tissue-paper and laid it in Lela's arms. Carefully she carried it home, right up to her room.

She set the pot down at the window. Bright and cool. She had hardly taken the paper off before the scent of the flower filled the whole room.

"Darling flower," she said in a low voice. "Do you need a drink?" She felt the damp earth. "No, the lady has had all she wants," she said, laughing. The thick head of blossom seemed to nod in answer. Lela ran downstairs whistling.

Her high spirits, however, received a check. There was a constrained silence at the dinner-table. That often happened. Either Papa had "worries" or "bills," or Helling had been having a row with Marie, or Bertram

had been up on the carpet for bad behaviour. Lela was
not going to bother about it, and spooned up her soup
with quiet contentment.

The soup tasted marvellous to-day; Lela was hungry.
But since no one else seemed to have any appetite, her
capacity for food provoked astonishment and had almost
the appearance of a social error. To-day, however, she
did not give a fig for anything. In an hour's time she
would be with Mother Inge, and then everything would
be all right. What would she say to the Lady Hyacinth?
Would she be pleased? Would she read in the gift how
much Lela was pining to do for her at all times, whenever she could; all that Lela would do for her one day
when she was grown up at last? . . . The chairs were
pushed back from the table, and Lela had already
grasped the door-handle when her father called her back
in answer to a significant look from Fräulein von Helling. He had to clear his throat; he seemed embarrassed.
Bertram made himself scarce and Helling sailed out.

"Yes, Papa?"

Papa wiped his mouth with his napkin and mumbled
a piece of toast. He did not look at Lela.

"Where are you running off to now? Can't you spare
a minute or two for your father?"

Lela, conscience-stricken, sat down opposite him.

"Of course, Papa, I only thought that Helling . . ."

"Oh, Helling," he said contemptuously, and then,
remembering himself: "No, Fräulein von Helling has
no time to-day, and I have something to say to you."

Lela felt a shock of premonition. Something dreadful
was going to happen to her, at this very minute; whatever could it be? . . .

She did not have long to wait. Meinhardis had

rehearsed the scene thoroughly. And as if he were repeating a lesson by rote he said:

"You see, this kind of thing can't go on, my dear. You're running quite wild. I've been hearing tales about you that make my hair stand on end, and it's my duty as your father to point out that your conduct is most unbecoming. Not that of a young lady. You're in danger of losing your reputation through the way you're behaving."

Lela felt hot: Helling, it must be Helling—this wasn't Papa speaking, it was Aunt Luise, it was . . .

"Your aunts, who are very fond of you, and Fräulein von Helling, who is thinking of your good, have decided that you must be sent to boarding-school."

"Me, Papa?" Only one frantic thought: not now, not now, please, please, not just now! A few days earlier she would not have cared, but not now, not good-bye to Mother Inge.

"You don't need to look at me like that; it's nothing so very terrible. Your mother was in a school of that kind, and most girls have to leave home at some time or another. We thought of Hochdorf. It's said to be rather a pleasant place, and you'll be quite near to Aunt Irene, who'll keep an eye on you."

Lela pulled herself together.

"Papa?"

"Yes, my dear?"

"Please, please, dear Papa—please not just now!" She could not say another word.

Meinhardis smiled a little. That proved how right Helling was; the girl was certainly in love. Soothingly he laid his hand on his daughter's.

"Come, it doesn't really matter when. Why not just

now? Soon you'll have got over the worst of it and
everything will be settled."

"Please, Papa, I can't go away just yet. You don't
know . . ."

"But, Lela, my dear, I do know. It's Fritz Lennartz
who has turned your head. And I won't have any
young fool suddenly sending my daughter crazy."

Lela stared dumbly at her father, then shook her head
and answered with firmness:

"No, Papa, it's not because of Fritz—it's because of
his Mamma. . . ."

Meinhardis burst out in an explosion of laughter.
Still laughing, he stood up, grasped Lela by the
shoulders, and said:

"My dear, you're priceless, you're just exactly like
me! Always an excuse handy—anything rather than
be cornered! You're an amusing kid. But let me tell
you this, you'll have to learn to think up better excuses;
that excuse wouldn't take anybody in."

Lela collapsed speechlessly upon the chair from which
her father in his enthusiasm had swung her. Now he
went round the table again, poured out a mouthful of
wine and pushed it over to Lela.

"Here, that deserves a little drink."

Mechanically Lela clinked her glass against his.

"There, now go and see Helling. You've plenty to
arrange with her; perhaps there are things you need to
get before you go. . . ."

Something had to be done at once and quickly. And
Lela summoned all her resolution.

"But, Papa, I have to go out this afternoon—I've been
—I've been invited out."

Meinhardis looked out of the window.

"Well—where is it you're going?"

"To Frau Lennartz's."

"No, my dear, there's to be no more of that. Anywhere but there."

"But I promised!"

"Oh, well, then, we'll just send Minna along with a polite note of excuse. I'll write it now," and he sprang to his feet energetically.

But he got a shock when he saw that Lela's face, as she wearily rose up, had turned grey and suddenly like an old woman's. Effusively he cheered her up.

"Come, come, my dear, it isn't so bad! It doesn't last, you know. By the time you've got to Hochdorf you'll have forgotten all about it!"

At the door he turned round again, for an idea had struck him.

"Lela," he said, looking at her gravely, "you're not to do anything silly, do you hear? Promise me that you'll be good. Confined to barracks, you understand, and not to go out except with Helling."

Tonelessly the answer came back:

"Yes, Papa."

PART FIVE

"No, you can say what you like, Bettichen, this coffee's
not up to much."

"And what if it isn't? Haven't we got to be thrifty
here? I'm sure you've heard that often enough from
Kesten. Thrift's good for the character, she says, says
she. And she's right enough there."

Two tin spoons wandered round and round in the thin
white coffee, among the black grains and small white
shreds that floated on its watery brown surface. One
of the hands, "Bettichen's," was lean and scrawny and
emerged from a tight-fitting sleeve; the other, a huge
paw, belonged to Herr Alemann, who was at that
moment sitting in his shirt-sleeves. For it wasn't worth
his while to wear his good uniform while drinking "such
muck" as that coffee. His uniform was for putting on
whenever the bell rang. And even then there was "no
need to hurry"; for anybody who rang a bell here did
so modestly and without insistence, waiting meekly until
Herr Alemann had donned and buttoned up his jacket,
an operation which took some time, since there were lots
of buttons on his uniform and a high collar to hook.
It wasn't every janitor who was so grand. And after all
the buttons were fastened he had to smarten up his
whiskers with a little comb. Herr Alemann's chin was
clean-shaven, and that made his long whiskers all the
more imposing. Herr Alemann was "up to Guards'
standard," and in Hochdorf that was the ambition of

every man. It was an old tradition that for the ruling sovereign's regiment of Guards none but the tallest fellows were eligible; the Guards' standard was a fraction over six feet, and anything short of that was of no account whatever. Frau Alemann, on the other hand, was small, and looked even smaller than she was because of her stoop. Her thin black woollen dress was tightly stretched across her bowed and bony back. Her pointed chin stuck out. Her straggling hair was covered by a flat white lace cap, and a pleated white apron was tied firmly round her scraggy figure.

They were sitting at the well-polished table in their narrow quarters. By the wall were presses divided into many lockers, with a telephone exchange beside them. One window looked out on the front garden and the street, while a peep-hole on the other side gave on the hall. It was dusky there and not unlike a mausoleum, with dark stained-glass windows and a marble bust of the royal foundress who had given her name to the establishment: "Princess Helene's Seminary."

For the moment the house seemed to be asleep. And yet it was the very middle of the day. No sounds, however, could have penetrated these firmly closed doors. White doors; white corridors; white rooms. Rooms for sleeping, for eating, for learning, for reading. Long, bright corridors, carpetless and curtainless. Stairs upon stairs: back stairs, ordinary front stairs and a ceremonial staircase in the middle of the building, adorned with a thick red carpet for the use of visitors, for the use of royal visitors. A chapel and a gymnasium.

On the spotless, well-scoured planks of the upper corridor footsteps were easily heard, but the grey figure that now flitted busily from door to door had a sound-

less step. These shoes were designed not to betray the
wearer; they had rubber heels. Nor did the grey dress
betray the presence of a body; it hung in straight folds
and looked almost as if it were held in place merely by
the elbows pressing stiffly at its sides and the hands
folded across its waist. Stooping a little, but with a
quick eye darting into every corner, Fräulein von Kesten
steered her course towards a low doorway. Like all the
mistresses she wore a small lace cap, and it was skewered
to her scanty hair by enormous hair-pins. Her hair was
colourless and so was her face: only the pupils of her
indefinite eyes made a dark and striking impression.
Yet even these Fräulein von Kesten often sought to
conceal, although her colourless eyelashes hardly veiled
them. She opened the small door without knocking,
and, without paying any attention to the woman sitting
hunched over a sewing-machine, walked up to a clothes-
stand and inspected a bunch of dresses that were hanging on it. A stale odour of dress-making materials lay
heavy in the room.

"Marie, there's a new girl coming to-day."

"Yes, Fräulein von Kesten, I know."

"Get a uniform ready for her."

"Yes, Fräulein von Kesten. But there's no good ones
left," came the husky answer from the corner. "I hope
it isn't some princess or other that's coming."

"No, a free scholar."

"Oh, poor child."

"Why do you say that? She won't be made to feel
her position here."

"I know, I know, Fräulein von Kesten, of course.
Well, there's some dresses that aren't too badly worn,
this one here, for instance. . . ."

The old woman hobbled up to the clothes-stand.

"That's the one young Fräulein von Brockenburg had, if I'm not mistaken: yes, we'll see what can be done, Fräulein von Kesten. . . ."

"Better call her attention to the way she has to do her hair. . . ."

"Yes, yes, of course, gracious Fräulein. . . ."

The door shut again behind the small grey lady, and again she flitted busily along the corridor. Her hand passed lightly over a window-sill . . . and an angry frown furrowed her brow. She ran her eye over the window-panes, but they were spotless and gave an uninterrupted view of the laughing blue sky. Yet as if even that were undesirable Fräulein von Kesten shook her head. Now, however, she heard something: she paused and listened. No—was it possible? Swiftly she pounced on a closed door behind which, in merry trills and cascades, the strains of a waltz were resounding; her pale hand wrenched it open, and a startled child leapt from the piano-stool to face her.

"Marga—do you call that practising?"

There was no reply for a second or two.

"I have been practising, Fräulein von Kesten—I had just finished," came the timid answer at length.

"I want to talk to you about something."

Marga drew a breath of relief and guiltily smoothed back with both hands her rebelliously straying hair. Then, as was the custom, she stuck her hands in the bib of her black apron and took up the pose of a soldier who has just been told to stand at ease. Her face was still flushed with alarm, but her high-bred and somewhat bony features assumed a deferential, almost servile expression.

Fräulein von Kesten's eye rested approvingly upon her.

"Well, of course, I know *you*, Marga." She screwed up her eyes a little. "I'm never mistaken in my judgment of you girls."

Politely, in a low voice, Marga replied:

"I beg your pardon, Fräulein von Kesten, I'm very sorry. . . ."

"Very well, my child. But another time confine yourself to the tasks that are set you, do you hear?"

"Yes, Fräulein von Kesten," and Marga dropped the little bob known as a *knix*. A *knix* was a small genuflexion, rapidly made, and could be performed in a standing position or even while walking: it was the smallest change of courtesy. More impressive was the Court *knix*, due to visiting princesses—a deep, sinking curtsy and bow—but even that was far removed from the lowest genuflexion of all, paid only to God Almighty. Between these extremes came the *knix* for the headmistress, and the *knix* for one's parents or one's aunts. It was not usual to expend a *knix* on an occasion such as this, but Marga von Rasso liked to perform little services for Fräulein von Kesten when nobody was looking on.

"Marga, there's a new girl coming to-day, and I wanted to ask you if you would care to be her foster-mother."

Marga felt honoured. She nearly dropped another *knix*, but that would have been a little too much, and so she merely answered quickly:

"I should be very glad, Fräulein von Kesten."

"Then I must ask you to watch over her carefully and to see that she fits in as quickly as possible with-

out any trouble. It's not exactly convenient to have
to admit a new girl in the middle of a term, but there
are reasons for it."

"Yes, Fräulein von Kesten."

"Well, I see you understand me. . . ."

"Oh, yes, Fräulein von Kesten."

II

"HERE's the new girl. The new girl. . . ."

One voice made the announcement, but four girls
went rushing to the window. Ilse von Westhagen got
there first, and in flat disobedience to rules flung the
window open so that all four heads could be thrust
out. Down below there was drawn up one of the cabs
that spent weary days waiting by the station at Hochdorf. An elderly lady was in the very act of alighting:
the step bent low under her weight. From a large
but shabby *porte-monnaie* she extracted some money
and paid off the cabman.

"Don't you want me to wait, lady?" he inquired.

"No, no—I shan't need you. I can walk. . . ."

From the upper window the whole transaction was
closely observed.

"Look, she's coming out now . . ." whispered Ilse
excitedly, pinching her nearest companion, Lilly, in the
arm.

"Ow, stop it. . . ."

"For goodness' sake don't make such a row. . . ."

But recriminations were forgotten at the sight of
Manuela emerging from the cab.

Her first glance was towards the great building in front of her. At first she thought the cabman must have made a mistake and brought her to some barracks; for it was nothing but an immense stone box with windows and more windows, row upon row, and a huge, tightly shut gate. . . .

"What are you thinking of? Pick up the valise!" cried Aunt Luise, interrupting her meditations.

Frau Alemann, however, was already hurrying out, since Herr Alemann was far from quick at getting into his uniform; she now unlocked the latticed gate and took possession of the luggage. Behind her the aunt and niece advanced through the front garden. Manuela had observed the curious eyes that were watching her, and bent her head down; but the peeping girls also withdrew their heads in a hurry, for Fräulein von Kesten had come upon them from behind, and with an energetic: "What is the meaning of this?" put an end to their entertainment. She marched up to the window and shut it with a slam.

"You know that it's strictly forbidden to open windows and look out. What are the people in the street to think if you're all gaping out like . . . like kitchenmaids? Ilse, have you tidied up your wardrobe?"

"No, Fräulein von Kesten."

"This afternoon is inspection . . . so I think . . ."

One after the other they slunk out of the room, silent and embarrassed.

Fräulein von Kesten had not been a governess her whole life long, although to look at her it was difficult to believe that she had ever been young or even had a childhood. General von Kesten, her father, was a soldier of some distinction. His broad red stripes and his grey

walrus moustache were regarded with all honour and
respect. His three sons had been sent into a cadet corps,
as a thrifty preparation for a military career, while his
small daughter, Armgard, had gone to a school where
she was known as "Bunny." The nickname stuck to
her as she grew up, and when her brothers held commis-
sions in various regiments and were required to take
"Bunny" to the regimental balls, they sighed. Armgard, indeed, sighed too. Her low-necked ball-dress of
cheap silk, with a bunch of artificial forget-me-nots that
an aunt had given her to pin on her corsage, looked
pretty only in the dark mirror at home by the light of
the paraffin lamp. In the great ballroom, among all
the trains and jewels and uniforms, its wearer was ex-
tinguished, and cowered against the wall until some
junior lieutenant or ensign was firmly told off by a
superior officer to go and dance with Bunny. Other
girls might have armfuls of bouquets and be escorted
by laughing officers all the way down the broad steps to
their carriages, but Bunny, with a few miserable
flowerets, shrank where possible behind the footmen's
backs, and had to go home alone on foot, or submit to
the quite superfluous chaperonage of her parents. When
further invitations came she refused them. It was only
a torment.

But what was to be done with Bunny? The
old general and his wife held a consultation. Bunny
wanted to learn something. But what? It cost money
to learn things, and, in any case, what use could she
make of it if she did learn something? To take a situa-
tion among strangers, to work for wages at all, was un-
ladylike and impossible. No, no, the best thing would
be to get her into some institute; as a nursing sister in

a hospital, for instance. Yet Bunny seemed fragile and
had no real vocation for sick-nursing. It was a great
relief to everybody when the chance came to establish
her in the Seminary. That was no disgrace and Bunny
had a career now for life. Congratulations poured upon
her, and the poor girl herself believed that it was an
honourable distinction for her to be appointed to a post
which hundreds of other Bunnies had applied for. With
all her strength she set herself to master her duties, to
fulfil and enforce all the rules and regulations of the
house, to devote her small, frail person entirely to the
good cause. Every order from above should be punctiliously obeyed and as punctiliously enforced upon others:
whatever came from her superiors was right, and whatever she herself did was right. Life outside these walls
had never had any attractions for Armgard, and she
belonged now to the Seminary, heart and soul, without
any regrets or longings. So at the age of twenty Bunny
donned the grey uniform, whose unyielding material
apparently hindered her body from developing, and so
she parted her hair in the same place to the very end of
her life.

"Dear me, hasn't that janitor's wife announced us?"
wondered Her Excellency von Ehrenhardt, sitting
stiffly upon a chair in the reception-room. The door
had been left open, and the janitor's quarters were
just across the passage. "Go and find out, Manuela,
I haven't any time to waste, I have to be at your Aunt
Irene's by one o'clock. . . ."

Timidly Manuela knocked at the janitor's door. She
almost jumped with alarm at the bellowed "Come in"
of Herr Alemann.

"Oh, is Fräulein von Kesten not down yet?

Well, we'll give her another ring," he said good-humouredly.

He plugged in and announced, standing at attention before the telephone:

"Her Excellency von Ehrenhardt is waiting in the reception-room. . . ." Then he smiled pleasantly to Manuela: "There, now she'll soon come sailing down!"

And, indeed, as Lela came out of the door she ran plump into a lady who rounded on her without a greeting:

"The janitor's room is out of bounds for the pupils: it is strictly forbidden for them to have anything to do with Herr Alemann. . . ." And then, in a somewhat friendlier voice: "So you're the new girl, are you?" And without waiting for an answer she steered Lela into the reception-room as if she were removing her from danger.

III

HERR ALEMANN shut the great gate behind Her Excellency von Ehrenhardt. She walked off with an air of having done her duty. Her conscience was at ease; she had done her best. Or could one do better for any girl than to enter her at the most elegant seminary in the whole country? Now the girl was safe. Now she would become that most desirable thing, a well-behaved young woman; and there was this further advantage in the arrangement that it would not cost the family a penny, since thanks to good connections a free place had been secured for Manuela.

For the next few years the problem of Manuela could be shelved. Thank God that Meinhardis had at last come to his senses. Yes, the girl was unfortunately very like her father; the same temperament, the same irresponsibility—the same love for all kinds of superficiality. . . .

Not a trace of Käte, my poor dear sister, thought Luise von Ehrenhardt, sighing and looking up at the sky. It was a pity she hadn't let the cab wait after all, for rain was beginning to fall slowly.

Lela was in the dressing-room, lost in a sea of girls. Her first impression was that they all looked alike and that she would never be able to tell one from the other. They all wore their hair modestly sleeked back; they all had the same dark frock with old-fashioned little pleats on the bodice and a tight waistband; they all had the same hideous black apron and stuck their hands under the bibs when they were idle, just as if they were all freezing.

Marga had at once energetically taken up her task. She was raking with both hands in Manuela's trunk. Manuela had to stand before her empty wardrobe and dispose her things as she was told. Nervously she kept a smile ready for the owners of all the hands, some friendly, some casual, that were stretched out to her with a more or less pleasant greeting. She was resolved, come what might, not to betray her feelings. The one thing she must not do was to burst into tears of fright. Anything but that.

"Put that away." Marga held out a garment and Lela obeyed. It was a simple sailor dress, nothing remarkable about it, but all eyes were drawn to it as by a spell.

"Oh, how nice! " sighed the little dark girl, who was called Ilse.

"What's all this here? "

"Books."

"Books have to be given up," said Marga severely.

"Given up? But why? "

"Not allowed, my dear."

"No time for reading, anyway, except perhaps on Sundays, and then you can get books out of the library. . . ."

Ilse had snatched one of the books from Marga, rushed off to the window with it, and began to turn its pages.

"Hand that book over, Ilse! " cried Marga.

"Nothing of the kind. I say, this is marvellous! "

"Hand it over, Ilse, or I'll tell Fräulein von Kesten."

"All right, sneak, tell away. But you be careful—if what Manuela's brought with her comes out she'll get into a terrible row."

Manuela was growing uneasy. She went up to Ilse.

"I say, give it back, will you? I took it from Papa's bookcase and I haven't even looked at it yet."

Ilse seized Lela by the shoulders and drew her aside, whispering in her ear:

"This is a great old book, by Emile Zola. 'Le Ventre de Paris '—what a ripping title! I'm going to hide it in my wardrobe. Don't you be taken in by Marga, she's a pusher and sucks up to Kesten."

"But, Ilse, if it's forbidden . . ."

"Look here—I'll tell you what: make me a present of it. . . ."

Manuela laughed. "Delighted! "

Ilse tucked the book under her arm and with a grave face stole out of the cloakroom on tiptoe, right along the corridor until she came to a door that could be bolted from the inside. Through that door she vanished. In that place one had peace and privacy, and could read forbidden books undisturbed.

Marga had arranged Manuela's wardrobe. Manuela's head was spinning with all the things she had to remember. The first thing to learn was the list of forbidden articles. Eatables of all kinds, especially chocolate, fruit and sweets, were forbidden; jewels and money had to be handed over; pocket-money was doled out, but had to be strictly accounted for; hair-washes must not be used, and any soap of one's own had to be given up. All one's underwear had to be marked with one's full name sewn in red on a white tape. Chemise must lie tidily on chemise, knickers on knickers, handkerchief on handkerchief. The wardrobe must be kept locked, the key carried always on one's person and never lost. The key had a number.

"You're No. 55," said Marga.

Manuela looked up at the number above her wardrobe: a black "55."

"Your clothes will be marked 55. Your shoes will be in box 55 in the boot-room. Your coat and your hat will be hung in the cloakroom by the hall, in compartment 55. Your wash-basin is No. 55, and so is your bed."

Manuela felt herself slowly turning into No. 55.

"Well, now I'll take you to Marie to get your dress. Just tell her you're No. 55 and then she'll know."

Marie knew well enough. Manuela stood apprehensively in the doorway. How heavy and oppressive was the air of this room! How small the window! The walls were not visible at all; nothing but rows and rows of garments whose exhalations were like those of many

people soaked to the skin and crowded together in a
narrow space.

"Come along, No. 55, I know all about you already.
Goodness, what a face to make. No need to be scared,
my dear: this uniform's been the death of nobody yet.
Come along, now."

A claw-like hand grabbed at Lela and drew her into
the circle of light that spread beneath a lamp burning
in the dark room although it was day-time. The glass
lenses of a pair of spectacles reflected the light as they
looked up at Manuela, and she had the impression that
this woman had no eyes at all. Innumerable small plaits
of incredible tightness covered her head, and innumerable dry, sinewy wrinkles ran from her collar up to her
chin.

"There, now off with your things. . . ."

Two hands peeled Manuela's frock from her body.
It lay on the floor, and she stood there, white and
uncovered.

"Now step out of it, I can't wait all day! "

Marie pushed her away so that she could get at the
garment. She picked it up, together with the hat which
Manuela had been holding all the time, and carried both
off without a word. Indignant and helpless, Manuela
cried:

"What are you doing? Where are you taking my
clothes? "

She could hear a door creaking and a key turning in
a lock. With a complacent grin Marie returned.

"There, my little Fräulein, that's all right. You'll
get your frock again when you have permission to go
out. And all the rest of the time you'll just wear your
uniform like a good girl."

"All the time?" escaped Manuela's lips. She had, of course, known that a uniform was worn here. But these hideous garments—it was simply unthinkable that one should wear them *all* the time. . . .

"Of course," replied Marie, and her toothless mouth spread in an ugly smile, "that's the rule and there's good reasons for it. If you try to run away, you see, then everybody knows your uniform, don't they? Well, then, they bring you straight back to the Seminary, you see."

Manuela stared at her in horror.

"What, has anybody ever wanted . . ."

The old woman laughed delightedly, and it was like a screech.

"Wanted? Ha, ha, ha—*wanted* is good. . . . There's more than one has tried it. But it's no good trying. The police nab them, and even if they do get home their people just send them back. . . . Wanted, I dare say, many a one has wanted. . . . Now you just sit down there." She pushed Manuela on to a stool and took hold of her hair, giving it a painful tug.

"No, no, don't do that!"

"Deary me, it has to be done, and what has to be done just has to be done. Your hair has to lie flat, quite flat. And if I don't manage it then Kesten will take your head off—and then you'll see a thing or two. When she sets about you with a brush and comb it's a different story, I can tell you."

The hairpins hurt. Manuela felt as if the skin were being torn from her scalp. But she made no more objections. A hard hair-brush, a scratchy comb, mishandled her head, and Marie's bony fingers held her hair tightly, plaiting it into a pigtail and pinning it up.

The dark blue dress that the old woman slipped over her head felt damp and fusty. Manuela resisted.

"Come along now, what's the matter? It's not a new one, certainly—but it was a fine, clean young lady that had it before you. Look for yourself: not a single sweat-mark under the arms. You can think yourself lucky to get it. Don't be so finicky—that kind of thing won't take you very far here, let me tell you."

In spite of herself Manuela's hands began to tremble. A grey horror invaded her; she felt suddenly as if she were no longer herself. As if she had lost her own skin. The sleeves of the frock were too short at the wrists. The skirt was wide and crumpled. The black apron was scratchy; it was of cotton moire and stuck out in front of her like a board.

"See how well that fits you!" said Marie, unmoved. "So now we'll put on a cockade, and then you're ready."

"A cockade?" Manuela looked inquiringly at Marie.

"Yes, of course—everybody has to wear one . . ." and she brought out a box filled with coloured rosettes. Yellow, red, black and light blue, for each class there was a different badge. Of course; all the girls downstairs had been wearing these carnival favours. . . .

"It's a red one you need, pick yourself one. These aren't new either, none of them, if you can bring yourself to put up with that."

Manuela turned them over, and picked out a red cockade, observing that on the back, where the ruche was attached to a white piece of stuff with a safety-pin on it, there was something inscribed in ink. She held it to the light to decipher the inscription.

"Marie?"

"Yes, gracious Fräulein?"

"Marie, what does this mean? Here's a heart and an arrow and three letters: E. v. B.?"

The old woman suddenly thrust her face close to Manuela so that the girl felt her breath, which reeked of coffee. One of her brown, wrinkled hands fell on Manuela's arm, and she leered into Manuela's face to observe the effect of her words.

"What does it mean? It means Elisabeth von Bernburg. One of the ladies. The ladies, they're the mistresses, you know." And since Manuela showed no trace of comprehension she added in a whisper, as if it were a profound secret: "The young lady who used to wear this cockade seemingly had a fancy for Fräulein von Bernburg."

Manuela stared in some bewilderment at the old woman, who opened her eyes wider and with her forehead wrinkled into a thousand creases peered suggestively at the girl.

"In love, she was, in love with her. . . ."

"In love? With a governess?" Manuela could not understand that.

The old woman burst into a shrill cackle.

"Just you take the cockade, little Fräulein—it doesn't matter—you'll soon learn—you'll soon find out about the 'governess.'"

Marie laughed so much that she began to cough. Manuela regarded the inky heart and turned the cockade in her hand. She could not bear to look at Marie again, but she allowed her to pin the thing on. The proper place for it was on the apron-string over the left shoulder, a little above the heart.

IV

UNCERTAINLY Manuela descended the white staircase. Her small hand clung timidly to the iron balustrade that led from post to post. For the first time since her arrival in this place she was quite alone. With a despairing gesture she put her free hand up to her hair, and then, standing still, pulled at her apron-strings, which were too tight, and tore at the stiff, high collar that threatened to chafe her neck. If Papa were to see her like that—and Fritz—and Mother Inge . . .

The electric lights illumined the house but sparsely. Manuela hesitated, not knowing which way to turn. She could not tell where she was, where the dressing-room was, where the corridor was or the dormitory. A chill struck through her from the damp, white walls. Then she heard light, rapid footsteps ascending the stairs and a clear, pleasant face laughed up at her.

" My name's Edelgard—what's yours? "

" I'm No. 55."

Edelgard laughed.

" No, what's your name, I mean. . . ."

" Oh! " Manuela passed her hand over her face as if to remove a veil. " Manuela."

The other girl took her by the arm in a warm and comradely fashion.

" I say, what a lovely name. Are you always called that? "

" No—my—at home they always called me Lela, and sometimes Lel."

Edelgard bent over quickly and looked into Manuela's face.

" May I call you Lela too? "

Manuela was confused by so much friendliness. She could make no other answer but " Yes, please do," although she would have liked to say much more, yet there was something rising in her throat again, almost suffocating her.

" Have you unpacked your things already? "

" Yes."

" Then we've plenty of time. Sit down a minute. We're not allowed to sit on the stairs, but there's nobody about."

Manuela obeyed. But she was immediately aware that this submission was the last straw. She had to snatch out her handkerchief, for her sobs could no longer be suppressed. They rose up in spite of her. They mastered and shook her. Edelgard laid her arm right round Manuela's shoulders.

" Come on, have your cry out."

Manuela was ashamed. If she could only stop—but she simply couldn't.

" All the girls cry when they come first, Lela. It doesn't matter. We don't think anything of it; you needn't be ashamed. Have your cry out, and then you'll feel better. And you'll sleep all the sounder after a good cry."

The sobs gradually subsided. Manuela blew her nose. Edelgard's quiet voice did her good.

" You know, it's the first few days that are so unbearable. But that soon passes off. And after that you won't have to stand being asked so many questions, either."

Lela pressed Edelgard's hand.

" Thanks, you're very good to me."

"That's only because I'm sorry for you."

"Oh, don't mind me, it'll soon be over; I'm a terrible slacker, that's all. Do forgive me."

Edelgard tried to turn the conversation.

"Do you know which dormitory you're in?"

"Yes. Dormitory One, Marga told me."

"Oh, I say, you're in luck."

"How's that?"

"That's where everybody wants to be—because of Fräulein von Bernburg. . . ."

This was the second time that Manuela had encountered the name. But she did not want to ask any questions—indeed, there was no necessity, for Edelgard went on of her own accord:

"We all like Fräulein von Bernburg immensely, although she's very strict. But, you see, she's so frightfully just. All the other teachers have their pets, but Fräulein von Bernburg likes all of us the same and makes no favourites. I wonder what you'll think of her."

At that moment a bell rang and a shrill cry echoed along the lower corridor:

"Take your places! Take your places!"

Edelgard took Lela by the hand.

"That's Kesten; come on, it's prayers now. I'll point out the teachers to you beforehand," and both of them ran downstairs and were lost in the throng of a hundred and fifty girls who came flocking in answer to the bell from every room in the house.

There was much chatter and laughter and shouting and running to and fro. On a bench by the wall sat several ladies in the same kind of grey dress that Fräulein von Kesten wore. They all wore the badge

of the Seminary on a blue ribbon attached to their
bosoms. They all had white lace caps on their heads.
At the second bell the ladies rose and the children
arranged themselves in columns, two by two along the
wall. The various classes were separated from each
other: nothing but the colour of the cockade distinguished one column from its neighbour.

Edelgard stayed beside Manuela, and they found
their places in their class. Fräulein von Kesten was
standing beside a door, her hand on the bell ready
to give the third signal. But first she ran her eye over
the waiting files of children. On the command " Left
turn " they all turned round so as to face the door and
the row of grey ladies standing before them. On the
third stroke of the bell the door opened.

This is like a theatre, thought Manuela, trembling
as she stood in the line.

" That's the Head," whispered Edelgard, who was
secretly holding Lela's hand. Low as the whisper was,
it was immediately reprimanded by a severe glare from
Fräulein von Kesten.

The tall figure of an elderly woman appeared—a
massive figure, for it moved forward only by the help
of a stick; yet one could feel at once an enormous force
of will that reduced the importance of the stick to a
minimum. In her arm she bore a Bible. Her dress
was grey, a deeper grey than that of the other ladies.
Her lace cap was black with two lace ties hanging
down at the sides. Her vast bulk almost filled the
doorway. She carried her head high. Her small grey
eyes ran searchingly over the ranks of the curtsying
children. Her skin was yellowish, and the prominent
cheek-bones gave her face a hard look. Her chin was

energetic, her mouth narrow, and firmly compressed. Now she handed her stick to Fräulein von Kesten and opened the Bible. The bare corridor carried her voice well; it was a firm voice, distinct and almost masculine.

"In the name of the Father, the Son and the Holy Ghost."

A low "Amen" from all present answered her.

There followed the reading of a chapter from the New Testament. Until this moment Lela had not been able to tear her eyes away from those of the Headmistress. A cold shudder ran down her spine at the thought of what this woman must be like when she was angry. Lela found it more comfortable to gaze at the "ladies." The small old creature with the somewhat Chinese face was Mademoiselle Oeuillet, the French teacher; beside her was a pretty young woman, Miss Evans, the English mistress. Next to her, if Lela had not mistaken Edelgard's instructions, was Fräulein von Gaerschner. Tall and energetic, she stood very straight, but in spite of her severe appearance was supposed to be not half bad. Fräulein von Attems was also popular, especially since she did no teaching; she had something to do with the housekeeping.

At the end of the line stood Fräulein von Bernburg. Lela's eyes rested attentively on her face. Fräulein von Bernburg was gazing obliquely at the floor. Her eyes seemed to be half shut; her strong, beautifully arched eyebrows were slightly raised; her broad mouth, full of character, had a hint of arrogance about it at the moment, and her slightly curved, aristocratic nose seemed to be somewhat dilated. One got the impression that her jaws were locked very firmly on each other,

for the muscles under the fine skin of her lean face
were plainly visible. Her forehead was high and
narrow, with hollows at the temples. Her ears lay close
to her head. She had a resolute chin. It was a face
with something unyielding about it. Her black hair
was severely parted and brought low in a knot at the
back of her neck, a style which suited the noble contour
of her head. Her neck was slender but the muscles were
strong that supported it and vanished into the high,
well-fitting collar. Her shoulders were broad, her hands
well-shaped; long, narrow, somewhat bony hands, bare
of ornament.

" We shall now sing the hymn: ' Take Thou my hand
and lead me. . . .' "

The altered pitch of the Head's voice awoke Manuela
from her meditations. Low and hesitating at first,
then more and more assured rang out the hymn which
Manuela tried to follow from a hymn-book held out
to her.

> " Take Thou my hand and lead me,
>   Do Thou go on before;
> Until the end I need Thee,
>   And evermore.
>
> I need Thee to befriend me,
>   Alone I cannot go.
> Oh, let me but attend Thee
>   To and fro."

Manuela's voice began to falter. She could not go
on; her lips could frame only a syllable here and there.
Involuntarily her eyes sought again the face of Fräulein
von Bernburg, who had now lifted her head and seemed

to be gazing far beyond the children and the corridor
and the whole school.

> " I need Thy love to shelter
>   My faint and trembling soul,
> To hold me when I falter,
>   To keep me whole.
>
> At Thy dear feet I lay me,
>   Thy humble child am I.
> Blindly I will obey Thee,
>   Oh, let me lie."

sang the clear, unthinking young voices. The walls
re-echoed the song. The children liked singing, and
it was all one to them what they sang. The letters of
the last verses flickered before Manuela's eyes; her
mouth was shut; the sobs that had receded were returning now with dreadful force.

> " And even if I mistake Thee
>   And fail to know Thy might,
> Thou wilt not yet forsake me
>   In darkest night.
>
> Take Thou my hand and lead me,
>   Do Thou go on before;
> Until the end I need Thee,
>   And evermore."

The melody died away. The Head shut her Bible
and folded her hands, saying in a low voice:

"Let us pray."

With bowed heads the children all joined in the
Lord's Prayer:

"Our Father which art in heaven . . ." Then all
heads were raised again while the Head pronounced
the benediction:

"The grace of Our Lord Jesus Christ and the love of God and the fellowship of the Holy Ghost be with you all now and for ever. Amen."

"Amen" came echoing in response. The Head handed the Bible to Fräulein von Kesten and received again her stick with the silver crook handle. As if she had turned into a different creature her voice now changed, her face reddened, her eyes widened. Sharply these words cut the air:

"I have a few things to say to you." Her eyes pierced the children before her. "It has come to my ears that disobedience is becoming rampant again. Rules are being ignored. Some of you are sending out letters without submitting them first for inspection, letters which contain, of course, groundless complaints about the conduct of this establishment. I have instructed the servants to report to me at once every infringement of this regulation. Anyone who is found guilty of such disobedience will be severely punished, and will be made to wear a special dress for walking in the town. Take note of that. The new pupil, Fräulein von Kesten?"

An impatient wave of the hand holding the stick dismissed the children, who bobbed timidly and quickly vanished from the corridor. Manuela remained before the Head with Fräulein von Kesten.

"Manuela von Meinhardis?" asked the Head, holding out a bony hand.

Manuela collapsed in an alarmed curtsy without understanding Fräulein von Kesten's look which intimated that she was to kiss the proffered hand.

"Well, I hope you'll soon settle down among us, my child. You have just heard that infringements of the regulations are severely punished. You will note for yourself that children who behave themselves properly have no cause for complaint here. I shall expect you to bring me a regular report, Fräulein von Kesten."

"Very well, ma'am," replied Fräulein von Kesten significantly. She thoroughly understood the Head's meaning. This little Meinhardis was no ordinary case. But the Head would be satisfied. All this was implied in the tone of her reply and in the gesture of her reverently folded hands.

V

AFTER prayers came supper. Again in orderly ranks, two by two, the children were marched to the dining-room, an enormous square, high, bright room, empty save for the four long tables at the end of which the mistresses sat in state while the hundred and fifty pupils of the Seminary were ranged down the long sides.

It was a cold supper, and beer was served along with it. The girl next to Manuela, Ilse von Westhagen, observing that the new-comer was eating hardly anything, said cheerfully:

"Pocket some of it. You're sure to be hungry later on. Even if you don't like it now, you'll be glad of it afterwards when it's that or nothing. We all do it."

How can you put bread in your pocket, without any paper, thought Manuela, it'll crumble and be full of fluff. And yet she was soon to learn to cram all kinds of things in her pocket—scraps of meat, bits of sugar,

rolls buttered and unbuttered—and, in truth, even if
one didn't fancy the stuff oneself someone else was
always glad to get it.

Another shrill bell—grace after meat. You stood up
to thank God for your evening meal, and all the time
your pocket was weighing you down; it felt exactly
as if you had been stealing.

And after another interval the bell rang again, this
time for bed. In the large corridor all the "ladies"
stood in a row and shook hands with each one of the
hundred and fifty children. To the French mistress
one said "Bonne nuit, Mademoiselle," to the English-
woman "Good night," and to the others "Gute Nacht."
Now they were all in the dressing-room.

"Manuela, quick, come over here—I want to show
you something."

Ilse hauled Lela along by the arm.

"Just come over here, you'll laugh till your sides
split."

Lela let herself be pulled across to Ilse's wardrobe,
that stood almost opposite hers. Ilse threw both doors
wide open and watched Lela's face eagerly to see the
effect. At first Lela was stunned: the display was so
unexpected. Both doors of the wardrobe, outwardly
so white and simple, were lined with fiery red crêpe
paper adorned by a medley of pictures, Japanese fans,
postcards of every kind, Christmas-tree ornaments and
artificial flowers.

"It's beautiful," Manuela managed to say.

Ilse was delighted. Lela was obviously overwhelmed.

"And now look here—this is the knock-out."

Carefully Ilse lifted a pile of underwear, and lo! there
was Lela's book. "Le Ventre de Paris." Ilse beamed.

"There you are; and now just tick off all the things
that are forbidden. Go on."

Embarrassed but smiling Lela complied with the
request.

"Chocolate."

Ilse unrolled a pile of stockings and a package wrapped
in silver paper appeared.

"Money."

Ilse opened a box with a false bottom, in which
letters were lying innocently. But underneath there
was the chink of metal.

"Jewellery," said Lela, feeling all at sea but unwilling
to spoil Ilse's pleasure.

Ilse took out a drawing-pin and pulled down a flap
of the red paper on the door. And there hung a gold
chain, a bracelet and a narrow golden ring.

"But, Ilse!" Manuela's fears rose up. "Whatever
happens when it's inspection and your wardrobe's
examined? Fräulein von Kesten . . ."

"Won't find a single thing!" said Ilse, in great glee
over Lela's alarm. "We manage it like this. When
my wardrobe's up for inspection I park all my stuff in
Ilse von Treitschke's wardrobe, for she's in a different
dormitory, and when it's her turn to be spied on she
parks hers with me. Good idea, isn't it?"

"Magnificent," said Lela, and meant it, too.

Ilse was enjoying herself in the rôle of enlightener.

"I say, if you want to get round the regulations at
any time just ask me, and I'll tell you what to do. I
won't split, and you won't be caught. For instance,
if you have too many bad marks, what happens? You
don't get leave to go out. But good marks can make
up for the bad, and you get good marks, for instance,

if you darn a stocking well. But, of course, there are
never enough torn stockings to go round, for everybody
who has bad marks grabs a stocking to darn. Well,
then, I just help myself to one, and cut the heel off—
that makes a glorious hole and an enormous number
of good marks. . . ."

"Thanks very much," said Lela, laughing.

"Don't mention it. And I know a lot of other
tricks—about letters and so on—don't you be taken in
by all that the Head said to-night. Besides, you see,
when she's really up in the air and I feel downright
afraid of her, I know what to do. I simply imagine to
myself what she looks like when she's got no clothes
on . . ."

Lela burst out laughing—and so did Lilly von Kattner
and Ilse von Treitschke who had just come up. Their
giggles drew others into the group.

"Girls, Ilse's made a first-class joke. . . ."

The joke was repeated and renewed peals of laughter
shook the dressing-room.

VI

"WHAT are you doing, Manuela?" inquired Ilse. They
were all lying in bed, except Manuela, whose demeanour
was making Ilse shriek with laughter, for she stood
gazing at her cold, white bed and suspiciously fingered
the coarse, patched hospital coverlets into which she
was now supposed to step.

Manuela, however, did not laugh. She sat down
hesitatingly on the edge of the bed and did not venture
to put her feet under the bedclothes. The iron frame

of the bedstead was cold against her bare legs, and there was no spring in it. I'll never be able to sleep on this ghastly thing, thought Manuela. And so many people in one room. . . . Ever since she could remember she had had a room to herself, and her bed at home was of lovely, warm brown wood, with dreamy, soft pillows, and was so comfortable that in all her childish illnesses she had been happy to stay in it. And then . . . a long time ago . . . there had been another bed, into which one sank blissfully, a bed with a silken coverlet that tucked itself round her when as a small, shivering child she snuggled in beside the softness of a quietly breathing bosom, beside the warmth of the body that had borne her, and that filled the sheets and pillows with its sweet and wonderful fragrance.

Lela drew her icy-cold knees under her chin and stared into vacancy. That fragrance was gone—it could not be retained in memory like pictures, or like words, like the thousand and one things that brought Mamma back to her and lay so deeply embedded in her mind; but still, once upon a time, oh, God, how long ago it seemed! there had been a mother for Lela; for a brief space only, now past and gone.

"Manuela!" called Edelgard in a low voice, "you must lie down. Fräulein von Bernburg will be here in a minute."

So Manuela slid her feet under the bedclothes and lay down obediently. The pillow was hard, the blankets thin. The light burning high up near the roof dazzled her eyes. Bed No. 55 was in the middle of the room; a narrow gangway separated it from Edelgard's bed, and on the other side lay Mia von Wallin who had not yet addressed a single word to Manuela.

Suddenly, in expectation of Fräulein von Bernburg's arrival, they were all hushed and solemn in their beds. Manuela could not help thinking that for the first time they looked really like children in their long-sleeved nightdresses from whose cuffs the scrubbed, reddened hands protruded, and with their long, loose plaits which at night were released from hairpins. Only Ilse, with her bobbed head, looked like a boy among the others.

A door that Manuela had hitherto overlooked opened, and a sigh went round the room; Fräulein von Bernburg was coming in.

"Well, children, are you all right?" she asked, and then began to go round the beds, saying good night to each occupant.

Ilse, whose bed stood at the foot of Manuela's, sat up and whispered over her shoulder:

"Watch, Manuela, see what happens now. . . ."

Her eyes were shining. She knelt in her bed, and Manuela saw that a whole row of girls were already kneeling like Ilse, waiting for Fräulein von Bernburg, who paused beside each of them a moment, took their heads in both hands, and dropped a kiss upon their foreheads.

"Good night, Edelgard! . . . Good night, Ilse!"

She was coming nearer and nearer to Manuela's bed. Manuela's heart beat thick and fearful. She did not know whether she was doing right in continuing to lie down. Perhaps she, too, ought to have been kneeling. Was it a regulation? No, of course not, the others were doing it of their own accord—but she, a stranger, what was she to do?

So she lay quite motionless, waiting, her hands on top of the bedclothes. Her heart beat more and more thickly; she began to tremble; she could feel her clenched teeth chattering a little.

And then the problem was solved quite simply. The grave lady who was walking round the room stopped close beside Manuela's bed and took in her warm, comforting hands the ice-cold hand of the agitated girl.

"We haven't really spoken to each other yet, Manuela," she said. "I hope you sleep well on your first night among us."

And before Manuela could reply—ah, she could not have made any reply, for her eyes were dim with tears, and her lips were trembling as if in fever—the hands came nearer, nearer came the voice, a warm breast, a living woman bent over her, and Fräulein von Bernburg kissed Manuela's forehead, quite as if she did not see the tears that now were rolling down both cheeks.

"Thank you, Fräulein von Bernburg," stammered Manuela, but she did not know whether her voice had been heard. For Fräulein von Bernburg was already at the door, switching off the light.

"Good night, children," she said once more, and was gone.

The twelve white beds lay in darkness. Only in one corner there burned a tiny night-light. All the windows were shut, and for moments at a time the silence in the room was profound. Manuela lay with wide-open eyes staring at the door which Fräulein von Bernburg had closed behind her.

VII

DAYS fly rapidly when one has no time for reflection, when each day is the same as the next, when one does not act but is acted upon. A day that is governed by the ringing of an electric bell is a mechanical affair, and one tends to become as mechanical as the bell. That bell roused Manuela from the deepest morning sleep; it urged her downstairs for morning prayers; it shrilled: nine o'clock, school, and again: twelve o'clock, walk; it rang for dinner and once more for school, once more for a walk, once more for a meal; and then, finally, it announced bed-time. It interrupted trains of thought during school hours and gossip in the play-interval; it parted friends in the garden, set hearts beating at the imminence of a disagreeable lesson, and snatched the cup from one's lip at the breakfast table. The bell was authority; the impersonal, ruthless, eternally impassive organizer of an uneventful existence.

Where one day is exactly like another, all days are indistinguishable. That was why the girls kept calendars inside their wardrobe doors, on which each day was crossed off in black. Another day gone, and one reckoned up how many remained till the summer holidays, till Christmas, till one could go " home."

Manuela had no calendar. She had no longer a home. The house in Dünheim had been given up, and she might well never return there again. Of Fritz and his mother, who loved her, she no longer dared to think. Her heartache over them had ceased; she had not even a feeling of homesickness for them. Nothing was left but defiance—defiance and rage at her incarceration in this place—and an undefined, incomprehensible preoccupation which she could not have put into words, but which kept her awake many a night, lying with wide-open eyes. Her father was touring in Italy. Brightly hued postcards displaying blue sea, sunshine, oranges, donkeys and old churches, slowly covered the inner side of Lela's wardrobe.

Fräulein von Bernburg had examined the first batch of these postcards when she inspected Lela's wardrobe. Then she had turned to Lela with the question:

" And your mother? "

In silence Lela had brought out a photograph and laid it in Fräulein von Bernburg's hands.

" My mother is dead. I have no mother. Or else I shouldn't be here. . . ."

That sounded bitter. Fräulein von Bernburg had looked long at the photograph before returning it. Then, with one hand on Manuela's shoulder, she had gazed gravely into the girl's eyes.

" But you have settled down quite well among us already, Manuela. Haven't you made some friends? "

" Yes, Fräulein von Bernburg—only—— "

" Well? You know that you can always depend on me."

" Yes—Fräulein von Bernburg—but if "—and then at last it had come out in a gasping rush—" if you weren't here it would be simply unbearable. . . ."

Fräulein von Bernburg's expression did not change. She went on gazing searchingly at Lela and said, slowly and emphatically:

" You mustn't suggest such an idea to yourself. Whatever is done here is well and rightly done. Even although you don't understand why many things are

not different. It will take time before you begin to
understand. It's not for you to criticize, but to obey.
The greatest Christian virtue is humility. You know
that already, don't you? "

Falteringly the words came from Lela's lips:

" Yes, Fräulein von Bernburg."

" If you shut yourself up in defiance you'll never
find your own place among us. You must have the
conviction that we are all striving to do what is best
for you. Then everything will be easy."

" Yes, Fräulein von Bernburg."

Elisabeth von Bernburg's hand slid from Manuela's
shoulder down to her arm: she held the girl firmly,
she wanted to shake her awake.

" Will you try? "

And Lela looked up into the face that was inclined
towards her, into the dark eyes that seemed to search
her very marrow, and some resistance within her
collapsed. As if she were taking a solemn oath she
gave her word, gazing into those friendly eyes:

" Yes, Fräulein von Bernburg."

Since that moment everything had been different;
everything had acquired a meaning; everything had to
be done for *her* sake, to please her, Fräulein von Bernburg. There was nothing whatever that was uncon-
nected with her, and the day was governed no longer
by the ringing of a bell, but by the voice of Fräulein
von Bernburg. Her voice was not always kindly; it
was often hard and commanding. But Manuela knew
that what she commanded was right: to rise from bed,
to dress, to pray, to learn, to go walking, to wait, to eat,
to sleep. Fräulein von Bernburg was there, and everything was done for her sake.

VIII

ELISABETH VON BERNBURG, like Fräulein von Kesten and
nearly all the mistresses in the school, was the daughter
of an officer of high rank. She was twenty-eight years
old and had spent five years already in the school,
after, as was rumoured, her engagement to a young
lieutenant of dragoons had been broken off because of
her coldness and reserve, which had driven the lieutenant to renounce the connection on the very eve of
the wedding. There were others, however, who argued
that Fräulein von Bernburg herself had informed the
prospective bridegroom that she could never marry
him or any man, an announcement that was supposed
to have raised much dust and to have been construed
in the most shocking manner. This version was
current even among the pupils of the Seminary.
Nobody knew precisely who had started it, but there
was a suspicion that Ilse had brought it back from
Berlin, where she collected much curious information
during the holidays, chiefly from the youthful step-
father she had acquired after her Mamma had divorced
her Papa.

"Girls," she said, "the Bernburger—just imagine, she
could have been married and she chose to come here
instead! She didn't want any children of her own, she's
supposed to have said—and then she simply gave the
man a push—like that—right in the chest, when he was
trying to kiss her."

Oda and Mia exchanged a look and giggled their not
quite innocent giggle. But Manuela rose in wrath.

"Ilse, you've no business to call her 'the Bernburger,'

and besides—these are her private affairs—and nobody
can know what really happened."

"But only think!" said Ilse, much offended, "a
lieutenant of dragoons! You wouldn't catch me
behaving like that."

Everybody laughed, except Marga, who hissed out
"Silence!" having heard Fräulein von Kesten's stealthy
step passing the door.

IX

But Manuela remained reflective. On more than one
night, after Fräulein von Bernburg had switched off the
light in the dormitory, and the girls had all begun to
whisper and to fish out the little electric torches from
under their pillows, Manuela lay tormenting herself with
the question: What was Fräulein von Bernburg doing
now, alone in her own room? Was she happy? Did
she long sometimes to have a husband and children of
her own? Children, yes, Manuela could understand
that, but a husband—no, that was hard to imagine—
and to think of Fräulein von Bernburg in connection
with any man was simply impossible. Miss Evans, now,
she had a sweetheart somewhere in England, and was
supposed to be merely making some pin money before
her marriage; that was quite understandable; and it was
easy enough to imagine Fräulein von Attems, too, as a
country squire's wife, bustling about the kitchen and the
cellars. But Fräulein von Bernburg?

Elisabeth von Bernburg seemed to have no inkling of
all these childish and yet knowing rumours and alarms

that circulated about her. She was always there, silent, authoritative, strict and kindly, moving through the children's days with her serene and graceful bearing; she taught, gave orders, listened, advised—but she remained aloof, closed in upon herself and solitary.

Only once for a single moment was Manuela permitted a glimpse into her heart. It was a Sunday evening and Fräulein von Bernburg had as usual traversed the dormitory, giving each girl a good-night kiss and answering stray questions or administering brief counsel. She was detained also by Manuela.

"Fräulein von Bernburg," said Manuela timidly, "I don't know, there must be something wrong with me— I think I'm ill."

And hesitatingly it all came out; how she had been feeling queer all day with pains in her back, sickness, headache—and now she had just observed that she was bleeding.

Fräulein von Bernburg did not smile. Gravely she sat down on the edge of the girl's bed.

"That's not an illness, Manuela," she said gently. "It's nothing but a sign that you are growing up and have almost ceased to be a child. If that blood did not come you would never be able to have children when you are a woman. All women bleed like that every four weeks. And now I see that I must talk to you like a mother for a little, and tell you what you must do whenever this happens. . . ."

"Thank you, Fräulein von Bernburg," said Manuela. She lay pale and lovely on her pillow and listened more to the sound of the voice than to the instructions it was giving her. When Fräulein von Bernburg rose to go she held her fast.

"Fräulein von Bernburg . . ."

"Yes, what is it now, Manuela?"

"You said—all women. But there are women who never have any children, all the same."

"Yes, my dear, of course, all those who have no husband."

"Fräulein von Bernburg," gasped Manuela, and her hot hand sought the hand of the woman bending over her, "I—I must ask you something—I think about it such a lot—are you happy?"

Elisabeth von Bernburg lifted her head. Without the slightest trace of surprise, as if the question had been the most natural in the world, she looked Manuela in the eyes.

"Yes, my dear," she replied, "because I have all of you."

Perhaps she should have said: "Because I have you." But this daugher and granddaughter of soldiers who had been schooled all their lives to be sparing of their emotions and to despise outbursts of feeling, this virgin daughter of a puritan mother, bred in the fear of God, this young woman who had vowed to herself that she would do her duty truly and uprightly by the children entrusted to her care, could not have brought herself to make such a statement. She had to think here only of "the children"; she dared not let one single child usurp her heart. And now that she had done so in spite of everything, from the very first moment that her eyes had encountered Manuela's, she dared not contemplate anything but self-discipline and renunciation.

It was like a solace, like an undeserved and unhoped-for blessing, the love that this child gave her, so much more genuine than the spectacular worship and adoration of the other children. It was a love that spoke in every gesture and every faltering word of Manuela's. But she would not have been Elisabeth von Bernburg had she not punished herself for feeling happy because of the child, for returning that love boundlessly, with all the strength of her heart.

X

PAPA MEINHARDIS had plenty to do. A capacious basket was standing on the table before him and the head waiter was helping him to pack it. Neither of them had a glance to spare for the brilliant blue sea behind them, or for the palms that were waving gently in the morning breeze.

Attentively Meinhardis inspected the various packages. Cold chicken and caviare on ice. If only it doesn't melt, he thought. Then toast. Then wine—rough, red Sicilian. The first ripe tangerines—how fragrant they were! He was wearing a light grey suit; his face was tanned brown and the light grey hat emphasized the tan. The ladies, of course, weren't ready yet. He hadn't really expected them to be ready, but in any case the carriage was waiting at the gate. The jingling of the bells could be heard even here in the hall.

The waiter bestowed the basket in the vehicle, and when Meinhardis turned round the ladies were already in the doorway. Shrill cries of pleasure greeted him over the gaily bedecked horses, the jolly-looking driver, the bunches of flowers that adorned the carriage, the

silken cushions and dust-rugs. Once more the Lieutenant-Colonel had thought of everything. While they
were getting into the carriage the porter handed Meinhardis on a silver salver two letters which he quickly
shoved into an inside pocket, for he had to tuck the
rug around Ray Cammar's feet.

"Your feet mustn't get dusty," he observed, and set
his own small, light-shod foot on the floor of the
carriage. The two ladies sat facing the driver; he
established himself opposite them and called: "Avanti,
avanti," whereupon with much cracking of the whip
the equipage moved off.

"What were you up to last night after we went to
bed?" inquired Ray, speaking as if to some youthful
sinner whom she had to mother and train in the right
path. She was large and blonde; her lovely summer
frock, her large, light straw hat and the white veil round
her shoulders made her look younger than she was. It
seemed as if Miss Hill, a dried-up little creature, had
been engaged for the same purpose.

Apparently Meinhardis liked to be addressed in that
kind of tone, for a gratified smile flitted over his handsome face.

"Oh, Ray, don't be so hard on me! I was quite good.
I only had a little glass of wine and went off to bed too."

"And who was drinking wine with you? I'm sure it
must have been Miss Booth—I know you, Lieutenant-
Colonel. . . ."

"Oh, Miss Booth!" pouted Meinhardis. "How can
you say such a thing! Miss Booth and I . . . ?"

"Well, she always blushes when you toast her.
Nothing escapes my eye, my dear. . . ."

"Nonsense," disclaimed Meinhardis modestly, "she

wouldn't dream of it." Yet he was flattered by the suggestion, for Miss Booth was very pretty, considerably prettier than Ray. She was so strictly guarded by her old parents, however, that there was little chance for a man who preferred to be left alone with young women.

"But, Ray, you know quite well that it's only you I love. . . ." He raised her gloved hand to his lips with what was intended to be an ironical gesture.

"Haven't I staged it all perfectly for you?" He waved his hand lightly towards the sea and the town of Palermo now lying below them, as if it were all his own creation.

"Beautiful, wonderful, sweet," gushed the two ladies. "That was a brilliant idea of yours, to have a picnic on Monte Pellegrino—so poetical! You're a marvellous man," they assured him, and he was pleased.

"But you got two love-letters just now, and you haven't looked at them yet. Aren't you burning with curiosity?"

"Oh, it's only ladies who are given to curiosity. You mean that you want to know whose letters they are! Well, one is from Marchesa Trani in Rome who is languishing for me, and the other is from the Mafia, threatening to kill me if I go on loving you."

Both ladies laughed.

"Maybe," said Ray, "we women are inquisitive. But such liars as men are we can never hope to become. . . ."

Meinhardis, growing serious, took the letters from his pocket. He had recognized Manuela's handwriting on one of them; the other letter also came from Hochdorf, but he did not know from whom, and so he opened it first. Attentively, with an expression that was unfamiliar

to the ladies, he read it through. One sheet, and then
a second. Suddenly he exploded with laughter.

"This is first-rate—no, absolutely first-rate—I do like
this. Do you know what the Headmistress of the school
where they have put my little girl says about her? She
writes that my daughter is a talented child but tends,
unfortunately, to be rather impertinent!"

Meinhardis slapped his thigh, and the two ladies
giggled.

"Her father over again," was Ray's comment.

And Meinhardis, as if he had done a deserving deed,
admitted:

"Yes, the girl's like me, what? She's not to be taken
in by the crazy old hags. Right she is, too! God knows
what these old women have been trying on with her. . . ."

Hastily he opened the other letter from Lela.

"DEAR PAPA," he read. "This is Sunday, the only
day on which we are allowed to write letters. There's
not much else that we can do on Sundays. I'd like it
very much if you could come here some time, only I
can't tell you why. I'm learning a lot of French so as
to be able to travel later on, like you, and speak lots
of languages. I know English quite well. Our Miss is
very nice. Please send me lots of picture postcards for
my wardrobe.

"Can you speak Italian? That's a language they
don't teach here.

            "Many greetings from
                    "Your affectionate daughter,
                            "MANUELA."

Meinhardis sighed. A funny kind of letter. The

ladies, too, were disappointed. At last he concluded, with another sigh:

"Yet what can the poor child do? All the letters are read before they're sent out. And that's a mean trick. But she must have got into a row"—he laughed again—"when she displayed her tendency to be rather impertinent."

Once more the ladies' laughter pealed out, but it did not ring quite true. They only laughed, indeed, to help their escort to a better frame of mind, for it was not much that Ray could do with a worried father. And Miss Hill came to the rescue.

"It's a good thing for a girl to be sent to boarding-school."

"Yes," said Ray, "I was at a convent school."

Meinhardis pricked up his ears.

"What, you in a convent school? That's something I can hardly imagine. . . ."

"I was exceedingly pious," she hastened to protest against his insinuations.

None the less they were all rather silent for a while. Then they came to a seat with a good view, and Meinhardis suggested a rest. The ladies alighted and the Lieutenant-Colonel extracted a round bottle and some glasses from the basket. Three glasses clinked and were emptied to the health of the small Manuela, with the cheerful wish that her impertinence might long survive in her.

"To-morrow I'll send her some tangerines," said Meinhardis.

XI

" MANUELA! " said a curt voice in a tone of authority. In the dormitory Manuela was busy turning down her bed, the last among the girls. " Come here at once."

Manuela's knees loosened; Fräulein von Bernburg's voice rang hard. At once she dropped her hands and obeyed the summons. As she stood with downcast eyes before Fräulein von Bernburg, she had difficulty in holding herself upright, and her heart thudded until she fancied it must be audible.

" Manuela, what's this I hear about you? Since when have you been given to rudeness? "

No answer came; Lela's head only drooped lower on her breast.

" You have been rude to the Headmistress."

Manuela nodded.

" How did that happen? Tell me."

Haltingly and with anxious fear Manuela began to give an account of herself.

" We were going through the corridor—Ilse and I. And then—and then the Head came past and called to me—and Mademoiselle Oeuillet was there too. And the Head told me to hold myself straight and . . . and I did hold myself straight."

" You were impertinent in your movements, weren't you? "

Manuela nodded guiltily.

" And why, Manuela? "

Manuela had to think back.

" Because—because the Head said we should walk like German soldiers, and I thought she only said that because Mademoiselle was there, and that Mademoiselle would be offended. And so I exaggerated it, and then the Head said I was marching like a boy."

"And you put out your tongue at her? Is that true?"

"No, Fräulein von Bernburg. I only made a face."

"Why?"

"Because"—suddenly Manuela's calm deserted her—"because I want to be a boy, I hate being a girl. I loathe my hair and my skirt, and at home I always wore shorts when I did gymnastics with my brother, and I'd like to wear them all the time."

Now she glanced up at Fräulein von Bernburg, as if pleading for help.

"I don't want to be a woman—I want to be a man, and to be with *you*, Fräulein von Bernburg, and that's why *she* mustn't interfere—not the Head—not *her*."

"Manuela!" Pale and unyielding Fräulein von Bernburg towered over the agitated child. "Words like these must never pass between you and me, do you hear? Now you'll go at once to the Headmistress and beg her pardon."

That was an order and had to be obeyed. Two minutes later Lela was standing before the huge grey figure that regarded her with a frown.

"I have come to apologize and beg your pardon. . . ."

"Did Fräulein von Bernburg send you?"

"Yes, ma'am."

"Indeed. Are you another of her enthusiastic adorers?"

Lela stared large-eyed at the woman confronting her.

"No, ma'am."

"That's all right, then. You may go."

A deep bob; a hollow sound that came from the

Headmistress's stick striking the floor violently; and
Lela was out of the room.

XII

"FRAULEIN VON BERNBURG—one moment, please." That
was the Headmistress's voice, breaking into sharpness
almost before the last echoes of the concluding " Amen "
had died away at the close of " prayers."

"Yes, ma'am? "

And Fräulein von Bernburg vanished behind the
Head into the room which mistresses as well as the
children always entered with sinking hearts—except,
possibly, Bunny, who was no longer a person and so
had nothing more to fear in this world.

"I must ask you again, Fräulein von Bernburg, not
to encourage in any way the hysterical feelings among
the children of which you seem to be the object, and
which apparently tend to arise at their age."

"I assure you, ma'am, I do all that is possible."

"I hope so, Fräulein von Bernburg. But how do
you account to yourself for the obvious preference that
the children show for you? "

Groaning a little, the Headmistress lowered herself
into a chair. The mistress remained standing, studiously
ignoring the gesture which indicated that she too should
sit down. Her voice shook almost imperceptibly, as she
answered:

"I love the children, ma'am, and I try to deal justly
by them."

Darkly the old woman looked at the young one,
standing before her with irreproachable correctness.

"That little Meinhardis in particular seems to me to have an utterly extravagant temperament. I want her to be subjected with special severity to the restraints of discipline. You are young, Fräulein von Bernburg, but if you had my experience you would know that such natures can become a poisonous influence if they are not kept in check."

Fräulein von Bernburg did not flicker an eyelash.

"I shall do my best, ma'am."

"Very well, Fräulein von Bernburg. I shall depend on you."

XIII

Two by two the girls walked through the park. They all wore the same old-fashioned hats, the same old-fashioned cloaks. There was but little conversation. Mademoiselle Oeuillet brought up the rear. This was a French day, and anyone who relapsed into German got a bad mark.

Lilly and Lela were walking silently side by side. Suddenly Lilly nudged Manuela:

"Look!" And she pointed out a squirrel scuttling up a tree.

Manuela halted. She loved animals passionately, and, rapt into forgetfulness, took a step out of the column.

"Manuela!" came a reminder from the rear. The girls behind were already treading on Lela's heels; the whole column was being thrown into confusion.

"You are not permitted to stand still. Go on, there, and keep in line . . ." came in authoritative French from behind.

So they went on, always keeping at the same distance

from each other, always having the same objects to
look at, a pinned-up pigtail under one's very nose, a
hat, a cloak, a dark skirt, a pair of thick black stockings
and a pair of black boots.   Only the leading couple had
any freedom of range, and so there was always great
competition for the privilege of going first.

Many girls liked to lead the column into the town,
past the shops.   One could then have at least a glimpse
of the shop-windows.   It was delightful to peep at a
confectioner's window even although one could not buy
anything.   And it takes a girl with an old-fashioned
hat on her head to have a real appreciation of milliners'
models.   Moreover, in certain circumstances, it was just
possible to slide a letter into a letter-box without being
observed by the supervising mistress.

Even an externally humble little town has its charms
for those who pine, as these children did, for change
and distraction.   One might even encounter the Crown
Prince furiously driving a gig with a fast trotter over
the cobblestones, slim and elegant in his tight-fitting
uniform.   Then the whole column of Seminary pupils
would drop a deep Court curtsy, which amused the
young gentleman so mightily that he had to pull up at
the first opportunity and come back again to enjoy, if
possible, the spectacle once more.

Hungry and weary one returned home.   But dinner
was just as silent a function, for there, too, one had
to speak French—or English, according to the day,
Thursday or Saturday.   Only on Sundays was it
possible to babble freely as one did at home.   The food
was usually lukewarm or cold, because the kitchen was
so far away.   And one usually got up with one's
stomach only half satisfied.   Then came a short

interval during which one could saunter at will through the garden or the sitting-rooms, corridors and dressing-rooms.

XIV

IN small beds by the bare garden wall the first spring flowers were blooming. The bushes were sprinkled with young green. A girl here and there was busy digging and planting. Others were wandering about with books, reading. Manuela had discovered a quiet corner for herself and was declaiming half aloud verses from a hymn-book. She had her hands over her ears to avoid hearing the shouts and cries of the others. Then she laid the book beside her on the seat and called:

" Edelgard, Edelgard! "

Edelgard, without answering, appeared slowly from behind the bushes and drifted towards Manuela.

"Hallo," called Manuela eagerly, "I think I know it now. What about you?"

"Oh, Lela, I don't know any of it—none at all."

Edelgard listlessly sat down on the seat, and Manuela moved up beside her.

"Edelgard——" But at that Edelgard began to weep.

"Edelgard, are you crying again? Is there anything wrong with you?"

But Edelgard shook her head.

"Homesick?"

That word released a pent-up storm of sobs. Manuela laid her arm round Edelgard.

"Edel! Edel! Don't, I can't bear it—I'll have to cry too. Don't, Edel, please stop it."

"Oh, God, Lel, if I could. But I can't, do forgive me. For days I've been wanting to cry, and held myself in the whole time, but now I can't, I simply can't keep it in any longer. Do you know, when I see the snowdrops here and the pansies . . . You've no idea how lovely it is at home just now. As soon as you go into the park there are long borders of early tulips. And before my window there are birches and masses of crocuses, white crocuses that look like eggs, and yellow crocuses and mauve crocuses, and farther over, under the trees, there are violets. . . . It's too silly "—she began to sob again—" but only to think of the birches makes me miserable."

Manuela sat very still. Then she said reflectively:

"Look here, Edelgard, why don't you write and tell your mother about it? Perhaps you could manage to put it so that nobody here would . . . see what you meant. Then probably your mother would let you leave here sooner, once she knows that you're un-happy."

"Oh, she knows it all right. But she says I've just got to stick it. She was here for years herself. And Grandmamma too. That's the way things are done in our family. Papa, for instance, was in the cadet corps, and now my brothers are there too. They don't like it at all, but some time or other they'll be officers, and so they have to stick it."

"But you're a girl. . . ."

"Yes, but I'll probably marry an officer, and my sons will be officers, and my mother says we mustn't be slack."

"My mother," said Lela, as if to herself, "my mother . . ." She could not go on, for a frantic heart-

ache oppressed her, and she could hardly, after all, say
to Edelgard: "If my mother were alive I shouldn't be
here. . . ."

XV

ILSE and Oda were flushed with giggling over a note
that they were deciphering together in a dark corner
of the dressing-room.

"'Beloved and only Oda,'" they read, "'I have
chummed up with Eva von Brettner and we do nothing
but talk of you. . . .'"

They both went off into shrieks of laughter.

"What do you think of that, Ilse, they've chummed
up simply to talk about me! Enough to make you
die, isn't it?"

And Ilse: "How long has Eva had a craze on you?"

"Oh, goodness, I don't know. But she's quite off
her head, I do assure you. Every day she sends me
a present. Where she gets the money from I've no
idea. But yesterday I found a silk handkerchief and
some scent in my bed. The day before that it was a
slab of chocolate. A lordly wench, isn't she?"

"Read the rest."

"Well: 'It makes me frightfully sad that you're not
at all kind to me. Please come, just once, before bed-
time, into the corridor by the boot-room as you did
the other night. . . .'"

"What were you doing then?"

"Oh, I just happened to be passing, and there was
she watching me get out my boots. . . ."

"Well, what else . . . ?"

Ilse was all eagerness, but just as the narrative promised to become interesting an energetic: "What are you doing there, you two?" made them both jump. Fräulein von Bernburg stood confronting them, and with scarlet faces they tried to conceal the letter.

"Give that to me, Oda," came in icy tones from Fräulein von Bernburg's suddenly tight-lipped mouth.

Oda wavered.

"How long are you going to keep me waiting?"

A throng of inquisitive onlookers was gathering at the doorway. Lela was leaning with round eyes against her wardrobe, unconsciously clutching Edelgard's hand.

"Hand it over at once."

At long last Oda decided to give up the crumpled note. Fräulein von Bernburg took it in her hand and without so much as a glance at it, tore it into small shreds. She kept her eyes fixed on the culprits before her, who joined in the general sigh of relief.

"Take this and put it in the waste-paper basket!" She handed the scraps to Oda. "And remember, once and for all, that you are strictly forbidden to write notes to each other."

She turned and went. Lela's tenseness relaxed.

"Oh, Edelgard, wasn't that marvellous? She's a gentlewoman. She won't read other people's letters. If it had been Bunny or Mademoiselle who found that letter! They would have revelled in reading it. But she—she won't even look at it."

And Edelgard nodded thoughtfully.

"Terribly decent, that's what she is."

XVI

ON Sundays the week's routine was upset. To begin
with, Herr Alemann had to polish up his medals. He
had a whole row of these, won when he was a gallant
soldier in the war of 1870-71. Later he had become a
lackey in the service of the Dowager Princess, and since
that involved receiving many royal visitors, he had not
been forgotten in the distribution of favours. Herr
Alemann's hair was faultlessly parted, his black Sunday
coat speckless; Frau Alemann's apron-strings were so
stiffly starched that they stuck straight out, her hair
was sleeked down with water, her dress freshly ironed.
Thus attired, the old couple waited at their door for
the solemn procession coming down from above.

The bell of the small school chapel was ringing. With
noiseless footsteps on the red carpet the Headmistress
descended the stairs, Fräulein von Kesten close behind
her. The other ladies followed one by one. They had
plenty of time, for the children had yet to arrive by
the side staircase. Two and two they filed down, the
first form leading, all of them wearing grey cotton gloves.
Fräulein von Gaerschner took up her position at the
head of the first column and led it along the corridor
to the chapel. The second column, distinguished by
light blue cockades, fell to Fräulein von Attems, who
was still struggling with her white kid gloves. The
pealing of the organ could now be heard in the corridor.
Fräulein von Bernburg took over the third column, and
Mademoiselle and Miss joined the last. Then came
Marie in a black dress with an enormous brooch on
which a monogram was visible with an imperial crown

above it, Johanna the housemaid, two other housemaids with shining red faces, and the cook. Frau Alemann brought up the rear.

Herr Alemann withdrew to his post as door-keeper. There was always a chance that Her Royal Highness the Princess might turn up to divine service in the school chapel, and he had to be ready to fling open the gate at once. A Court pew was always vacant in the chapel, reserved for just such an occasion. Slowly the sound of singing grew fainter: Frau Alemann had closed the doors.

After the service there was only a short break before visitors began to arrive and escorts for the girls whose turn it was to have leave of absence. To the envy of all spectators these lucky ones got into their own frocks, undid their plaits and looped their hair with gigantic bows of ribbon. In the prevailing dark blue and black of the uniforms they made splashes of colour, red, pink, white and bright blue. Their movements were rapid and excited. They rattled their bracelets and counted the coins in their little purses. Injunctions were whispered in their ears to bring back this, that and the other from the town. Their heads kept jerking, often without cause, for they enjoyed feeling the silken softness of the loose hair that swept their cheeks. The lookers-on, too, liked to have a tug at it and said admiringly: " What lovely hair you have. . . . Is that silk, your frock? Is that the latest fashion? " One girl was pirouetting round so that her pleated skirt flew out around her like a disc: when she stood still it fell again into its respectable folds. Frau Alemann called out the names; a quick kiss, an " Adieu, hope you enjoy yourself! " and off they careered downstairs to meet their relatives. Herr Alemann could not open the gate fast enough for them.

The "enjoyment" that awaited them and made them such objects of envy to their friends was usually of this nature:

A walk through the town, in the course of which the escorting aunt usually met countless acquaintances who all said the same things and spoke the same Hochdorf lingo. In Hochdorf there were certain words that had to be slurred carelessly in pronunciation just to show that they were in familiar use. The long phrase "First Guards Regiment," for instance, had to be enunciated in one syllable, and any genuine Hochdorfer could do it. For the Hochdorfers, by virtue of having been born in Hochdorf, were superior to all other people. They had the privilege of referring to the Princes of the ruling house by their Christian names; indeed, if the Prince were called, for instance, "Hubert," and happened to be married, he and his whole family were simply called "the Huberts." The ruling family itself received the appellation "our lords and masters," in generous recognition of superior status; still, whenever the old Prince was ill the town ladies liked saying: "Poor old man, he has a lot to do," or "His poor wife nurses him devotedly," and if a little Prince took the measles Hochdorf was really quite pleased. That was so human!

"My niece . . ." the aunt would murmur by way of introduction.

"Oh, you're in the Seminary, are you? What a lovely time you must have there. . . ."

Then at the aunt's house there was a hearty and, it must be admitted, satisfying midday meal, after which

one withdrew to the "best room" for coffee. . . . In
Hochdorf the best rooms, too, all looked the same.
They were, without exception, adorned by trophies con-
sisting of antlers and horns or, alternatively, of pistols
and sabres. Stuffed birds, the skins of animals slain by
one's own hands, polished skulls, wild beasts' teeth and
such-like ornaments also bedecked the walls. Those that
came from the royal hunting-grounds were the most
highly prized. Many articles in ordinary use, moreover,
were contrived out of animal remains: ash-trays made of
an elephant's foot, more ash-trays of butterfly wings
stretched under glass, antlers set up as clothes-stands.
And buttons made of stag's teeth were worn on one's
clothes.

All these things were befittingly admired by the pale
little visitors from the Seminary, who were mostly
tongue-tied from excessive shyness. It was a change for
them and they thought it all lovely, and if an aunt took
them out for coffee in the afternoon to the open-air
military concert they were completely happy.

Those who were left behind went back listlessly to the
uncomfortable chairs of the sitting-room or lounged
about the schoolrooms writing letters. All over the
building, equally distributed, sat the ladies, one in each
room as supervisor. The ladies were just as bored
as their charges, and on this day were more inclined to
take part in a little gossip. But the pupils who availed
themselves of the privilege, such as Marga, who liked
to fawn on Kesten, belonged to the ostracized tribe of
"pushers." Most of the girls were glad to avoid seeing
a grey dress on Sundays.

It was always possible to stand looking out of a
window, provided one escaped notice. On Sundays

there was always somebody passing. Families coming
home from church—usually an officer accompanied by
his wife, with children in sailor suits, which had been
adopted in Hochdorf as a kind of uniform for children.
Otherwise it was considered good taste in Hochdorf to
wear the fashions of the day before yesterday. It did
not matter what kind of outmoded excrescence one
adopted, it needed only to be outmoded. If the fashions
of twenty years ago had demanded masses of false hair,
for instance, one stuck to false puffs of hair and a simple
coiffure was "impossible." The reason for this was that
the reigning consort of the princely family was nearly
always an old lady who, from sheer force of habit, could
not abandon the fashions of her youthful prime, and so,
automatically, her style of dressing represented good
taste in the family and therefore in Hochdorf society,
which, of course, considered itself a part of the family.
Whenever any member of the ruling house died, all the
Hochdorf ladies went into mourning as if they had lost
one of their own uncles.

True, all that was not exactly exciting to look at, but
to exchange one state of boredom for another can be in
itself an excitement.

Manuela and Edelgard were looking for a private
corner, for they wanted to be alone. And precisely that
was the most difficult desire of all to satisfy in this house,
where one had to live the herd life. There was always
somebody behind or in front of or beside one, at bed-
time, at lessons, at meals, or on walks. The two girls
sought out a store-room near the gymnasium where
apparatus was kept—their own discovery—but on this
day they found it already occupied. Oda and Mia were
sitting very close to each other with flushed red faces,

and started away from each other as soon as the door
opened. Angrily they flashed out:

" We were here first."

" Well, we're not thinking of disturbing you," returned
Edelgard, also flushing, and betook herself up a narrow
ladder that led to a garret. The garret was so low that
one had to go stooping, but in the middle of it rose
the tower clock. The clock itself, of course, was not
visible from that point. It had a little tower all to itself
with a roof on top, but from below that looked like a
four-square cupboard of rough wood with two large holes
for windows. One could crawl in there and sit down
at the windows. There was a loud noise of ticking and
the immense weights hung just over Manuela's head, so
that if one of them were to fall she would have been
killed on the spot; but they were not likely to fall, for
they descended very slowly on heavy chains, and one
knew that it was growing late when a weight grazed
one's head.

It was too much to expect Frau Alemann to track
Manuela up there. Aunt Irene had come on a visit and
had to sit waiting in the lower corridor until Manuela
could be informed. But at long last the shrill cries
reached Lela's ear, and rapidly, to avoid her retreat being
discovered, she scuttled down.

Aunt Irene had brought many small packages with
her, and Manuela, still hungry after her breakfast, could
not wait until her visitor's departure, but sank her teeth
eagerly into the cakes. On all the seats around sat
visitors with shy or bored or beaming Seminary pupils
beside them, and Bunny patrolled the corridor watch-
fully, dealing out polite greetings and occasional warn-
ings. Gifts of chocolate and sweets had to be handed

over to her, and it took all Aunt Irene's skill to smuggle
a packet into Lela's expectantly emptied pocket while
carrying on a pretence of conversation. Tenderly she
ran her hand over Lela's head.

"But you're getting on quite well, are you?" she asked
kindly.

Lela looked up with a happy face. At this moment,
with a friendly voice inquiring for her welfare, she found
that she was really content; besides, Aunt Irene had
Mamma's very voice and said the same kind of things
as Mamma, and when Lela looked up in her face it was
Mamma's face that became visible rather than Aunt
Irene's.

None the less Lela cast an embarrassed glance round
her before answering:

"Thank you, quite well. . . ."

Aunt Irene seemed relieved. She was often worried
about the child. She did not approve of institutional
training. And Manuela always looked so pale whenever she saw her, and was so curiously reserved . . .
still, that might be natural enough at her stage of
development.

Now Fräulein von Kesten came over to greet Frau
von Kendra.

"I believe it's next Sunday, Fräulein von Kesten, that
Manuela is to be allowed to visit us?"

And Bunny bowed with a polite smile.

"If she's a good girl and gets no bad marks this
week. . . ."

"We'll hope not, certainly!"

Aunt Irene took leave of Fräulein von Kesten and
embraced her niece. Once outside the door she drew a
long breath of relief. Every time she came to the place

she found the atmosphere oppressive, but, of course, it was possible that the children did not feel it so badly. . . .

Somehow or other Sunday always came to an end Manuela had met Fräulein von Bernburg in the upper corridor and she had caressed her hair, saying: "Well, how are things going?" And Lela's heart had risen to her throat because she thought of all the forbidden chocolate in her pocket.

At night, however, when all twelve girls were lying in bed before the light was turned off, an unexpected apparition stood in the doorway of the dormitory. It was Bunny, holding a large wooden receptacle, a drawer from some chest, which was already full of a medley of things, chiefly sweets, chocolate and fruit—but there was also perfume and jewellery and money there. Petrified with terror the children stared at her.

"Who has any contraband hidden in the bed?" she inquired, almost gaily.

One could not banish the impression that this pirate expedition rejoiced Bunny's heart. At first she met with silence and embarrassment, but she began to call out one by one the names of those she suspected, all those who had had visitors or had paid visits to friends in the town.

"Ilse!" and Fräulein von Kesten's eye fixed poor Ilse.

Ilse, however, maintained her composure, and like a gambler who knew how to play a losing game, felt under her mattress with a cool: "Well, this is my lot . . ." and fished out three cream tarts, a little squashed, certainly, but enticing enough to the spectators.

All the confiscated property was supposed to be laid aside and restored to the owners when they had leave to go out or when the holidays came round, but, after all, much of it perished by keeping and in the end seemed to have sadly diminished. For the moment it was certain that the good things the children had looked forward to enjoying in the silence and peace and darkness of night were as good as lost.

Fräulein von Bernburg was not there. That was a comfort to Manuela as she advanced in full view of everybody, just as she was, in her nightgown with her bare feet shuffling in slippers, to hand over her chocolate.

PART SIX

I

"WELL, to be quite frank, ma chère, I don't understand you." Mademoiselle was sitting in a comfortable chair in Fräulein von Bernburg's room. Both ladies were drinking tea and nibbling at cakes. Fräulein von Bernburg was leaning back, apparently absorbed in the picture hanging on the wall above the Frenchwoman's head. She did not try to stem the flood of Mademoiselle's adjurations, although it was by no means the first time she had heard them. All Mademoiselle's zealous arguments drew merely an amused smile from Fräulein von Bernburg.

"Eh bien, you're a handsome woman. You're young, and I have been told that you have money. You have fascination. You're clever. You could play a great part in social life. I don't understand you. An aristocrat, too. You could appear at Court. You could marry..."

Fräulein von Bernburg laughed in her face.

"Why should that make you laugh, Fräulein von Bernburg? I'm telling you the truth. You're a personality, and what are you doing with yourself? Turning sour in this barracks for girls. Enfin, as for me, I'm old. I've always been a teacher. But some fine day I'll take my money and go back to Paris. Oh, Paris—that would be the place for you; not to sit here until you're old and withered. . . ."

"But, my dear old Nelke, I like being here. . . ."

"Mais non, never—don't tell me that!"

Now Fräulein von Bernburg became serious.

"I do, my dear. Not only do I like it, I love this kind of life."

"Mais comment—always the rude children, always Kesten, always this Headmistress—it's not a life at all."

"It's a full life, a good life, a lovely life. I love the children. They gladden my heart."

"Sans doute, but—you're so very strict with them. Seldom do you laugh with them or make a joke. . . ."

"They have plenty of jokes among themselves. What they need is seriousness. They need something to hold on to. We have to be both mother and father to them."

"But you're never intimate with them. You keep your distance. Always aloof."

A shadow crossed Fräulein von Bernburg's face.

"Oh, no, I think that they look on me as a friend in need. They all know that they can come to me in the last resort."

"Well then, what about you yourself? You're living a life of complete renunciation—to what end? There's so much . . ." The little Mademoiselle grew agitated.

"Not for me," said Fräulein von Bernburg gently. "For me there's only one thing: the love of these children. You see, Mademoiselle, the children need someone they can believe in."

"Ah ça"—and Mademoiselle shrugged her shoulders —"if that's enough for you. . . . I was once young myself, and I should never have fancied being an ideal for nobody but some little girls."

Fräulein von Bernburg rose to her feet and leaned both hands on the table.

"It's enough for me," she said. "An ideal is something incredibly lofty. To be an ideal for all these poor girls who are sent out among strangers, so young —away from home, away from brothers and sisters and mothers—that would be for me the highest thing I could achieve."

The small, wrinkled Mademoiselle also rose to her feet.

"You are very unselfish, Fräulein von Bernburg. In general I look on unselfish people with some suspicion, for they are usually the most self-interested of all, but as for you—I must admire you. I can't see where self-interest could enter into your actions at all."

Fräulein von Bernburg blushed to the very roots of her lovely hair, that was but poorly concealed by the lace cap of the Seminary uniform.

"There is certainly self-interest in enjoying one's happiness—the happiness of loving, Mademoiselle—and that self-interest leads us into one mistake after another."

The shrill summons of a bell was heard.

The little Mademoiselle gathered up her handwork.

"That bell drives me crazy. Believe me, I'd often like to put my hands over my ears simply to avoid hearing that bell."

And then, as no answer was forthcoming, she shook her head.

"You shouldn't take this school so much to heart. You'll be sick of it one day—always children coming and going—always leaving you behind."

"Yes," said Fräulein von Bernburg, finding it impossible to smile at this moment while Mademoiselle pressed her hand in farewell, "always leaving me behind. That's true. But I don't forget them. And some of the children, believe me, Mademoiselle "—and for the first time her well-schooled voice trembled curiously—" there are *some* who won't ever forget me. . . ."

II

It was the Scripture lesson, the first lesson of the day, which Fräulein von Bernburg herself conducted for the third form. In the room dead silence reigned. During this hour there was never any misbehaviour. Fräulein von Bernburg stood tall and straight before the class and listened to the recital of a hymn which had been set for the day's task. With familiar fluency the hymn was reeled off. Each child learned well; that was a matter of course. Manuela was gazing at Fräulein von Bernburg, waiting her turn for a glance from her. But it did not come. Everybody was called upon save Manuela. Why? Lela's eyes took on a boundlessly yearning and sorrowful expression: her hands played nervously with a ruler. Fräulein von Bernburg was so aloof. . . . At last it rang out:

" Manuela! "

Quickly she jumped to her feet.

" Third verse."

Manuela felt giddy. The whole room swam round her.

" ' Oh for a thousand tongues to sing . . .' " she began; no, no, that was the first verse—the third—the third— yes, that was it:

" ' Why do ye fail me, all my powers . . .' "

Go on—go on—she could feel Fräulein von Bernburg's eyes upon her, she could hear Ilse prompting her in a whisper, but she could grasp nothing; she only stood gazing up into Fräulein von Bernburg's face and had forgotten every word.

Fräulein von Bernburg returned the look sadly and opened her hymn-book. "Again you've learned nothing! " and Lela had to sit down.

Yet the hymn-book was never out of Lela's pocket. At every opportunity throughout the day she extracted it and learned from it. At night she kept it under her pillow, and learned from it as she was dressing in the morning. But as soon as Fräulein von Bernburg said: " Manuela! " everything vanished. Then her head was empty, her knees faint, her hands cold and damp. If she could but once manage to tell her about it! She yearned for the evening to come, and rehearsed to herself a hundred times what she would say and how she would say it. That she couldn't help herself, that it was only fright, and that she really did learn ever so much—all for her, only it was in vain. Trembling she knelt in her bed. Fräulein von Bernburg had turned the light out and was going softly from bed to bed. Only two more and she would be at Lela's.

Lela's heart thudded as if it would burst. She gave herself her word of honour that she would " tell everything " this time. And instead, she opened her arms and in a sudden collapse of weakness threw herself on the neck of Fräulein von Bernburg, who nearly lost her balance and in alarm held the trembling child fast.

" But Manuela, Manuela," she said, in a low, soothing voice.

Gently her hands tried to loosen the clinging arms.

Lela eagerly snatched those hands, remembering what
she had pledged herself to do, and pressed her hot
face into them. The hands did not resist. They let
her do it. They received the tear-wet face of the child,
and Fräulein von Bernburg bent down and kissed a
quivering mouth.

" Steady, Manuela. . . ."

Her hand caressed the head lying on her shoulder,
and the child did not guess that she herself in that
moment was perhaps even more in need of comfort.

" Steady, my darling—don't get so excited."

Carefully she took Manuela by the shoulders and
laid her back on her pillow.

" Sleep well," and from Lela came a low " Thank
you."

III

For weeks now the preparations for the celebration of
the Head's birthday had brought some variety into the
monotony of life. As every year, this event, which
took place in May, was to be crowned by a dramatic
performance staged by the pupils, and this time, in
pursuance of an unwritten law, it was Mademoiselle
Oeuillet's turn to direct the proceedings and to super-
vise the production of some French play. After much
hesitation she had pitched on Voltaire's " Zaïre," a
classical piece, distinguished for the rhythm of its lines
and the lofty chivalry of its tone, that touched on
no problems unfitted for the youthful years of the
performers.

During these weeks the mistresses somewhat relaxed their exacting requirements, and wherever one went one encountered children zealously studying and memorizing their parts.

Manuela, who seemed to be a favourite of Mademoiselle's, had been given the role of the crusader Nerestan, whose sister Zaïre, represented by Edelgard, had been taken captive by Orosman, the sultan reigning in Jerusalem. The character of Orosman, passionate in love and second to no Christian in magnanimity, had been assigned to Ilse, and she was never done declaiming with fire-flashing eyes the long, rolling French Alexandrines.

Even in the garden, where the children laboured from time to time with spade and hoe, the eager rehearsals were carried on, until work was forgotten and enthusiasm flamed high. Edelgard herself, so recently drowned in tears because of her springtime homesickness, was as enthusiastic as anybody.

Manuela was standing on a seat with one arm stretched high into the air. One foot advanced in a knightly posture, the spade with which she had just been digging flourished like a sword, she was reciting in a loud and thrilling voice, as if intoxicated by the sound of the syllables:

" Vous, le sang de vingt rois, esclave d'Orosman!
   Parente de Louis, fille de Lusignan,
   Vous, chrétienne et ma sœur, esclave d'un soudan! "

She stopped and waited. Now Edelgard should have come in, the lovely Zaïre, in love with the Moslem Orosman and ready to become his bride. But Edelgard did not seize her cue. Edelgard and Ilse stood staring

at Manuela as if awakening from a trance; Edelgard
and Ilse began to laugh.

" What's the matter? Was it so awful? " asked
Lela anxiously.

" Oh, Lela, you're a perfect scream! " Ilse doubled
with laughter. " You're ranting just like an actress—
do it again properly."

But Lela flourished her spade in the air. Her hair
was untidy and almost falling down; she raised her
glowing face towards the sun and cried:

" Nonsense, I can't do it any other way, I'm much
too happy! Everything's glorious, the garden and the
sun and you and everything. And for the first time
in my life I'm going to be myself, as I really am."

She jumped down from the seat and put her arm
round Edelgard.

" Just think of it, Edel—my hair flying loose and a
silver tunic, and silver tights—no skirt at all! And
I'll be standing there and Oda has to say to me:

> ' O brave Nerestan, chevalier généreux,
>   Vous qui brisez les fers de tant de malheureux.' "

Ecstatically she flung her arms in the air.

" Girls, you won't be able to help liking me—then,
when I'll be able to laugh and cry as I've never done
before, so free, so . . ."

" Let me tell you," interrupted Ilse, " you can laugh
and cry well enough as it is."

" Never enough, Ilse. Never so much as if I were
pretending to be someone else and yet were myself,"
and, coming close to Ilse, she added in a low voice: " I
say, Ilse, do you think Fräulein von Bernburg knows
much about the theatre? "

" Not a scrap."

"Oh, Ilse . . ." Manuela was obviously dejected.

" But I assure you," persisted Ilse, enjoying Manuela's discomfiture. " Just the other day when she was inspecting my wardrobe she said: ' Well, Ilse, you have a funny taste—nothing but photographs of actors.' "

" Oh, that has nothing to do with what I mean."

" Quite unprofessional, anyhow."

IV

THE round-cheeked housemaid, Johanna, was dragging a heavy basket of laundry upstairs. On every landing she stopped and took a rest. Then she entered Dormitory No. 1 and laid on each bed a parcel of freshly washed underwear. When she came to bed No. 55 she lingered, turned over Manuela's things, held a nightgown up to the light, examined the stockings and finally laid everything down again with a sigh. Slowly she quitted the room.

Fräulein von Bernburg heard a knock on her door. "Come in," she called, and as she turned half round from her desk she saw Johanna, who began awkwardly:

" I've brought the laundry, Fräulein von Bernburg."

" Very well, Johanna, then you can go."

But Johanna did not go; she stood still and went on:

" Fräulein von Bernburg . . ."

" Yes, what is it, Johanna? "

" I only wanted to say that No. 55's laundry's not in very good condition."

" Oh! "

" Yes—nearly in rags."

" Well, then No. 55 will just have to mend it."

Johanna was embarrassed. She brought all her courage to bear.

" I'd be glad to do it for Fräulein Manuela."

" Nonsense, Johanna; you've enough work of your own. You've no need to take on other people's work."

" But I'd like to do it for Fräulein Manuela."

" Indeed? "

" Yes—I don't know—she's such a nice girl—and besides, I'm sorry for her. She cries so much in the night. Her pillow's often soaked through in the morning."

Fräulein von Bernburg's voice became incredulous.

" Oh, Johanna, you must be imagining that! "

" No, not at all, Fräulein von Bernburg—she's homesick, very likely."

" Yes, very likely."

For a moment there was silence. Johanna waited, crumpling her apron in her hands. Fräulein von Bernburg seemed to be meditating. Then she turned to the maid:

" Bring me No. 55's laundry."

Johanna's kindly eyes shone with satisfaction now that she had achieved what she wanted. She ran back to the dormitory, eagerly gathered up Manuela's pile, and laid it, article by article, before Fräulein von Bernburg, with a compassionate murmur for each garment.

Fräulein von Bernburg closely examined the things that Johanna handed to her.

" Tell Fräulein von Meinhardis to come up and see me now. She's in the garden."

"I'll be very glad, Fräulein von Bernburg!" Johanna, beaming with relief, actually dropped a *knix* before rushing off.

Breathlessly she conveyed the invitation, and Manuela, escorted by Edelgard, mounted the stairs in trepidation.

"I say, Edelgard, what can she be wanting? I'm frightfully scared."

Once at the door she would have turned and fled.

"If only it isn't something dreadful. If only she's not angry. . . . Edelgard—no——" She clung to Edelgard's hand, which was about to put an end to this scene by knocking at the door. "Don't; I say, wait a minute," and she sought to gain time by smoothing back her untidy hair.

"But she's waiting, Lel . . ."

"All right." Manuela drew herself up and Edelgard knocked at the door.

For a moment Lela stood hesitating in the doorway, waiting for a word. Fräulein von Bernburg was writing at her desk with her back turned.

"Come over here," she said at last, in a dry tone of command.

Obediently Lela advanced to the writing-desk. Then Fräulein von Bernburg raised her head.

"Tell me, child, did you not get a new outfit of underwear when you first came to school?"

"No, Fräulein von Bernburg." Manuela felt ashamed.

"Where were you, then—at that time?"

"At home, Fräulein von Bernburg. Our housekeeper thought the things I had would do."

Fräulein von Bernburg lifted a chemise and held it up between herself and Manuela. The shoulder-straps were torn off, and a large triangular tear decorated the

lower portion.   The scanty lace trimming was in tatters.
Fräulein von Bernburg smiled.

"And what do *you* think?"

Over Manuela's face flitted a shy smile.

"It *won't* do any longer, Fräulein von Bernburg."

"Indeed it won't. It might serve to wipe the black-
board in our classroom. . . ."

Manuela laughed.

"That's just about what it's good for."

"But then you'd be one chemise short."

Fräulein von Bernburg got up and went over to her
wardrobe.   After some searching she found what she
was looking for.   With a chemise in her hand, she came
back to Lela and proffered it.

"The shoulder-straps will have to be taken in a bit;
it'll be a little large for you, but you're still growing. . . ."

With both hands Manuela clutched what was given
her, holding it to her bosom.   Tears of joy welled up in
her eyes.

"For me? No, it can't be . . ." she stammered.
"A thousand, thousand thanks!   But it's a shame to
give it to me. . . ."

Fräulein von Bernburg laughed to see Manuela's
delight.   She did not make any objection, either, when
Manuela seized her hand and kissed it.   But when
Manuela tried to say something else her voice failed
in her throat.   Losing all self-control she burst out
sobbing, and Fräulein von Bernburg had to support the
reeling child in her arms.   This kindly action brought
down Manuela's last barrier, and Fräulein von Bernburg
had to lead her to a chair and set her down on it.   Wordlessly she waited until the child should somewhat recover
herself.

Lela struggled for composure.   Still sobbing and gasping she tried to apologize.

"I really don't know why I'm crying.   I'm not really unhappy.   Not the least little bit."   And wiping her eyes, in which the tears welled up again and again, she looked timidly up at Fräulein von Bernburg.

"Let the tears flow, child.   That won't do you any harm.   But, tell me—does this often happen?   Are you homesick? "

"Homesick? " repeated Lela in amazement.   "No. . . ."

"And yet you simply do this kind of thing without any reason, all of a sudden. . . ."   Fräulein von Bernburg's voice was warm, grave and tender.

"Oh, I don't know why—and just to-day I've been so happy—but sometimes . . ."

Fräulein von Bernburg pulled out a chair beside Manuela's and sat down quite close to her.

"Sometimes? " she prompted gently.

But Manuela could not go on.   What she had to say could not be said to *her*, to her above all people. Fräulein von Bernburg waited, and then, somewhat disappointed, remarked:

"Haven't you any confidence in me? "

"I—I do," stammered Manuela.   "But it's—it's too difficult to say."

"Will you not try?   Not if I tell you that I very, very much want to hear it? "

Lela clung to her hand and gazed at her bosom.

"When I go to bed at night and you shut the door behind you, then I . . . have such a longing for you because you're gone, and I have to keep looking at the door, and then I think: no, I mustn't, and I hold myself down in my bed. . . ."

Fräulein von Bernburg jumped up and turned her back to Manuela, whose eyes followed her.

" You're always so far away, so distant, I can never be close to you and never hold your hand and never kiss you, never get near you. . . ."

" But, my dear—tell me——"

Lela would not let her go on. She had suppressed herself too long. With both arms round the hips of the woman beside her she poured it all out.

" I can't, I can't help it. I love you, darling Fräulein von Bernburg. I love you so much, as much as my mother and ever so much more. Whenever I see your hands I feel drawn to touch them. Your voice when you call my name makes my heart turn over and carries me away—I can't help it, I love you, I love you. . . ."

Now Fräulein von Bernburg energetically seized the child's hands and freed herself. She walked away from her as far as possible, to the very wall, while Lela, panic-stricken over what she had done, followed her with her eyes.

By that time Fräulein von Bernburg had got herself in hand.

" Listen to me, Manuela. I can't have you saying that kind of thing to me. I think you are exaggerating your feelings, without intending to; things can't be as bad as all that. You must pull yourself together. One should be able to control oneself. Do you understand me? Every single person must exercise self-control, Manuela. I do so too! "

Manuela's eyes opened widely. She was too much of a child even to guess how much an admission of that kind cost the woman confronting her. She heard only

the reprimand and submitted to it. Trembling and
with a final sob she gave her promise.

"Yes, Fräulein von Bernburg."

"And now there's something I must say to you, and
you must take it sensibly."

Her voice sounded gentler, and she again approached
the child.

"I am very fond of you, Manuela, but all the same
I cannot pay more attention to you than to the others;
you know that, of course. Still, if ever you are in trouble
you can always come to me."

Gently she took Lela's head in her hands and tilted
the girl's chin so that they looked in each other's eyes.

"Are you content now?"

"Thank you, a thousand thanks!" and once more
Lela shyly and reverently kissed the beloved hand,
that beautiful hand whose fragrance reminded her of
lavender and of her mother.

V

LELA got as far as the staircase and there stood still.
On her right was a window from which one could see
far over the tops of the neighbouring trees without even
a glimpse of the wall encircling the Seminary garden.
Once more, but more strongly than ever before, she had
the feeling that until now she had never really lived.
Only when one felt like this, soaring and uplifted, only
when one was apparently not there at all, when one was
transformed into a new creature, was one wholly alive.
As soon as she went downstairs she would have to relapse
into being only Lela again, and that she did not want

to do. Her hands were twined in the white linen garment, holding its coolness to her breast, as if to prove
that she had not been dreaming. She would have liked
best to stand quite motionless for ever, so as not to lose
the fragrance of that room and of the woman in it, so
as not to destroy by one movement the reality which
had just taken shape.

Slowly she descended step by step, pausing on each
to observe if her ecstasy were vanishing. No, it still
remained. She went on down the stairs, but she was
still up there in the room, sitting in the chair, her arms
round Fräulein von Bernburg. That was really real.
The figure descending the stairs and going into the
dressing-room and opening a wardrobe was not herself;
it was a dream.

Lela folded the gift and laid it like something holy
in her wardrobe. Now the bell was ringing; Oda, Ilse,
Lilly and Edelgard came rushing in. Life went on.
Lela felt serene and undisturbed. All that now seemed
to have no relation to her at all and did not prevent
her from remaining where she really was—upstairs in a
room on the fourth floor, sitting in a chair.

VI

OLD Marie's cloakroom was in wild disorder. Card-
board boxes, too frail for their heavy contents and now
hauled down from the garrets, were bursting all over
the place and letting gold braid, white muslin, green silk
and vivid red oddments trail over the floor. Whenever
an interval came a throng of girls came scurrying up

stairs, threw off their uniforms and got into the most
fantastic costumes.   Black-haired Oda with the sleepy
eyes that were never quite open was examining herself
in a mirror; the light grey tights and close-fitting red
tunic of the knight Chatillon suited her to perfection.
A white lace ruff forced her to carry her chin high,
a broad leather girdle hung loosely about her narrow
hips, and her hand played seriously with the hilt of a
sword.   Lela came up behind her, all in shining silver.
Oda regarded the figure behind her in the mirror, and,
as if she were only acting in a scene, laid her arm round
Lela and drew her close.

"I say, Lel, do you know you're very handsome?"

"Oh, Oda——"

"No, seriously.   Just have a good look at yourself.
Besides, I'm not the only one to say that.   My sister who
was here yesterday said that you would be a rare beauty
one day."

A fire of joy darted through Lela, but she did not want
to betray it.   Oda went on, with practical calm:

"Just look at your legs.   Simply marvellous."   And
Oda ran her hand down them, as if she were a man
appraising a horse.

"Stop it, Oda!"   Manuela felt ashamed.

"And your hips are so marvellously slim.   Very, very
like a boy's.   I could let my hands meet round your
waist if I liked . . ." and Oda did so.

"But, Oda, you're pinching me!"

A giggle sounded behind them.   They both whirled
round.   Marie croaked:

"No, no, don't let me disturb you, ladies.   Why
shouldn't you have a bit of a peep at each other . . ."
and once more she giggled.

But for the two girls their pleasure was spoilt. Silently they stripped off their costumes, drew on their uniforms, tied the stiff apron-strings in the prescribed bow, and arm-in-arm began to descend the staircase. Suddenly, however, Oda seized Manuela fiercely in her arms and pressed a warm kiss on her lips.

"Oh, how I like you!"

Oda's hands closed like iron on Lela's breast.

"I say, let's be chums. Let me stay with you always, please, please do."

Lela struggled furiously, so that Oda staggered and had to hold on to the balustrade. In Lela's eyes there were tears of rage and disgust. With a burning face she hissed at Oda: "Stop it, will you?" Feverishly she shook out her disordered apron and caught up her hair, which was on the point of falling down.

Oda remained standing with her eyes fixed on Lela.

"You silly baby—you're glad enough to let me touch you!"

"No, that's not true!"

"Well then, perhaps glad enough to let somebody else touch you?" and slyly, quietly, watching the effect of her words: "Perhaps . . . Fräulein von . . ."

She got no farther. Manuela stamped her foot on the floor and in another moment she would have fallen raging on Oda. But just then the voice of Mademoiselle floated up from below:

"Est-ce qu'on parle français là-haut?"

And both girls went on downstairs in silence.

VII

EACH wardrobe had two compartments: one on the
left for hanging clothes in, with a shelf for hats above
it, and on the right another filled with shelves on which
underwear, stockings and spare shoes had to be ranged,
while special shelves in the middle harboured family
photographs and other souvenirs. Sewing materials,
embroidery, and even harmless games had their proper
places there. Many of the children had lined these
shelves with coloured paper, for the wardrobe was one's
"home," one's sole private belonging. In the evening,
just before prayers, there was a break during which one
could potter about in the wardrobe; and since the
dressing-room boasted no chairs, nothing, indeed, but
wardrobes standing side by side without any intervening
spaces and with only small gangways between the rows,
there was nothing for it but to sit down inside the wardrobe itself. The short frocks hanging from the hooks
did not reach far down, and one could very well sit in
the clothes compartment with one's legs sticking out
into the gangway or tucked up underneath, Turkish
fashion.

Manuela was rearranging all her shelves, for there
was one possession of hers which had to have a worthy
setting. Ilse was sitting inside her wardrobe, secretly
occupied under cover of an open work-basket in polishing
up her rings and bracelets for next Sunday.

"I say, Manuela," she whispered to the neighbouring
wardrobe. "I've really done it this time," and in a lower
voice she continued: "I've smuggled out an awful letter,
a tip-top letter, I tell you."

" But, Ilse, how did you manage it? "

" Oh, I met the cook; this is her afternoon out. I stuck the envelope in the front of her bodice, and she didn't half squeal. But I gave her my best postcard as a bribe; you know, the one marked ' Le Baiser '—where there's a lady sitting on a sofa in a ball-dress and a gentleman in a smoking-jacket bending over and nuzzling at her. Liese simply loved it."

" What did you say in the letter? "

" Oh, everything I could think of. That the food's rotten and I'm always hungry. That there's so many pious prayers that I'm sickened. That it's always cold and we freeze to death. That we're not allowed to lie down when we're unwell, and so on and so on. When my little Papa sets eyes on that he'll be jolly sorry for me, and if he doesn't hike me out of the place at once he'll at least send me something to eat. Then we'll have a gorgeous spread one night. I'm looking forward to it already."

When parcels came from relatives they were opened and the contents displayed to their owners, but not handed out until the next Sunday, when all eatables were doled out in rations. But anyone as skilful as Ilse could enlist the help of Herr Alemann, who was not above being suborned, on commission, to abstract a portion of the whole.

" If only it's not found out, Ilse! " said Lela timidly.

" Oh, nonsense; if the worst comes to the worst I'll be chucked out, and that's what I want, anyhow. I don't care."

" But what will you do after that? "

" Do? God, I don't know. Marry soon, I suppose, not an infantry officer, at any rate, they're too boring.

I like Hussars best. Of course, it *might* be an actor.
And what about you, Lela, what will you do? "

" I—I shan't get married, anyhow."

" But why ever not? " Ilse was amazed.

" I don't know."

" Well, you must have some kind of reason for saying
that."

" I don't like men."

" Oh, I could tell you—I say, you just haven't met
any decent ones."

" Yes, I have."

" Have you ever had an admirer? "

" Oh, yes." Fritz, thought Lela, and felt quite woeful
about the heart.

" Well, what? Wasn't it nice? "

" Yes, but marrying's a different story."

" Of course, it's much nicer. I was once kissed quite
madly. I pretended not to like it, but it was lovely,
all the same."

" Shut up, Ilse, you make me feel ill."

" But what will you do, then, later, if you don't mean
to get married? "

" Don't know. Probably remain single."

Ilse shook her head, rose up, and silently took a postcard from her wardrobe door. It represented a red
poppy-field, through which a blinded maiden was
groping her way with a stick. Ilse handed the card to
Manuela.

Lela looked up, took the picture, regarded it long and
said pleasantly:

" Many thanks, Ilse."

Ilse bestowed a drawing-pin upon her and Manuela
fastened the card to her own wardrobe door.

VIII

THE Headmistress was sitting at her desk—reading a newspaper. Fräulein von Keston stood waiting beside her. At last the Headmistress laid down the newspaper and Bunny had the opportunity of bowing for the third time since entering the room. Bunny had a file of papers in her hand. She flinched under the eye that was turned upon her.

" The accounts—for your signature—ma'am."

Graciously the Head accepted the file. But without her pince-nez she could make nothing out. From her bodice, from the place where countless mother-of-pearl buttons fastened up her bosom, she extracted her pince-nez and mounted them on her nose.

" Hm . . ." She brought down a stamp with her signature on one of the sheets. " Economy, Kesten, economy."

" Yes, ma'am," and Fräulein von Kesten flinched again.

" The butcher's bill is too high."

" We do our utmost, ma'am. . . ."

" Utmost?" The word came incredulously from the desk.

Fräulein von Kesten writhed.

" To tell the truth, ma'am, the children often complain of hunger. . . ."

" Hunger? "

Indignantly the Head removed her pince-nez and stared at poor Bunny, who was already regretting her unheard-of boldness.

"Hunger? Children are always complaining—have always something to grumble about. You mustn't pay any attention to that, Kesten. Besides, to go hungry strengthens the character. We can't have any pampering here," and the stamp descended forcibly on another sheet of paper.

"Yes, ma'am," and then, timidly: "I only thought . . ."

"Don't think, my dear, obey! We Prussians have grown great through obedience. Not through pampering ourselves."

"How true, ma'am! How true!" sighed the devoted little Fräulein. She lifted the file and whispered discreetly: "May I consult you about some other matters for the theatricals?"

"Well, well, what is it?"

"Here is the list of the ladies to be invited. And here the menu . . . and a little estimate for the decorations. . . ."

The Head perused all of them attentively.

"Very good, yes—what does the menu say? Hockcup?—how does that come to be there? Surely the kitchen staff isn't suddenly going to start innovations? For as long as I can remember we have had a small glass of Swedish punch there, and nothing else."

"Very well, ma'am."

"And see that the children don't shout too much. Surely they can amuse themselves without making so much noise."

"Certainly, ma'am. Quite right, ma'am."

"By the way, Kesten, can't we cut down the coal? It's always much too hot all over the building."

"But it's turned so cold outside, ma'am. And the

class-rooms have to be aired every hour, and until
they get warmed up again . . ."

"Makes no difference. The children must not be
pampered! And you might try to see that our sick-
rooms are not always crowded. That's sheer nonsense.
I've never been ill in my life."

Against her will Bunny dropped her eyes to the
ailing foot of the Headmistress. But she hastened to
make good her sin:

"You have a wonderful constitution, ma'am."

"Tut, constitution! It's will-power that one needs.
To pull oneself together. That perpetual coughing
among the children at prayers, for instance, is nothing
but rudeness. Quite superfluous, tell them that, Kesten
—emphasize it!"

"Certainly, ma'am, I shall. . . ."

"You will, will you? You're always going to and
going to. But I can wear myself to the bone and still
I have to keep on telling you. Hold the reins tighter,
Kesten . . . tighter. . . ."

The Headmistress rose to her feet, and Kesten, dismissed, scuttled backwards towards the door as best she
could, and with a concluding: "Thank you very much,
ma'am," disappeared.

IX

"No, no, there's something fishy about that letter
. . . better leave it," and Herr Alemann detained his
wife in the kitchen. "It's been written in pencil, see?
and it's all got rubbed out so's the address can't be
read, and the Post Office has returned it. I tell you,
that letter's been smuggled out, as sure as my name's
Alemann."

"If it's been smuggled that's all the more reason
for handing it over, Alemann. That's the rule. And
rules is rules."

Herr Alemann squinted at the envelope and looked
at the back flap. "Sent by Ilse von Westhagen" could
be deciphered clearly enough.

"But, Bettichen, that'll get little Westhagen into a
row—no, I'm sorry for the kid. Why shouldn't a young
thing like that write and tell her mother how she's
growing out of her clothes?"

Bettichen was of a different opinion.

"That's not your business or mine. What the postman brings in here has to be handed over. Even if it's
a bomb, see? That's doing your duty faithful, see?"

"Oh, I know all about that—but it's not so easy to
know what your duty is. For instance, in the war, if
a soldier . . ."

He got no farther. The house-telephone shrilled,
and Frau Alemann, who was quicker in her movements
than her husband, was already at the instrument.

"Yes, Fräulein von Kesten . . . Just this minute
arrived, the post . . . yes, I'll bring it up . . ." And,

hanging up the receiver, she added: "She knows to a minute when the postman's due. . . ."

Alemann, taken by surprise, allowed the letter to be snatched from him without a struggle, and Bettichen vanished upstairs with it.

For the moment Herr Alemann had nothing to do, and why should he not repair to the kitchen to see what old Liese was concocting for the evening? As the sole male inhabitant of the establishment, living, moreover, in constant though unavailing opposition to most of the regulations, Herr Alemann was rather despised by the womenfolk. But on this occasion there was something brewing that might require a man's judgment, to wit, the Swedish punch which was to be served up at supper.

In matters like this Herr Alemann rightly considered himself an expert. Liese, the fat cook, had her own opinion about that, but simply to convince him that he was superfluous she ladled him out a sample. Herr Alemann sipped it, mumbled his lips over it, wiped his moustache with his handkerchief, and then uttered one long-drawn, suspicious monosyllable.

Herr Alemann said: "We-ell . . ."

X

In the lavatory beside Dormitory One there was a riotous bustle. True, every cubicle had a curtain which it was forbidden, on pain of punishment, to leave open, but on this evening there was too much general excite-

ment for the observation of rules. The girls who were
taking no part in the performance stood round or
helped to sew up a seam here, to finish off a head there,
or were dispatched at the last moment to fetch something that had been forgotten.

Manuela was very calm. At least she showed no
external agitation, unlike Ilse, who was already got up
as Orosman the Turk and was running like a mad thing
from one cubicle to the other.

"I say, look here, my beard. . . . Tell me, what do
you think of my trousers?"

The trousers were funny enough. They were
obviously too large for Ilse, for they reached up to her
arms, and although girdled tight were of an impossible
width. Her turban, however, was the chief thing. It
had been sent to her by her youthful Papa, and was an
enormous round structure, although quite light, so that,
of course, let Ilse shriek as she might, it had been rolled
as a ball along the narrow passage between the cubicles
and tossed from hand to hand. At long last Ilse had
managed to fix on her long beard, with the help of
Edelgard, who, draped in floating veils, was supposed
to look like a kind of odalisque, but in reality, with
her broad Gretchen face, looked much more like a
mediæval German saint. Ilse was really a martial figure.

Manuela stood before her looking-glass and looked
into her own eyes. Her hair hung loose, the silver tunic
sat pleasantly close to her body, and tautened her
shoulders almost as if she were carrying a load. The
lack of a skirt gave her a feeling of having grown taller.
Her very walk was altered. The way in which she set
one foot before the other had suddenly become important—there was a responsibility attached to it. And

yet it was good to be so free. No skirt hindered her
now to set one foot on a chair when she wanted to
lace her shoe: she could use her legs quite differently.
She used her foot to kick to one side the boots she had
taken off. Muttering a few lines of her part, she knelt
down and stood upright again. Then she braced one
foot on a stool and propped an elbow on her knee.
How lithe it made one feel. Little by little she was
turning completely into Nerestan, the noble knight.

Finally she sat down on the stool and crossed her
right leg over her left. But not as one did it in a skirt.
Only her right ankle lay across the left knee, and her
left hand rested on her hip, where she could feel the
hilt of her sword. She leaned her head against the
wall and dreamed herself into her part.

" Manuela, that's not the way to sit! "

Quite unexpectedly Bunny had come bursting in, but
she did not linger over Lela, for she had more important
work in hand. There was such a confusion in the
lavatory that at first she was not remarked. Ilse was
standing with one arm round Edelgard, declaiming at
the very moment two lines of her part:

> " Le voilà donc connu ce secret plein d'horreur,
> Ce secret qui pesait à son infâme cœur! "

when Fräulein von Kesten suddenly confronted her.
As if a bomb had just exploded, there was an immediate
hush in the room. Bunny had a letter in her hand
and thrust it out under Ilse's nose.

" Do you by any chance recognize this handwriting? "

For sheer horror Ilse could not answer a word, only
her great ball of a turban slipped a little to one side, as
if in sympathy, without her remarking it. Fräulein

von Kesten turned the letter over, and, indeed, the address, written in pencil, was almost illegible.

" Open it."

Ilse first took off her turban and then pushed to one side the long beard that was fastened by a wire round her head, apparently because it hindered her from doing as she was requested. She opened the letter—but she was not required to read it. Fräulein von Kesten snatched it from her and ran her eye over it. Then she darted another glance at Ilse, who stood there dumbfounded in her trousers, impatiently pulling at her beard, because it seemed somewhat out of place for such a performance.

" So! " Bunny hurled in her face. " Now I'll tell you something. Children who smuggle letters out of the house and write down lies about the school needn't think they're going to act in a play. Do you understand me? "

The spectators' eyes widened in horror. But so long as Fräulein von Kesten was standing there they did not dare to utter a word nor even to move a finger. Only Manuela had risen to her feet, and regarded the scene, leaning against the wall. It almost looked as if she were minded to draw her sword and drive it into Bunny's back between the shoulder-blades.

Bunny sensed the hostile atmosphere and scurried out. None of the girls recovered the use of her tongue for a moment. Ilse tore off her costume and rushed out. Only then did the storm break from all sides.

" They won't allow us a single bit of fun."

" Might have waited till to-morrow at least."

" Who's to play Orosman now? "

" Somebody will have to read the part."

" The star part? That'll ruin the whole play! "

" Fräulein von Bernburg would never have done a thing like that! "

" Of course not! "

" Oh, I'm fed up, I don't want to act at all. . . ."

At that moment old Marie appeared on the horizon, sailing in with great excitement.

" Come on, girls, Fräuleins, it's time to begin! "

Down below everybody was feverishly restless. Mademoiselle Oeuillet was flying to and fro. The drop-curtain was hung across a wide folding-door that divided the common-room from one of the class-rooms. The stage was a broad platform, cut off by large screens from the room behind it. Some carpets and green pot-plants were supposed to give it an Oriental character. The children were all in their seats already, only the first row of stalls was still vacant, being reserved for the ladies, for the Headmistress, the chief figure of the birthday celebrations, and her guests.

XI

ILSE had rushed headlong into the empty dressing-room. Violently she tore her wardrobe open. With a crash her trunk bounced down from the top of it and lay open at her feet on the floor, while she pitched into it headlong all her clothes, shoes, and books, flinging them in with both hands. The drawing-pins gave her some trouble, for she did not want to leave her portrait-gallery of actors behind. They were to come with her. Now was her chance to get away, for everybody was at

the performance. She had seen even Herr Alemann
sneaking in there. And if the doors were locked she
could get out by a window. She, Ilse, had had enough
of the whole business. She wasn't going to stand that
kind of thing, not she! She would simply take the
next train to Berlin. Her little Papa would understand.
And that was that. Ilse swore out loud and encouraged
herself by ejaculations. " Every word of it true. That
damned Kesten! This is the last straw, anyhow . . ."
She stood on her trunk to get it shut. The trunk, however, refused to shut. She sat on it, but that, too,
proved unavailing. Ilse was red and hot with exertion,
and, in her preoccupation with the trunk, did not
observe that someone had come up behind her.

" What are you doing here? "

Ilse was petrified. But Fräulein von Bernburg looked
quite friendly. Ilse stood up straight and gave her
gaping trunk an angry kick.

" But don't be so hard on it, Ilse—the *trunk* can't
help it. . . ."

" No," wailed Ilse. Her fine, tearless rage was beginning to break down, and that annoyed her dreadfully.

" Come here a minute," and Fräulein von Bernburg
put an arm round Ilse.

" You've got yourself into trouble again quite unneces-
sarily. Must you always run head-first into everything
that's forbidden? "

" I can't help it if it's forbidden . . ." sobbed Ilse.

Fräulein von Bernburg had to smile. True, Ilse was
not able to see the smile, since her head was drooping
in miserable dejection on her breast.

" But you know that what you did was very
naughty? "

" Yes," said Ilse in a small voice.

" And so you must stand up to the consequences, mustn't you? "

" Yes."

" And not run away like a little savage? "

" No."   Ilse's voice was growing still smaller.

" Isn't it much more honest to face the consequences when one has been naughty? "

" Ye-es."   Ilse broke down in tears.

" You have deserved your punishment, don't you think?   And it's quite unjust to lay the blame for it on anybody but yourself.   Do you see that? "

" Yes. . . ."   Ilse was at the end of her resources.

" Well, now do what you like about it.   I'm going to leave you alone and go downstairs.   If you want to run away, you have a splendid opportunity.   But if you decide to think better of it, wash your face, comb your hair, and don't spoil your friends' fun by pulling a resentful face."

A good-humoured little cuff on the side of the head, and Fräulein von Bernburg was gone.   Only then did Ilse raise her wet face and send a smile, blissful and transported, after the departing figure.

XII

UNREMARKED, Fräulein von Bernburg slipped into her place again among the audience.   People were laughing at poor Marga, who had had to take the part of Orosman at a moment's notice, and was finding it far from easy to balance the turban on her head and read Voltaire's none too simple lines at the same time.

Everybody was giggling. But then Lela appeared upon
the stage. The girl was as if transformed. The
moment she appeared the stage seemed to shrink. She
more than filled it; she filled the hall; she seemed to fill
the entire building. Profound silence settled on the
audience. Her sombre voice carried far, without
apparent strain, even when she spoke low—perhaps then
most of all. Her force, her sincerity, her warmth,
gripped every person in the darkened auditorium. The
Head was already uneasy. Even Bunny was twisting in
her seat as if something were happening in defiance of
the regulations. But what could have gone wrong?
Should Mademoiselle perhaps have chosen a different
play?

The children followed Manuela's slightest movement;
their eyes hung on her as if spell-bound. Secretly they
squeezed each other's hands. Manuela was surpassing
herself. One believed every word she said, one suffered
with her, one sacrificed oneself when she did, rose to
her heights of nobility and courage . . . and finally
burst into tears with her because poor Edelgard lay
dead on the stage, pierced by the sword of the jealous
Orosman.

When the curtain fell a ripple ran through the hall.
Forgetting all their good manners the children rioted.
The Headmistress applauded benevolently. Mademoi-
selle Oeuillet bowed modestly. But from the audience
there came a roar: "Manuela, Manuela! Brava!
Brava! . . . " and chairs scraped and hands clapped—
and Lela, tottering on her feet, with one arm round
Edelgard and the other round Marga, made her bow,
very grave and very pale. Anxiously she sought
Fräulein von Bernburg's eye . . . and caught it. Un-

like the others, Fräulein von Bernburg did not send her
a smile. As if she were thinking of something very
serious, her gaze met and rested in Lela's.

The classes waited until the Head and her guests had
left the hall, then they stormed out. Everybody was
clutching at Lela. Everybody wanted a hand, a kiss, a
word.

Lela was pining to be left alone. But that was out of
the question. Everybody was pushing to get near her.
She had become unreal to the other children: they all
wanted to touch her and speak to her as if to reassure
themselves that it was really Manuela. Mademoiselle
Oeuillet, too, after acknowledging endless compliments
on the excellent performance of her pupils, felt a need
to address a few words of appreciation to Manuela.
She was indeed amazed at the child's powers of acting,
flowing elegance and musical enunciation, which had
never been displayed at rehearsals to such a degree as
to-night.

Manuela had first to be disentangled from a mass of
girls.

"Eh bien—you did very well, Manuela."

"Do you really think so, Mademoiselle? Now that
it's all over I have a feeling that I ought to have done
it much better. Don't you think so?"

Mademoiselle was unwilling to let herself in for a
serious discussion.

"Mais non, mais non, que pensez-vous? It was very
good as it was—we're not a dramatic school—we're not
actors here—much better?—but that wouldn't have been
the thing at all—not ladylike—mais Manuela—quelle
idée—you're not thinking of becoming a professional,
surely?"

"No, I would never dare to try that. I haven't enough talent for that. I was only thinking . . ."

"Tut, tut . . . never mind that . . . go off with the others and enjoy yourselves. . . ."

Obviously there was nothing to be gained from her. But now Manuela thought of something else. Without paying the slightest attention to the fact that both "shouting" and "running" were forbidden in the large corridor, she did both, and ran calling for Ilse. Ilse came into sight. Manuela put an arm about her and bestowed a kiss on her, which Ilse accepted, unaccustomed as she was to kisses from Lela.

"I'm all right again, Lel. I'm not needing any more comfort. At the first go-off I was simply bursting with rage, but then—then the Bernburger turned up. . . ."

"Ye-es?" asked Manuela, lingering on the word, "and then?"

"Oh—well—then I just went down among the others."

"Where were you sitting?"

"Just behind the ladies."

"I say"—Manuela dragged Ilse into a window-bay—"what did they say? . . ."

"Oh, Gaerschner thought you had learned your part very well, but your costume wasn't quite respectable. . . ."

Manuela was hardly listening.

"And Evans?"

"Evans, she said: 'Oh, sweet! Isn't she a darling?' But of course she didn't understand a word of it."

"And . . . the other ladies?"

"The Head went so far as to say that you had a very nice pair of legs."

Manuela stamped her foot.

"Oh, leave my legs alone. . . ."

"But nice legs aren't to be despised. I never really knew that you had nice legs! " and Ilse circled round Manuela, who irritably aimed a kick into the air.

Then Lela seized Ilse by both arms, and half laughing, half imploring, gazed into her face.

"Ilse, darling, please . . . what . . . ? "

Ilse screwed her eyes up.

"What did *she* say? "

Manuela nodded energetically, and Ilse replied, looking her steadily in the eye:

"Well, this is just the remarkable thing: Fräulein von Bernburg didn't say a single word."

Manuela blenched. Deep dejection was visible all over her face.

Then Ilse grabbed her.

"But you should have seen what *eyes* she made! Such *eyes*, I tell you. . . ."

At this moment Marga appeared.

"Girls, what are you doing? We've all been in the dining-room for ages, waiting for Manuela. . . ."

XIII

ONCE more applause thundered out when Manuela entered the dining-hall. Her seat was reserved, and Edelgard and Marga were at each side of her. Bunny came flitting into the room.

"Well, girls, to-night you're to have no supervision —don't get into mischief, now—behave yourselves properly—is that understood? "

A loud "Yes, Fräulein von Kesten," accompanied her out. Hardly was the room relieved of her presence when Ilse took the floor.

"Come on, everybody, let's all drink to the health of our hero, what?"

There was general agreement. They seized their glasses.

"Three cheers for Nerestan, the noble knight!"

"Hurrah! Hurrah! Hurrah!"

They set the glasses to their lips, but most of them in immediate disappointment put them down again.

"Foo! What the devil's this?"

Ilse was the first, Lilly followed suit.

"Is this supposed to be Swedish punch?"

"Hogwash," said a melancholy voice.

"Hairwash."

"Sugar and methylated," said another.

"Enough to make you sick. . . ."

All the glasses were replaced on the table again. Only Manuela had emptied hers, and Edelgard observed:

"But, Manuela, you've drunk it all up!"

Manuela laughed with arrogant excitement.

"Doesn't matter. I don't care a button to-night how anything tastes. I simply shut my eyes and taste nothing. Main thing: it's alcohol."

"Here, I say, if you like the stuff you can have mine too!" and Ilse von Treitschke pushed her glass across the table to Manuela.

"Mine too."

"Mine too . . ." and from all sides the glasses came in.

"Great, my dears. Thanks—all contributions gratefully accepted . . . !"

THE CHILD

Marga warned her.

"Manuela, we're supposed to have only one glass apiece. . . ."

"Oho!" came in indignant chorus from the others.

"Leave Manuela alone—let her, if she wants to," and Marga felt herself outvoted.

Manuela thrust her arm under Marga's.

"Come on, Marga, I'll drink this glass all by myself to the health of my foster-mother, and forgive you this day all the good you have ever done me. Here's to you!"

Everybody laughed, and Marga, protesting still but no spoil-sport, returned:

"All right then, do it, you mad goose!"

"Oh!" and Manuela threw out both her arms. "Why shouldn't I be a little mad?" And then, thoughtfully: "I think I'm really a bit off my nut, for I'm feeling amazingly happy—gloriously happy!"

"Well, we'll have to mark this as a red-letter day in our calendars."

This time it was Oda who had interpolated the remark. Since her last encounter with Manuela Oda had avoided her, but when she now sent a glance over the table Manuela lifted her glass again.

"Prosit, Oda—let's make it up, shall we?"

At any price Manuela wanted to be reconciled with all her fellow-creatures that evening. Oda stood up, ceremoniously carried her glass round the table, and begged in a low voice:

"Lela, tell me one thing: can't you really like me a little bit?"

Manuela recoiled slightly, but then cried aloud so that everybody could hear it:

"Yes, of course I like you—I like you all, without a single exception. . . ."

She turned and embraced Edelgard.

"Doesn't Edelgard look sweet?"

Edelgard's hair was very fair, and, indeed, the light veil and flowing white robe suited her admirably.

"She looks marvellous. But she's not nearly such a good actress as you are. She didn't speak loud enough." That came from Oda, who had returned to her seat.

"Oh, Oda, she had to speak low. She was a girl."

"And you, Lela, I suppose, were a man? Your voice was quite deep, and you suddenly had all the right move-ments. . . . We were inclined to believe to-night that you —that you're really half a boy. . . ."

"Here's to Oda!" and they both emptied their glasses. Lela was standing upright by the table, while all the others were sitting down.

"Oh, it was lovely, anyhow, to be able for once to yell out one's feelings. . . ."

"How's that? They weren't really your feelings," remarked Mia.

"Yes, they were. . . ."

"Go on with you. Edelgard wasn't your sweetheart at all; it came out that she was only your sister. . . ."

Manuela smiled.

"Yes, my sister—but that's lovely too, isn't it?"

As if they must all understand what she meant, she turned her gaze round the table. At that moment music struck up from the other side of the hall: Marga had sat down to the piano. Mia came up to Manuela.

"Come, sir knight, let's have a dance."

Manuela coolly put her arm round Mia. Together they advanced behind the table, where a space had been

cleared.   There were not many couples dancing; most
of the girls preferred to sit around and look on.   But
Manuela was always in demand as a partner because she
was so good at steering.   Mia was a dark-haired girl with
light grey eyes, somewhat gipsy-looking, and although
Lela slept in the next bed to her, she really knew
nothing about her.   Mia never said much.   She was
mostly sullen, went her own way, and seemed to care
for no one but Oda.   And even that friendship, it was
rumoured, was one-sided.   Mia, the girls said, merely
let Oda hang about her, but she never gave Oda a single
present.

Manuela's head was reeling a little.   But she guided
Mia among the dancers with skill and confidence, so
that everybody watched them admiringly.

"I say, Lela," said Mia suddenly, laying her head
beside Lela's.   (It was easier to dance like that.   The
two faces were very close together.)

"Yes?"

"I'd like to show you something, but nobody's to see
it except you."

"All right, Mia, what is it?"   Manuela was not very
curious, but to-night she wished to be on good terms
with everybody.

"Come out into the corridor with me.   Then I'll let
you see.   If we dance out now nobody will notice."

And Lela steered Mia skilfully outside, between the
tables.   In a half-lighted window-niche they came to a
halt.   Silently Mia unfastened the cuff of her sleeve, and
began to bare her left arm.   On her small white upper
arm there was a dreadful wound; the skin was red and
swollen.   At first Manuela thought it must be a badly
healing vaccination mark, but then she noticed that the

raw, red weals composed a monogram: E. v. B. Horrified she gazed at the arm and then at Mia.

"I won't let it heal up. . . ."

"But, Mia, doesn't it hurt frightfully?"

"Yes, of course, it's meant to hurt. Then I feel it all
the time, always . . . and to-night I wanted to let you
see it. . . ."

Manuela carefully pulled the sleeve down again and
her hand trembled a little. She did not know what to
say.

"Mia, darling . . ."

And then, as if a decision had suddenly ripened within
her, she dragged Mia back to the dining-hall and shouted
over the tables:

"Girls! I want to make a speech too! . . ."

Quickly she tossed off another glass that somebody
offered her. She wanted to climb on a chair and had
one foot already on the seat, when she suddenly felt
unsteady and had to be helped up. Then she stood
straight.

"My dear and honoured friends . . ." she began, high
over the heads of her audience.

They all laughed.

"Well, that's how speeches begin. . . ." Her head
was swimming a little and she really did not know how
to carry on in that vein. So she decided to try another:
"Oh, girls, there's something I simply *must* tell you. . . ."

"What is it?" They all came crowding about her.

Manuela bent to steady herself on Oda's and Edelgard's shoulders, for they were standing nearest her.

"She made me a present of something. . . ." The
words came tumbling out.

Single voices called:

"Who? What? . . ."

They were all beginning to feel interested.

"She gave it to *me*," and Lela stood upright again.
"To *me*. A chemise, and I have it on at this minute.
I can feel it here on my breast, on my body, cool—
pleasant . . ." and since she still encountered nothing
but incomprehension and questioning looks, she shouted
it aloud: "Fräulein von Bernburg's chemise . . . she
gave it to me. . . ."

At that moment Bunny's small grey figure appeared
behind the backs of the children.   Nobody remarked it.
All eyes were turned towards Manuela, who stood high
above them with flying hair, glittering in her silver
sequins.

"Yes, to me . . ." and then, in a lower voice, very
rapidly: "She went to her wardrobe and took out a
chemise and gave it to me, I was to wear it, to wear it
and think of her. . . . No, she didn't say that, but I
know all the same. . . ."

"What?   What do you know?" came in agitated
voices from the crowd.

Fräulein von Kesten vanished again. But Manuela
spread her arms wide.

"That she loves me . . . that's what I know." Shaking
her head in humility, she went on: "She laid her hand
on my head, her lovely white hand. That thrills
through and through you and is so solemn that you
want to kneel and . . ."

Now the Headmistress came in, followed by Fräulein
von Kesten. A few of the girls caught sight of them
and stood as if turned to stone.

Lela laid both hands on her breast.

"To feel it here makes one good. From now on I

want to have only good and pure thoughts. I want to
be good," and louder and louder: "There's nothing can
touch me now—she, she is there—she . . ." For a
moment Lela faltered, and then, as if recalling the
original purpose of her speech, she hastily snatched up
a glass. "To her we all love, to our holy, our good,
our one and only Fräulein von Bernburg. . . ."

Then at last she observed an uneasy agitation among
the children. The Headmistress was thrusting aside
those who were barring her progress until she came to
a halt close beside Manuela, who, summoning her last
strength, gazed fearlessly into her face.

"The whole world must know it—*she*, she is the
miracle—she is the love that passeth all understanding. . . ." With that her glass fell from her hand and
splintered. She herself shut her eyes and swayed into
the arms of Edelgard and Oda, who caught her.

An uncanny hush spread in the room. Horrified, the
girls cowered away from the Head. Fräulein von Kesten
ran bustling around.

"Water . . . lift her up . . . carry her away . . ."

Loudly the Head's stick beat on the floor.

"A scandal . . . a scandal. . . ."

The sister in charge of the "hospital," an outlying part
of the building, was already on the spot. She, Edelgard
and Ilse carried Manuela along the dimly lit corridor.
Herr Alemann was standing beside his lodge.

"Quick," shouted Fräulein von Kesten, "ring up the
Herr Surgeon-Major and tell him to come at once. One
of the girls is unconscious. . . ."

Herr Alemann, with the utmost calm, gazed after the
remarkable procession, and scratching his head, betook
himself to the telephone.

Arrived in the sick-room they laid Manuela, whose eyes were still firmly closed, on a sofa that stood ready. Sister Hanni felt Lela's pulse.

"You may go now," announced Fräulein von Kesten to Edelgard and Ilse. "Do you hear me?" Fräulein von Kesten was in a state of nerves. There was nothing for it but to go out quietly.

In the room Sister Hanni was attempting to take off the child's costume. Fräulein von Kesten scurried up and down. Sister Hanni laid a hand on Lela's brow, then, shaking her head, knelt down beside her, drew off her shoes and stockings and spread a white woollen blanket over her.

At long last the rattling of a sabre was heard outside in the corridor. That was the Surgeon-Major. The doctoring of the Seminary pupils was only a side-line for him, since he was really a medical officer for the soldiers. But he did not mind doctoring the girls: nice little girls, he used to say, nothing but children's ailments. . . .

As he entered he lifted two fingers to his cap. "Good evening," he greeted the company in a rasping voice. Then laboriously, with a few groans, he extricated himself from his grey military cloak and took off his cap, ran his hand over his white moustache, unbuckled his sabre and handed it to Sister Hanni.

"An unusual case, Herr Surgeon-Major," said Fräulein von Kesten.

"Indeed," growled the Surgeon-Major. And advancing to Manuela: "Well, what's the trouble?"

He felt for her pulse and bent over her.

"What, unconscious?"

Bunny nodded, her lips tightly set.

"Bless me, how has that happened? Out with it

now, Fräulein von Kesten. Has there been a rumpus
here? "

When the Surgeon-Major was alarmed he did not
bother to be polite. In jerky sentences Bunny stammered out a recital of the events preceding the fainting-
fit. When she came to the climax, Manuela's speech,
the contents of which she did not divulge for shame, the
old man bent over the child again and sniffed at her
mouth. Sniffed again to make certain, and then collapsed, roaring with laughter, into the nearest chair. He
rubbed his knees with delight. He wheezed until he
coughed. Horrified, Fräulein von Kesten and Sister
Hanni, who had been waiting in the background,
stared at his antics. Red as a lobster, he regarded first
one woman and then the other, beaming upon them,
and as if it were the best joke in the world exploded:

"Drunk—dead drunk! "

"What? " Fräulein von Kesten started forward.

Sister Hanni repressed a laugh and had some trouble
in keeping her face straight.

"Herr Surgeon-Major! " Fräulein von Kesten could
hardly speak. "How can you say such a thing! "

The old gentleman hoisted himself to his feet and
examined Manuela again.

"Can't help it, drunk she is—and she's done the job
thoroughly, too."

Then he looked up into Fräulein von Kesten's face.

"What kind of damned muck have the girls been
drinking? It simply stinks of methylated spirit! The
child's got a first-rate attack of alcoholic poisoning."

"But I assure you, Herr Surgeon-Major, you must be
mistaken. Each girl got only a tiny glass of Swedish
punch made by our own cook."

The old gentleman was not to be shaken.

"Leave the poor girl to sleep it off; to-morrow or the day after she'll be all right again, I hope."

"Herr Surgeon-Major—I can rely on your discretion?"

"What?—discretion? About her little spree? My God, Fräulein, that's nothing to get the wind up for. Why shouldn't a body go on the spree occasionally? . . . But let me see . . . Sister, put the child in the sick-room, and if anything happens just ring me up at once. I'm not over pleased with her heart. Watch her pulse carefully—she might need a small injection. I'll leave you something here," and he deposited what was needful on the table. . . .

XIV

UPSTAIRS in Dormitory No. 1 dejection reigned. Without a single word the children undressed in their cubicles. There was no sound but the splashing of water whenever a tap was turned on, and everybody was ready in less than the usual time. One after the other they scurried in noiseless slippers towards their beds. Fräulein von Bernburg said merely: "Good night," in a low voice, and switched the light off.

This was the end of all the celebrations. For a long time there was silence in the dormitory. Edelgard's low sobbing was audible. Between her and Mia stood the empty bed. Ilse slipped over to Edelgard.

"I say, don't howl about it. Nothing much can happen. Manuela will get a terrific pi-jaw, and maybe three days C.B. or the green cockade. But others have survived that before her."

Oda had fled to Mia, and Mia put her arm around her.

"I say, it was partly my fault. . . ."

"Yours?"

"I showed her my arm, and she suddenly got a queer look in her eye, and rushed off to the hall and . . . I'm so scared about her, Oda."

"Me too, Mia."

"Did you see what a look the Head gave her? As if she were dirt. I thought she was going to stamp on her."

"She'll do it yet. . . . But perhaps we could help her somehow? . . . I'll help her where I can. . . ."

Marga and Ilse von Treitschke took a different view. Marga felt herself involved in the disgrace because it was her charge who had caused such a scandal. It might easily happen that she, Marga, would be drawn into it.

"Do you think it'll ever come out how much she drank?" she asked despairingly. "And I told you . . . don't you remember, you're my witness—I said: 'Each of us is supposed to have only one glass apiece.' Did I say that, or did I not?"

"Of course you did. . . ."

"You'll see, to-morrow I'll get into a row with Fräulein von Kesten."

"Oh, nonsense—and you such a pet of Bunny's—but as for poor Manuela . . ."

XV

FRAULEIN VON GAERSCHNER and Fräulein von Attems were both agreed: "An impossible child. A girl like that should be expelled. This is no place for that kind of thing. Getting drunk! . . . It's really incredible. And all that hysterical adoration. . . ." They could not help smiling scornfully.

"Well," said Gaerschner, "I shouldn't like to be in Fräulein von Bernburg's shoes either. Everything has its drawbacks. All very nice to be worshipped by the children, but when a thing's beyond the mark it's beyond the mark. There's a limit, and I shouldn't care to be the cause of excesses like these."

Fräulein von Attems shook her head too.

"No, better to be rather less popular and to keep things within decent bounds. That kind of extravagant behaviour is vulgar."

They both strolled down the corridor, highly pleased with themselves, for nothing like that would ever happen to them: they were in no danger of losing their situations on the staff and the pensions that they could look forward to. . . . Warmly they bade each other good night, and, indeed, it was certain that they would each have an excellent night of sound sleep.

XVI

"Now, now, Lord help us, Johanna, don't take on like that."

Marie was stirring her milky coffee, and reading a

lecture to the weeping Johanna, who sat hunched up on a stool.

" There's nothing very terrible likely to happen. What a carry-on all over the house just because of a bit of loving! And a drop of drink! Deary me, the poor girl was unhappy enough—she's not one of the strong kind—she should never have been here, I always did think."

" But that's just it," burst out Johanna. " That's what's such a shame. If the likes of us can't bear the place we just give in our notice and say good-bye and go home to our mothers. But the Fräuleins here can't give notice. They're enlisted like soldiers and have to serve their time. And I don't know—but that little Manuela—she's so . . ." and Johanna had to feel for her handkerchief.

Marie found this distress exaggerated.

" Oh, put a stopper on it now. . . . Maybe they'll send her home, and she'll be happy enough if they do."

" No," struck in Johanna, " she'll never be happy in her life without Fräulein von Bernburg."

" Don't you start that line of talk next, my girl. Drink up your coffee now, and for goodness' sake go and get some sleep."

Johanna, accustomed to obedience, swallowed her cold coffee and stumped off to her room.

Muttering to herself, Marie fished about among her clothes-stands and boxes. For a meditative moment she stood under the lamp regarding Manuela's silver tunic.

" And she looked grand in it, too—like an angel from heaven. . . . Well, what can the likes of us do about it? . . ."

XVII

HERR ALEMANN was on his slow rounds through the
sleeping house. He opened each class-room door and
shone his pocket-torch into every corner. He had just
mounted from the basement, where he had made sure
that the taps were not dripping, that the gas was properly
turned off, and the outside doors locked. It was his
business to see that no lights were left on and no
remains of food or drink left lying about. Behind him
everything went dark, and all the lights still burning
were switched off. Herr Alemann rattled his keys like
a prison warder. Occasionally he stopped and listened
for any irregular sound, such as a shutter banging or a
curtain flapping; was that a voice speaking somewhere
at this late hour? Was someone groaning in her sleep?
Or was it a cough? Should it be reported?

In the large corridor, too, he stopped, for there was
still a crack of light shining through the Headmistress's
door. The sound of rapid conversation could be heard.
"Oh, of course," he growled and went on his way again.
Herr Alemann was not the man to eavesdrop when the
Headmistress and Bunny were having a conference.
Herr Alemann was tired and wanted to go to bed.

But Bettichen was still all agog with excitement.
Such unusual events as those of this day were not so
easily banished.

"Now did you ever . . . a child like that to go and
get drunk! No, if that were my girl I'd know what
to do. . . . I'd smack her behind for her . . . good and
hard."

Although Herr Alemann had made up his mind not
to discuss the matter, this was too much.

"Just let me tell you something. I'm the only one in this house who knows anything about them things, and, I tell you, the little Fräulein must be in a bad way, poor thing. That fiery stuff turns *my* head, and what can a poor little thing like that do to help herself, with her weak little stomach?" All this was accompanied by powerful blows in the air, that must have laid Betti out had they encountered her. "I saw the filthy muck they had to drink, and it was simply stinking. . . ."

Betti tried in vain to interrupt him.

"Stinking, I tell you, and when I say stinking I mean stinking. And God only knows what all Liese put into it. Arrack, she said it was—and white wine and sugar and some measly liqueur or other. The poor child'll be as sick as a dog all night, I hope for her own sake. And on top of that you'd blow the head off her, you would. That's the kind of thing you'd enjoy doing." And Alemann brought his great fist down with a bang on the bed-table.

That was apparently his last word on the subject, and so Betti ventured to cap it with a personal remark:

"Oh, well, if you're going to stick up for her, I must say she'll be well off . . . a fine champion you are."

Herr Alemann pretended to snore.

XVIII

THE door of the Head's room opened, and a shadow flitted out and closed it again. The shadow needed no light, for it knew how to find its way here in the dark.

It flitted to the staircase, glided noiselessly up, and knocked faintly at Fräulein von Bernburg's door. Someone inside must have been waiting for it; a word was exchanged, and the shadow flitted off round the corner and vanished into a room with " Fräulein von Kesten " inscribed on the door. A key grated gently in the lock, and there was a subdued rustling inside. On the bed lay a long, starched night-gown with long sleeves and a high neck, buttoning up to the collar. A drawer was shut, a few things laid ready for next morning. The lace cap was laid on the bed-table: the light was turned out.

XIX

" THE girl must be made an example of."

The Head's stick thumped on the floor. The Headmistress was stumping up and down the room. Fräulein von Bernburg, pale and composed, was standing by the lamp.

" That girl's a pest. She'll infect all the others. That kind of thing sets fashions. She's a danger to the house, to the reputation of the school."

Fräulein von Bernburg did not flinch.

" Reputation? " she repeated, with a faintly questioning inflexion.

" Our reputation is more important than anything else."

" May I ask what you have decided? "

" Decided! What is there to decide . . . ? Decide! "

Fräulein von Bernburg remained waiting. In a correct posture she stood before her superior, waiting to

hear her sentence—her sentence, for whatever verdict
was decided on would strike at her too. . . .

"You, my lady, are responsible for all this. If you
can take the trouble to remember, I mentioned it to
you before. You are encouraging for your own ends
an hysterical devotion."

"Ma'am . . ."

But Fräulein von Bernburg was not to be allowed to
speak.

"You should have nipped that kind of hysteria in
the bud. There's a limit to everything. You see now
what it leads to." And then, as if speaking to herself:
"An unhealthy business. . . . Decide?" She sat down
and stared at the motionless face of the young woman
before her.

"Above all things, of course, she must be separated
from you. Full stop. Finish. The end. Do you
understand?"

"Yes." The answer came like a breath.

"And from the other children too. Isolated.
Locked up. Not to make the other children as bad as
herself. I'd like best of all to write to her father and
tell him to take her away. But how could I explain
such an unusual step to Her Royal Highness? That's
the difficulty. The affair must be hushed up. The
servants are gossiping too much already."

"The servants!" said Fräulein von Bernburg, and in
spite of herself her tone was bitter.

"Certainly, that kind of gossip can have the most
unpleasant consequences. Scandal. Rumours. . . .
Well, to stick to our point: Manuela must be
isolated. . . ."

"But even so, ma'am, I beg you to consider—what

if the child has a nervous breakdown? She's a very nervous child—sensitive—she . . ."

Fräulein von Bernburg twisted her slim hands together.

"That means nothing to me. Nervous breakdown—what kind of expression is that to use? When I was a child no such thing was ever heard of. Fräulein von Bernburg, we are here to educate soldiers' children."

"I'm afraid for Manuela, ma'am; she is not strong. She'll take terribly to heart a separation from me and from the other children."

"And that will be her punishment. Fräulein von Bernburg, I expect you to obey me."

"I know my duty. But, ma'am, I beg of you, let me wean the child gradually from her devotion to me. . . ."

"Gradually? Devotion? Are you aware what we are really dealing with? Manuela is sexually abnormal." The Head took a step towards Fräulein von Bernburg. "And perhaps you know what the world thinks of such women—our world, Fräulein von Bernburg?"

Fräulein von Bernburg did not evade the look that was fixed upon her. Her mouth was closely compressed. Firmly she looked the old woman in the eye.

"I do know, ma'am."

And then, in a low voice, as if she were speaking only to herself:

"Manuela's not a bad child. But she has to grow into a free and independent woman . . . and therefore I want to detach her from myself."

"I'm glad you're able to see it. I think there's nothing more for us to say to each other to-night."

Fräulein von Bernburg remained standing as if she had not heard her dismissal; it was only the continued silence that told her the Head was waiting.

Still as if she were meditating on something, she walked slowly to the door.

" Good night, ma'am."

" Good night, Fräulein von Bernburg."

But in the very doorway fear clutched again at the heart of the departing woman—dreadful fear.

" Ma'am, suppose Manuela . . . suppose she can't bear it. . . . I mean, if the child falls ill . . ."

" Then we'll make that an excuse for sending her home."

And as if this were the final solution, the Head laid her stick on the table to intimate that she wished to be alone.

XX

In the sick-room a night-light was burning. A pale green glimmer illumined the bed and the sleeping girl. Outside a door was opened, and a low voice asked:

" How is she, Sister Hanni? "

" Better, Fräulein von Bernburg. She was tossing about a lot and her heart was very weak. I had to give her an injection. But she's still very exhausted. She must have absolute quiet and nothing to excite her, the Surgeon-Major says."

Sister Hanni opened the door wide and admitted Fräulein von Bernburg. She offered the visitor a chair, but it was declined with a wave of the hand.

Fräulein von Bernburg remained at the foot of the

bed, and Sister Hanni went out. Manuela's mouth lay
open, as if she wanted to speak, but her eyes were
tightly shut and encircled by dark shadows. Her face
seemed to have fallen in but looked none the less
childish. One hand lay on her breast, the other, in a
gesture habitual to her since early childhood, was tucked
behind her head. Frau Käte used to take it away from
there and lay it beside the other, but Fräulein von
Bernburg did not dare to attempt such a thing. She
folded her own hands on the cool white rail of the
iron bedstead as if she were going to pray. Her face
suddenly changed; her bearing relaxed; her severe
mouth softened and quivered a little. Her eyes hooded
themselves until the dark pupils were half hidden, but
she kept them fixed on the child although her eyelids
were closing. As if she were weary her shoulders
drooped.

With a last effort she turned to go, resting her hand
for a moment on the table. Outside there was nobody;
the passages were in darkness. Only swift shadows
played over the white walls, as the wind swayed the
slim, budding trees in the garden to and fro. The road
was wet, uncertainly lit by flickering lamps. . . . A
weary step dragged up the staircase. Two windows sent
rays of light into the surrounding darkness.

XXI

The sea was so dazzling that all the sun-blinds had been
drawn down, creating a soft twilight. The electric
ventilators hummed a faint tune, and palms and flowers

that stood about quivered slightly from the vibration and gave off a warm moisture. Lieutenant-Colonel von Meinhardis had thrown himself into a deep armchair, in which he was lying rather than sitting. This was the one hour of the day in which he simply did not know what to do: the hour after lunch. The ladies had withdrawn, but he would not take a nap; he feared that habits of that kind would make him grow fat. Thinking of that danger he pulled his waistcoat firmly down and regarded his new shoes. They were of white leather with brown toe-caps and brown seams. A new fashion, which, of course, one had to adopt. His coffee had grown cold, and Meinhardis was feeling for his cigarette-case when he heard light footsteps.

Looking half over his shoulder, he saw a bright frock gleaming behind the palms. With a smile on his lips, and without ceasing to light his cigarette, he called gently:

"Come along, little 'un. . . ."

The " little 'un " was indeed fairly tall, but her mother had a way of dressing the twelve-year-old girl that initiated her in the technique of looking younger than she was. Her silk frock was decidedly too short, her corkscrew curls were long on her slim shoulders, as if she were a three-year-old, and her enormous scarlet hair-ribbon, while acting as an excellent foil to her pale skin and coal-black eyes, was hardly suitable to her years. Unconsciously, too, her coquetry had taken on a childish tone which did not accord with her real nature.

Thus addressed, she sprang round the palms and flew to embrace " Uncle Meinhardis." He laughed and freed himself from the frail little arms.

" Well, you little monkey? What are you doing here? Why aren't you asleep at this hour? "

" Oh . . . I . . ." she answered hesitantly, and, letting herself sink into a chair, looked up into the man's eyes.

Pamela had passed nearly the whole of her childhood in hotels, for her mother was ailing and could not stay in her native climate. Wherever they went a Miss or a Mademoiselle or a Signorina was engaged to look after the child, and by now she was a completely grown-up little lady who was extremely insulted if she were invited to children's parties. But when it suited her to play the baby, as now, for instance, she did it with great skill. Meinhardis had not interested her very much at first; she thought him really too old—too much of an " uncle." The dancing professional, for example, who always bowed before asking her to dance and treated her exactly like any of the other ladies, was much more to her taste. But then that creature, Ray, was in the running. And Pamela considered Ray simply awful—and what a perfume the woman used! . . .

" How many sins have you been committing to-day? " asked Meinhardis.

" I've had an Italian lesson. And then I went walking with Signorina."

" Is she pretty, your Signorina? "

" Her? Oh, Signorinas are never pretty."

" Probably you're right. I think so too. Where are all the lovely Italians one hears of? Those that run around here are all fat and pasty."

" And have greasy hair," supplemented Pamela, with expert judgment.

Silence set in. Pamela sighed.

"What are you sighing for?" asked Meinhardis.

Pamela shook herself. "I've been wishing a wish"
—but she grew a shade darker—not redder, for her
skin browned a little whenever she blushed.

Meinhardis began to be interested. He sat up and
regarded her. But Pamela was not to be drawn so soon.
She had thought out exactly how she was to say it.
Yet now she was discovering that it was difficult after
all. . . .

In the evenings, when she was lying in bed and the
sea-breeze came in through the window, she was in
the habit of getting up and leaning out of the window.
One could hear the jazz band down below and see
the guests sitting on the terrace in smoking-jackets and
gorgeous evening frocks with bare shoulders. At one
particular side-table Ray and Meinhardis always sat.
Occasionally they vanished in the dusk of the hotel
garden. Then all that one could see was the glowing
tip of a cigar, but that was enough to tell whether
they were walking or standing still. All that made
Pamela feel pathetic, and she counted up: twelve,
thirteen, fourteen, fifteen—when, oh, when would she
be really grown up?

She stood up and snuggled close to her "uncle,"
again laying her arms round his neck. Meinhardis felt
her slender body pressing against his knees.

"Out with it, then, whisper it in my ear. . . ."

Pamela brought her face close to his sleek hair and
greedily sniffed the mingled fragrance of tobacco and
scented soap.

"I'd dreadfully like to go walking with you one
evening!"

Meinhardis laughed full-throatedly.

"You're very flattering. No, you're really flattering
. . . and shall we perhaps take a skiff out on the sea
in the moonlight—eh? "

Pamela had grown quite grave and solemn; her
heart was racing madly.

"Yes—and—and will you . . . make love to me? "

Meinhardis actually had to look round to make sure
that nobody had overheard. But there was nobody
there, and so he clapped Pam on the shoulder and
laughingly replied:

"Of course—I'm awfully fond of little girls! I've
one myself—a bit older than you, it's true . . ." and
hardly had the words left his lips before his face took
on a quite wistful expression.

This answer was hardly what Pamela had desired,
but she betrayed no disappointment.

"When? " was all she said.

"Whenever you like—to-night, as far as I'm
concerned. . . ."

XXII

"You're the worst girl who ever came into this
school! "

The Head thumped her stick on the floor. Manuela
was sitting in her narrow iron bed, convulsively holding herself erect.

"You've conducted yourself like the lowest of gutter-
snipes. Swaggering—brawling—screaming your sins
out at the top of your voice for everybody to know the

kind of creature you are. Have you no sense of shame at all? " The Head's voice became sharp and cutting. " A good thrashing's what you deserve; it's a pity you're too old for it."

Manuela's hands clutched at the mattress. She was hardly able to control herself.

" And "—more quietly and deliberately the words now fell upon her—" and . . . as for the wrong you've done Fräulein von Bernburg . . ."—Lela lifted her head and stared in horror at the angry face—" I don't suppose she'll ever be able to forgive you that! "

A dreadful trembling took hold of the child. But the Head did not observe it.

" I'll send the chaplain to talk to you. He'd better take you in hand. Perhaps then you'll begin to realize the depths of infamy to which you have sunk—and the infamy you have brought upon this school."

The Head turned to go. At the door she paused, and, casting another look at the bed, explained simply:

" Your punishment will be announced to you later."

The door opened and shut—and all that could be heard was the hollow sound of the stick—tack—tack —tack—dying away in the distance.

With a shriek Manuela collapsed upon her pillow. Sister Hanni rushed to her:

" Manuela . . . my dear . . ."

But Manuela was sobbing and crying beyond all measure. Her whole body was shaken with screams; her limbs were convulsed, her head jerked, her body writhed, as if she were in the grip of some merciless power that was torturing her. Incomprehensible sounds came gasping from her lips:

" Hanni, Sister Hanni, help me—help me! What is

it I've done? I didn't do anything . . . to hurt
Fräulein von Bernburg, she . . . I . . . love her . . . I
didn't . . . wrong her . . . I—I wouldn't do anything. . . ."

A wild peal of laughter broke from the distorted
mouth. Sister Hanni needed all her strength to hold
the frantic girl down.

"Hanni . . . I must go to her . . . I must go to
her . . . at once . . . now . . . she . . . she can't be
angry . . . I didn't do anything to her! "

Both her feet were already out of the bed. Hanni
seized them and forced them back. She could hear
someone coming.

"Manuela, hush, be quiet—my God, there's somebody
coming."

Suddenly the collapse of exhaustion set in and
Manuela was lying strengthless among her pillows when
the door opened and Fräulein von Kesten appeared.

Fräulein von Kesten had been running, and was
excited and hurried. An important telephone call had
just been received, and, as luck would have it, the Head
was not in her room when Her Royal Highness rang
up, so that she, Kesten, had had to take the message.
She had run all over the house to find the Head, and
after catching her in the corridor, was now racing round
to pass on the exciting news which superseded everything else for the moment.

"Sister Hanni, Her Royal Highness has been so
gracious as to announce that she will visit us this afternoon. The Headmistress wishes all the children to
assemble to receive her "—and with a look at Manuela,
"all of them! " I'm not going to address a word to *you*,
was what the look said. How degraded your behaviour

was you have probably realized by this time. "Sister
Hanni, Manuela must in any circumstances be fit by
three o'clock. Do you understand?"

"I'll do my best, Fräulein von Kesten, but . . ."

Bunny lifted her hand forbiddingly.

"Please, no buts—Manuela must!"

And as hurriedly as she had come she disappeared
again.

XXIII

FRAULEIN VON KESTEN'S *glacé* kid gloves reeked of ben-
zine, and were no longer specklessly white. They had
not the pleasantly cool smoothness and tightness of new
glacé gloves. Like old skins they were covered with
wrinkles which even a hot iron could not remove. They
had, indeed, seen much service and had not been too
well treated. For *glacé* kid gloves and agitation were
closely allied in this case, and the one, so to speak,
necessarily evoked the other. While Manuela, pale and
exhausted, was slipping into her freshly starched white
frock and drawing the hard, uncomfortable patent-
leather shoes on her still unsteady feet, Fräulein von
Kesten's bony red hands were slipping into their tired
coverings.

Frau Alemann ran up and down the corridors flicking
the last specks of dust from door-handles and window-
frames. Herr Alemann with great deliberation pushed
open the carriage gate. The Head fastened her Order
of Elisabeth, with its small red ribbon, on her left

shoulder. Johanna swept up the dry little laurel leaves
that had fallen down when the two clipped laurel trees
were carried in. Fräulein von Kesten examined the
screws holding down the red carpet that had been
extended to the entry, in case any of them should work
loose and ruffle up the carpet . . . for if there were
any wrinkles in it, the Princess—God forbid!—might
stumble.

In the upper corridor the clattering of wooden heels
attached to patent-leather shoes had ceased. In perfect
order, with sleeked-back hair, white cotton gloves and
brightly scrubbed faces, the children were standing
ready.

"They always line us up much too early," argued Ilse.

"Silence!" came a reprimand from Marga.

"Oh, shut up—I'd like to know, anyhow, what's bitten
you since yesterday, you're so blooming important
to-day. . . ."

"Leave her alone . . ." said Edelgard.

"I say, we look exactly like the Maids of Honour
escorting the Fire Brigade on a Sunday morning. . . ."
Behind Ilse a giggle rose and spread.

Mia began to squat on her heels.

"I'm getting tired. . . ."

"And these abominable shoes pinch my feet," groaned
Ilse von Treitschke.

"They're two sizes too small. . . ."

"No, your feet are simply two sizes too big. . . ."

Again there was a stifled giggle. This time Bunny's
voice cut the mirth short.

"Silence! Eyes front!"

She went close up to the waiting ranks, and with her
hand straightened them.

"Marga, a little back, Oda and Mia, forward. Keep the lines even. Hands close to the sides. Heads up. Edelgard, I said head up. . . ." Then she crossed to the bell and rang it.

An absolute hush ensued. The small grey lady drew herself up, ran her eye down the ranks, and in her shrill, sharp voice issued the decree, which it was her function to transmit.

"Before Her Royal Highness appears I have a communication to make to you. We have had an unheard-of and very regrettable case of insubordination among us. The Headmistress would be glad to spare you any necessity for association with the pupil concerned, but since the Princess has announced her intention of visiting us an exception has had to be made. Manuela von Meinhardis will come down from the sick-room to be present. The Headmistress feels she can rely on your tact and discretion, and strictly enjoins you to refrain from intercourse with the said pupil. Any girl who addresses a single word to Manuela von Meinhardis will be severely punished. . . ."

It was at this moment that Manuela appeared at the lower end of the corridor. In order to reach her place beside Edelgard she had to pass along the whole line of blank and bewildered faces. She made an effort to look straight in front of her, but her gait was uncertain. She was overwhelmed by a boundless feeling of forlorn-ness, and a dreadful hand of ice clutched at her heart. Dully she sensed her complete detachment from this community, and in her head the question hammered unceasingly: Why . . . oh, why? Edelgard and Ilse had to open ranks in order to let her take her place, and Manuela felt as if they were drawing away from

her. Only her sleeves lightly brushed those of her
neighbours, and no hand pressed hers to give her
courage.

"You know what is expected of you," said Fräulein
von Kesten, keeping a sharp eye on the girls beside
Manuela.

XXIV

THE open carriage on its rubber-tyred wheels rolled
noiselessly enough over the cobblestones of Hochdorf.
A faint gleam of spring sunshine after the long rains
had apparently tempted the ladies to this little drive
out of town.   Although there was only one lackey, with
but a modest allowance of gold braid, sitting with folded
arms beside the coachman, everyone in Hochdorf knew
who was hidden behind the sunshade, and tact, custom
and good breeding all required that a deep Court curtsy
should be bestowed on this equipage, in complete dis-
regard of the fact that the streets were rather wet.   Anyone who did not pause and salute the carriage advertised
himself at once as an outsider who was not received at
Court, and no respectable person would care to make
such an admission.   These matters were part of the
Hochdorf tradition, like the hunting trophies on the
walls of the rooms, like the staghorn buttons on the
coat-tails of the Hochdorf gentlemen.

The Princess was a good-hearted woman who would
have been very shocked to hear the shooting of a carted
stag described as murder.   She was a really good mother,
in so far as etiquette permitted, and as she now stood

before the ranks of white-clad girls, all making such an exemplary Court *knix*, her heart rejoiced. She was delighted by the spectacle.

"Oh, it's splendid to see so many happy faces. . . ."

Her Royal Highness could not guess that these girls were almost swooning with fatigue and had been standing there for a full half-hour because she was a little late. Nor could she have guessed that they were all wondering secretly whether the royal guest had brought them something to eat. . . . For if the great lady had asked them—not that such a question was likely to occur to her: "Do you get enough to eat?" every one of them would have answered mechanically: "Yes, Your Royal Highness."

Now the Princess was greeting the ladies. One after another sank down to kiss her hand, and for each of them she had a friendly word.

"How is the housekeeping getting on, Fräulein von Attems?"

"Thank you, Your Royal Highness," was the answer.

"Are the children learning their lessons, Mademoiselle?"

"Remarkably well, Your Royal Highness."

"And how are they all in health?"

The Princess turned back to the Headmistress, who was standing immediately behind her, ready to impart any information that might be required.

"In excellent health, Your Royal Highness, excellent. . . ."

Beneath the large hat and the handsome grey hair, rolled in an old-fashioned puff on which the hat reposed, a pair of kindly eyes smiled at the children.

The Countess Kernitz, the lady-in-waiting, now ad-

vanced and whispered something under the brim of the
hat.

"Yes, yes," nodded the Princess, "I haven't forgotten,
my dear Kernitz. . . ." Turning to the Headmistress
she said: "The little Beckendorf girl . . ."

Hardly was the name uttered when Fräulein von
Kesten called out the girl in question, and Anneliese von
Beckendorf bobbed to kiss the hand of Her Royal
Highness in its faultless *glacé* kid glove.

"Well, how do you like the Seminary?" and
without waiting for an answer the Princess nodded
amiably to the child: "Very well, of course . . ." and
Anneliese was dismissed.

Once more the Countess Kernitz advanced—but no
reminder was necessary, Her Royal Highness had
thought of it herself.

"The little Meinhardis . . ."

With an unsteady step, which the great lady
attributed to shyness and agitation and regarded with
double benevolence, Lela approached and sank in a
trembling Court curtsy. It was difficult to bend one's
knee so far. . . .

"Yes"—the Princess studied Lela, who stood with
downcast eyes—"yes, you're very like your father . . .
very . . . I knew your mother, too . . . a very pious
woman. I hope you'll be like her. . . ." Then she
started, and, forgetting Manuela, regarded the Headmistress with reproachful surprise: "But pale—very
pale. . . ."

"Only a trivial, passing ailment . . ." stammered the
Headmistress.

"Not infectious, I hope?" asked Her Royal Highness
in horror.

"No, not at all, not at all. . . ."

The Princess began to move off without paying the slightest heed to Manuela, who was still standing there in a kind of daze.

"Yes, one can't help being anxious when one has so many children of one's own. . . ."

"Of course, Your Royal Highness. Quite natural . . ." and both ladies vanished down the corridor into the Headmistress's room.

It was now the Countess Kernitz's turn to issue a vicarious decree. She was an old lady, grown grey in Court service. At such moments she showed no timidity. She turned to Fräulein von Kesten:

"The children may go now. . . ."

And Bunny passed on the order:

"The children may go now. Change dresses, return white frocks, make no noise and go to your classes!"

The girls obeyed.

"Yes—and the ladies may go too. . . ."

But the ladies had not waited for this permission; and so the old Countess sat down on a bench to await the return of her mistress. After she had sat down Fräulein von Kesten also seated herself.

"A lovely day to-day," began the Countess, and Fräulein von Kesten could only agree with her.

XXV

DURING the ceremonial royal visit Lela's eyes had sought in vain to meet those of Fräulein von Bernburg. She felt a chill run through her: Fräulein von Bernburg did not want to look at her. The face she was

gazing at remained cold and unmoving. Even a
reproachful look would have been a comfort. Manuela
had only one thought, one desire, one obsession: to
go to *her*. Beside her, she felt, everything would all
come right again. She must surely understand, she
must surely realize that I love her, and would do
nothing, nothing in the world, to betray her, thought
Manuela. And once more her gaze was baffled by
the unmoving, rigid mask of her beloved.

Nobody spoke to her, the children scattered without
looking at her. But that did not matter for the
moment. She must speak to Fräulein von Bernburg,
and so she rushed as if hounded up a side staircase to
intercept Fräulein von Bernburg before she could reach
her room.

Manuela had to climb three storeys high. The stairs
were steep and her knees weak. She felt as if each
step were reeling away beneath her, and to keep from
falling she clutched at a rail, but it yielded in her hand.
And her head was swimming. Yet she had to hurry.
Once back in the sick-room she would not find it easy
to get up here again, and she simply must see Fräulein
von Bernburg—at once—immediately.

How her head ached, and how difficult it was to
remember all she ought to say and wanted to say!
The chaplain had said . . . what was it? . . . to
apologize—yes, yes—she wanted to do that—she would
be glad to do it. Her breath gave out. Manuela had
to lean against a stone pillar. Her breast was heaving
rapidly. But she dared not lose any time, she must
go on. Oh, to hold her hand . . . and—oh, yes, that
was it . . . the wrong she had done her. She had
wronged her, of course—yet what wrong had she done?

she could not remember at all. But when Manuela was quite small Mamma had once said: "When you do anything wrong you must set it right again." And so she had given one of her dolls to a girl at school, the only doll she had really liked. Why she had done so she could not now remember. But she would remember it later; it wasn't important, anyhow. Now she could hear footsteps. It was half dark, but Lela knew who was coming. She was seized with fear, frantic, yearning fear, but she stood in the middle of the passage and Fräulein von Bernburg could not pass her by. She tried to speak, but could not—what had happened to her voice? And what was this?—her knees were failing. I mustn't fall, she thought.

"Well, what do you want?"

Lela stretched out her arms. She lifted her head and her mouth opened as if about to scream; her eyes, hounded and miserable, stared into Fräulein von Bernburg's face.

For one moment only Fräulein von Bernburg gazed with horror at the despairing apparition before her, and her promise not to speak again to Manuela was forgotten.

"Have you something to say to me, Manuela?"

Lela's head drooped: "Yes."

"Very well—come along. . . ."

XXVI

" I WILL repent with prayer and fasting for all the wrong I have done, so that my great sin . . ." Manuela paused, but nothing happened. She was hoping for a sign.

Dumbly she stood imploring the smallest gesture of acknowledgment. But nothing came; she waited in vain. Had Fräulein von Bernburg heard what she said? Her words, she knew, had no force. How could they have? They were alien words. She gathered herself together and uttered the last phrase she could remember: "So help me God."

A dull thud made Fräulein von Bernburg start in alarm. Manuela had collapsed on the floor—her head was lying on the hard planks.

"Darling . . . darling . . . come. . . ." Hasty, warm, loving little words were whispered in her ear, but Manuela did not hear them. Her eyes were closed, her face deathly white, her limbs powerless. Two hands raised her head and groped to find if her heart were beating; but she knew nothing of all that. She was lifted up and carried to a sofa: her temples were laved with ice-cold water—and at that she opened her eyes. Now she was at peace. She had forgotten everything, for she was gazing at a grave face close to her own, into dark brown eyes that were searching hers. She felt both her hands lying captive in the cool hands of Fräulein von Bernburg. Her frock had been loosened at the neck—she could breathe. It was, as if a nightmare had passed away. All was now well. To lie like that, to touch *her* and to be held by *her* hands, to see *her* eyes looking down—that was good, and should endure for ever.

Fräulein von Bernburg took the child's hands and laid them together on her breast. But after that she stood up. To say what she had to say, distance was needed.

"Manuela . . ."

The girl did not move. The hands still lay as she had

disposed them: Manuela would never move them again unless she were expressly told to do so.

"Manuela, you must exert all the strength you have. You must try to understand. . . ."

Why was she saying that? wondered the child. Strength? Manuela had no strength left. Nor did she need any: she only wanted to lie where she was. Unless she were expressly told to do so she could not even stand up.

"Manuela, we two must part."

It was so difficult to grasp what words meant when one was so tired. But Manuela made the effort. What was that? "We" and "part." Slowly the syllables took shape. Both these words were written visibly in the air: "Part" and "we." "We"—she thought—a lovely word. For the first time they were joined to each other by a word. Yes: "We." But "*part*"? Now that they were together at last?

"Have you understood me?"

No, obviously she had not understood.

"From now on you won't have anything to do with the other children. You will live in the isolation room. You won't eat in the common dining-hall; you will never see the others except in the class-rooms."

That did not affect Manuela. But a new thought struck her, and suddenly her fears returned, thrilling through her and jerking her involuntaily into a sitting position.

"And where am I to sleep?"

"Not in my dormitory any more."

"And . . . am I not to go for walks?"

"Not with the others, nor with me."

Manuela rose to her full height.

"And the Scripture lessons?"

"Not with me, but with the chaplain."

Like birds fluttering wildly round a room and beating
their heads against the walls, Manuela's thoughts flew
round and round.

"But I must. . . ."

"No. . . . You're never to see me again."

Manuela stood up on her feet. Knowledge had suddenly fallen into her mind like a red-hot, glowing stone.

"Never . . . to see you again?" The words came as
if torn out of her, searing and burning. This was the
end of everything. Never to see her again—and there
was nothing in the world but her. No country, no
home, nothing.

"No!" she heard her own voice crying. "No!"
Wild and defiant, as if she were a drowning man clinging to a boat. "No!"—until someone hacked off her
clutching fingers.

"You must do as you are told"—coldly and sternly
she said that, the woman standing there.

Manuela could not know that the woman's sternness
was a refuge from herself, that all she wanted was to
make an end as quickly as possible, without any evasions
—she had not strength enough left for anything but a
short spurt to the goal, and it had to be done quickly.

"You must do as you are told. You have to be cured."

"Cured? Of what?"

Heavy, deliberate, one by one the words came ringing
out:

"You must not love me so much, Manuela, that is
not right. That's what one has to fight, what one has
to conquer, what one has to kill. . . ."

In a low voice the child re-echoed the words: "One

has to . . . has to kill. . . ." But why? . . . Her eyes
wandered to Fräulein von Bernburg. "One has to," she
had said. She too? Had she to kill it too? She swayed,
she fell, she beat her head against the other's knees.
Swift, frantic, and as if burning with fever the words
came out:

"Dear, beloved Fräulein von Bernburg! Not that
—you didn't say that—you know all about it, you know
quite well I couldn't survive it, you know I would die."
And then, quite quietly: "Just tell me one thing, just
whisper: 'I won't give you up,' and then I'll be calm—
I'll do everything, I'll endure everything, I'll do all I'm
told and be good. . . ."

Manuela waited for a sign. Nothing came. Her
hands were gently but firmly detached and restored to
her; they fell on her own lap as she knelt. Fräulein von
Bernburg moved away. One step. She *must* make an
end of it, or else . . .

"Manuela, get up."

Now the child rose to her feet, but she was suddenly
no longer a child. She had become uncannily calm—
calmer than the woman before her.

"Yes, I'm going now," and with a wild smile she
looked into the other's face. "Dear Fräulein von Bernburg, I'm going. . . ." She made no move to kiss the
other's hand; it was as if she were past all feeling.

"Adieu, dear Fräulein von Bernburg."

As if in a trance she walked to the door, opened it
and shut it behind her.

XXVII

WITH an anguished face Fräulein von Bernburg made a swift movement towards the door, but when she reached it she stood still, holding her head with both hands.

"No," she said aloud, and then once more: "No!"

Manuela no longer heard her: she was as if walking in her sleep. Unconscious, seeing nothing, feeling nothing, she was drawn higher and higher; step by step the white staircase led her up. Manuela climbed with half-shut eyes: she dared not look down, for her head would reel; she dared not. . . .

"Our Father which art in Heaven—that is the end—that is the beginning—hallowed be Thy name. . . ."

Soundlessly, on her tiptoes, stealing along, then running, then breathlessly racing, Edelgard came flying along the corridor and reached the first landing . . . the second. . . .

"Edelgard!" A sharp voice called her back. "Where are you off to?"

Edelgard stood dumb, despairingly gazing up the stairs without paying any attention to Fräulein von Kesten.

"Come down at once; you have no business up there."

And Edelgard, trained to obedience, reluctantly turned back to stand with bent head before Fräulein von Kesten.

"What's the meaning of this, Edelgard?"

Edelgard summoned her courage.

"I—Fräulein von Kesten—I'm looking for Manuela," she stated, white to the lips.

"You disobedient, Edelgard?—this is a surprise to me. This is something quite new. . . ."

Edelgard lifted her head high.

"Manuela is not wicked, Fräulein von Kesten!" she said boldly, almost contemptuously, looking straight into Fräulein von Kesten's uneasy eyes.

Fräulein von Kesten struggled to find words. But there was to be no need for any. Down below suppressed cries were resounding.

"Manuela! Manuela!"

Fräulein von Kesten leaned over the balustrade.

"Silence down there! Have you all gone crazy?"

A wild agitation seemed to be overwhelming the children. Indignation was flaming up—panic—inexplicable panic. They were running all along the lower corridor: "Manuela." Opening all the doors: "Manuela. . . ." In the dormitory, in the empty classrooms low voices were echoing, asking: "Manuela . . . ?"

"Come back with me," said Fräulein von Kesten crisply to Edelgard, and hurried downstairs.

But the rush of children was coming nearer; they were already half-way up the first stair; they simply elbowed Fräulein von Kesten to the wall and stormed past her.

At Fräulein von Bernburg's door they halted.

No answer came to their knocking.

The door was locked.

With a last access of boldness Oda drummed on the door-panels.

"Manuela!"

But Manuela was far away. She did not want to hear anything again—or actually did not hear anything. Away up on the highest landing of all she was standing beside a window, from which one could see far over the roofs and tree-tops. It was a high, narrow, attic window, and the sill barely reached to Manuela's knees. With one hand she was opening the casement, with the other she was holding herself steady.

The fresh air blew gently on her forehead. Her mind was clear, unnaturally clear, like that of a dying person. It was a far cry down to the ground, but she would be free and cool—and she would be outside in the open— no longer inside—far—in the open—and free.

A breath of wind stirred the tall trees. The sun was sinking. In the street there was no sound. Unconsciously her lips framed the words:

> " And even if I mistake Thee
> And fail to know Thy might,
> Thou wilt not yet forsake me,
> In darkest night. . . ."

Then she flung her arms wide:

> " Take Thou my hand and lead me,
> Do Thou go on before;
> Until the end I need Thee . . ."

" Manuela! . . . Manuela! . . . Manuela! "
" Have you looked in the dressing-room? "
" Yes! "
" In the garden? "
" There too! "
" If only Fräulein von Bernburg . . ."
But suddenly a bell began to ring, a frantic bell; it went on ringing.
" What's up? "
" That's down below."

Why didn't it stop? Who was ringing it? Why were all the girls rushing downstairs?

Herr Alemann, his collar still unhooked, was tugging wildly at the front door. He could not manage it alone, he had to find a helper. Fräulein von Bernburg was beside him. Now!

And there was Manuela, lying on the hard stone steps in front of them. Herr Alemann spread his arms and kept the struggling crowd from following Fräulein von Bernburg.

Fräulein von Bernburg knelt down. Gently she lifted Manuela's head on to her lap. Her hand lay on Manuela's heart. But there was no movement there.

The house was as if frozen in silence. No one spoke. No one tried to push forward. They left the two of them alone: Fräulein von Bernburg and Manuela.

THE END

Also available in the Lesbian Landmarks series

WINTER LOVE
Han Suyin

'A stunning novel – resonant, penetrating and unsentimental'
– *Georgina Hammick*

Red is a married woman with children. But since adolescence she has been desperate to conceal from herself and others the true significance of her feelings for women. Now, with middle-age approaching fast, her thoughts turn insistently to her student days in that bitterly cold winter of the last year of the war when Mara offered – and Red rejected – love, desire, and trust. Painfully, Red relives the past, and comes to see the part that cruelty, loss and fear have played in the formation of her frozen sexuality. And with enlightenment, comes the possibility of thaw. . . .

Han Suyin, born in China in 1917, is best known for her novel *A Many Splendoured Thing*, and for her volumes of autobiography. *Winter Love*, her beautifully written and perceptive novel, was first published in 1962.

POISON FOR TEACHER
Nancy Spain

'An inspired craziness rules . . . Miss Spain has yet to write a better book' – *Elizabeth Bowen*

A nasty attack of murder has broken out at Radcliff Hall (aka Roedean) which brings, in the unlikely guise of schoolteachers, two most unorthodox detectives – revue star Miriam Birdseye (aka Hermione Gingold) and her Russian ballerina chum Natasha Nerkovina – hotfoot to solve it. Undaunted by the horrors of matron, mutton, Bally Netball and the pupils' endless recitals of *Innisfree* ('Ai will araise and go now . . .') Birdseye *et cie* triumph once more.

Poison for Teacher, first published in 1949, is one of Nancy Spain's most exuberant performances in the genre which she made triumphantly her own: novels of detection generously laced with comedy and high camp.

Nancy Spain, journalist, novelist and panellist on television programmes such as *What's My Line?* and *Juke Box Jury*, was one of the most witty and lovable figures in post-war Britain.

LOVE CHILD
Maureen Duffy

'A macabre tale of jealousy and possessiveness'
– *Daily Telegraph*

Kit's mother has just embarked on an affair with Ajax, her husband's secretary. Kit is murderously jealous, but of whom, her mother or Ajax? And what gender is Ajax, or Kit for that matter? It is impossible to tell. Why is the reader uncomfortable not knowing? Whether boy or girl, it is clear that Kit is a monster: a mini-adult whose freakishly sophisticated brain knows 'everything' and whose stunted emotions know nothing. The combination is, inevitably, disastrous . . .

Love Child, Maureen Duffy's teasingly brilliant exploration of the meaning of gender, was first published in 1971.

Maureen Duffy is one of Britain's most admired contemporary writers. Her work includes novels, biographies, plays and poems. Virago also publish *That's How It Was* and *The Microcosm*.

Also of interest from Virago

A MODEL CHILDHOOD
Christa Wolf

'This is a powerful book, a most extraordinary testament . . . it is her vision of the fundamental strangeness of what seemed at the time a fairly ordinary childhood, in the bosom of a normal Nazi family in Landsberg, which makes Christa Wolf's narrative so moving, so convincing' – *The Times*

In 1933, Nelly is four years old and lives in Landsberg; Nelly's family believes in Hitler's new order: her father joins the party, and she, as a matter of course, joins the Nazi youth organisations. In school Nelly learns of racial purity and the Jewish threat, and when the local synagogue burns, she feels not pity, only fear of an alien race. No voice of objection is raised, not even when the euthanasia programme dooms Nelly's simple-minded Aunt Dottie. It is only much later, when her family is fleeing westward before the advancing Russian army, that Nelly, now in her teens, tries to come to terms with the shattering of the fundamental values of her childhood.

Christa Wolf, novelist, short-story writer, essayist, critic, journalist and film dramatist, born in Landsberg, Warthe, in 1929, lives in West Berlin. Germany's most prestigious woman of letters, in this her fourth novel she explores the experience of Nazism as it was lived by ordinary people in an ordinary town. In doing so Christa Wolf has created a great novel which is also a plea to remember and to learn from the past.

THE QUEST FOR CHRISTA T.
Christa Wolf

'Undoubtedly one of the few great novels in the German language since the war' – *The Times*

Christa is a young girl in Hitler's Germany; she survives to embrace the new order but her enthusiasm and idealism wither as crass materialists corrode its splendid dreams. A teacher in a village school, a student at Leipzig University, a wife and a mother, the life of Christa T., here recalled by her friend, is the life of an ordinary, intelligent, sensitive woman. But this famous novel reveals much more: Christa's is the story of a whole generation, and a moving celebration of the unique value of each human being and all human life.

A FAVOURITE OF THE GODS
Sybille Bedford

'A writer of remarkable accomplishment' – *Evelyn Waugh*

One autumn in the late 1920s, a beautiful woman boards a train on the Italian riviera. Her name is Constanza, and she is *en route* to Brussels and a new marriage. With her is her young daughter Flavia, who is going to England for the education she has always wanted. An odd, almost meaningless incident interrupts their journey, and Constanza makes a seemingly abrupt and casual decision that changes the course of both their lives. Yet perhaps the pattern had already been set by Constanza's own mother, the American heiress Anna, who years before had left home for a strange marriage with an Italian prince . . .

A COMPASS ERROR
Sybille Bedford

Flavia, daughter of the *madame* Constanza is now seventeen. While her mother travels with a new lover to a secret destination, she lives alone in a Provençal villa, studying for Oxford entrance and dreaming of a life spent among books. But she is taken up and seduced by the wife of a fashionable painter, then moves into the arms of a fascinating, dangerous woman whose true identity she fails to comprehend. Doomed to betrayal, the idealistic Flavia discovers her true inheritance; she must bear the results of mistakes from the past, and face a future forever changed by the consequences of her own innocence.

Sybille Bedford, the author of seven books, was born in Germany in 1911 and lives in Chelsea, London. This complex, sophisticated novel, sequel to *A Favourite of the Gods*, was first published in 1968.